Praise for

1,000 COILS OF FEAR

"Olivia Wenzel's bold and exceptional novel, *1,000 Coils of Fear*, tells stories in many voices—of her estranged family, of female and male lovers, of her nation, once home to Nazis and the KGB, still inhospitable to immigrants, and to its Black German author. Wenzel's novel is not just of and from contemporary Germany, it proposes a different German novel. Her impressive writing, born of a brilliant mind, surprises—stylistically, and by its frankness and associations. An uncompromising consciousness leaps from sentence to sentence, city to city, in love, depressed, alienated, afraid, and contradictory. She is asked, 'Where are you?' She asks, 'Where am I?' I rode in the passenger seat, beside the beauty and strangeness of *1,000 Coils of Fear*."
—LYNNE TILLMAN, author of *Men and Apparitions* and *MOTHERCARE*

"This novel's mixed-race young narrator interrogates her own painful past and confusion of selves—German Angolan, child of an East Germany erased by unification, boy lovers girl lovers, badass and vulnerable, cowering and defiant—in a voice so exuberant, inventive, brainy, sensitive, and hilarious that it's like a pyrotechnic flare illuminating the whole woman, past and present, radiant, unique, a voice and a novel to take with us into the future."
—FRANCISCO GOLDMAN, author of *Monkey Boy*

"An audacious and disturbing novel."
—MICHELLE DE KRETSER, author of *Scary Stories*

1,000 COILS OF FEAR

A NOVEL

OLIVIA WENZEL

TRANSLATED FROM THE GERMAN BY
PRISCILLA LAYNE

Catapult  New York

This is a work of fiction. All of the characters, organizations, and events portrayed in this novel are either products of the author's imagination or used fictitiously.

ISBN: 978-1-64622-050-2

Cover design by Dana Li
Book design by Wah-Ming Chang

Library of Congress Control Number: 2021940579

Catapult
New York, NY
books.catapult.co

Printed in the United States of America
1 3 5 7 9 10 8 6 4 2

The translation of this work was supported by
a grant from the Goethe-Institut.

For K and O and S.

And for those who feel seen.

I

(points of view)

Quiet! Hush your mouth, silence when I spit it out
In your face, open your mouth, give you a taste.

MISSY ELLIOTT

My heart is a snack machine made of tin. This machine stands on some random train platform, in some random city. An isolated, industrial chunk of metal that's still unassuming. A machine; a rust-free, shiny, square colossus. Why does it stand there alone? Who created it?

The snack machine has a sheet of glass on the front so I can look inside and see all its snacks. I zoom in: the snacks are sorted meticulously. They laugh at me through their cellophane packaging. Market psychology probably played a role in determining how they would be placed. But that doesn't matter now. These tasty little snacks—from the morbid pig in a blanket to the coconut-chocolate bar—they are all there just for me and I can choose freely. I can choose how to look at them, buy them, salivate over them, and gulp them down according to my preference. I suddenly think, *My goodness, just fifteen more minutes, then the train will come,* and I feel my stomach growl.

My stomach growls again. It just wants attention; that's not real hunger. Even so, I start to look for some change in my bag. And as I consider whether I want coconut or pork—and my forefinger already stretches toward the buttons—my stomach starts all over again. The snack machine suddenly seems much bigger and begins to move. Even the train tracks that I'm standing next to begin to move, and the ground beneath me, too, along with the snack machine. Everything is swaying all of a sudden, even I am.

For a moment, I am disoriented. When I look above me, I can see that the sky has become darker, there's rust everywhere. My forefinger is still stretched out. *Coconut* shoots through my head. Then I fall to my knees and faint.

Maybe it would have been best if I had looked for shelter within the snack machine as soon as I stepped onto the platform. It may have been best for me to move right into this machine and live there for a few days. I would have covered myself in rustling cellophane and eaten whatever fell into my lap. Finally, I would have built myself a rustling toilet. I would have had peace and time, I mean, I love peace and time, and I would have been safe. I could have looked out through the glass pane and watched the people on the platform. I could have made faces at them and sung solemn songs. I could have synchronized their conversations live. I could have posed urgent questions to the people who might come to me for a snack. Or given them answers. I could have fallen in love. I could have forgotten my current occupations, my current life; just to have fun in the most eccentric ways.

I could have begun a new life.

But I want to go out into the so-called wide world, by all means.

WHERE ARE YOU NOW?

I'm in Durham, North Carolina, the second-northernmost of the southern states.

WHAT'S YOUR FAVORITE FOOD?

Yesterday I fell in love with a local specialty: thick, warm waffles with nuts, maple syrup, and chocolate cream topped with fried chicken. You could choose between four chicken wings and drumsticks.

WEIRD.

Yes.

WHERE ARE YOU STAYING?

In a massive hotel. There's air-conditioning and you can't open the windows. When the cleaning staff is finished, they turn on all five lamps whether I'm there or not. In the courtyard the pool is illuminated around the clock, even though it's much too cold to swim.

AND HOW ARE YOU? WHAT'S UP WITH YOUR EYES?

. . .

WHAT ARE YOU DOING TOMORROW?

Sleeping in.

TELL ME MORE ABOUT THE FOOD.

A well-frequented restaurant, some nondescript music is playing. The Black waitress asks me: *You want them wings or them drumsticks? Drumsticks, please,* I say. Then she says that she likes my hair. I say: *This was more of an accident, but now I like it.* We smile at each other as if we're friends. I suddenly feel at ease . . . like I belong.

NICE.

The food tastes good. The combination of waffles and chicken is wrong, disconcerting, perfect. There are no white workers in the restaurant, just a few white guests. At the table next to me, there's a mother sitting with her son, both are Black, both stare at their phones during the length of their stay at the restaurant. The boy looks like he's daydreaming, playing a racing game, his body is a little too big for himself.

YOU PUT THAT BEAUTIFULLY.

Ever since I got to the U.S., the first thing I notice about people is their skin color.

COOL.

No.

NOW YOU'RE MAKING THAT FACE AGAIN.

PLEASE STOP. THAT'S YOUR WHITE-PRIVILEGE FACE.

Sorry, I did that unconsciously.

IN ANGOLA THEY USED TO CALL YOU "COCONUT," RIGHT? BROWN ON THE OUTSIDE, WHITE ON THE INSIDE. WHEN YOU MAKE THAT FACE, I UNDERSTAND WHAT THEY MEAN.

Everyone always wants to talk to me about racism. That's not my life's work.

YOU'RE THE ONE WHO STARTED IT.

WHERE ARE YOU NOW?

Still in Durham, North Carolina.

WHERE ARE YOU AT HOME?

. . .

DID YOU SAY SOMETHING?

. . .

DID YOU SAY SOMETHING?

I say that a lot of Black people here can't afford a car, but this city was built exclusively for cars. I say that a Black couple was shot to death on campus last year by a racist who was well known in town. I say that the white people in rural areas have a lot of guns and I'd best not go out there. I say that there's a large statue on campus, on a pedestal, named Silent Sam. He was built in honor of all those who fought during the Civil War—for the South, against Lincoln. I say that the white people have threatened to take back their funding from campus if anyone disturbs the statue, and after protests by the Black community, a memorial was placed next to Silent Sam, for all the African American slaves who built the university. I say that the new memorial looks like a camping table: a large, round slab is propped up by figures the size of garden gnomes, holding it over their heads. I say that these slaves stand there embedded in the earth, as if they were sinking in quicksand, and that some people use the new, small memorial as a spot for sitting down. I say that, as a result, they built little stools around it, and with that it really became a table. A table that the Black enslaved people are holding up, out of the quagmire, an obvious tray, from which affluent white students eat their lunch during their break. I say that I didn't make any of that up.

THAT THE BLACKS THINK THEY ARE BLACK, AND THE WHITES THINK THEY'RE WHITE.

What?

THAT THE BLACKS THINK THEY ARE BLACK, AND THE WHITES THINK THEY'RE WHITE.

Yes.

WHAT'S UP WITH YOUR EYES?

Puffy from crying.

ATYPICAL.

Oh, well.

SINCE WHEN IS IT EMBARRASSING TO CRY IN PUBLIC?

Sometimes I come back to the hotel and I watch hours of HBO on a giant flatscreen in order to hide from my feelings. Until sleep comes.

At night, I dream of young Black men who jump out of planes to their death as they angrily call out the names of white American women.

Ashley, Pamela, Hillary, Amber!

Lots of clouds, lots of names, a long drop, no impact at the end, just me waking up.

THE WAY YOU SOBBED WHEN THE STEWARDESS ASKED YOU: *Do you want a cookie?*

I cried like a baby for a whole hour, totally plastered above the clouds.

YOUR SOFT, OBSESSIVE HEART. IF YOU COULD EAT IT, WOULD YOU?

It depends on who's offering it to me. How the service is. How it's served.

DO YOU FEEL GOOD IN PLACES WHERE PEOPLE SERVE YOU?

Yes, very. Service areas comfort me.

MAYBE BECAUSE THE WORKERS AREN'T ALLOWED TO TALK ABOUT POLITICS. THAT CREATES A SOFT AND HARMLESS ATMOSPHERE.

It's fine the other way around. Politicians are always talking about work.

Watch now: the ten most popular political topics of all time! Number seven: the future of labor!

We're so used to the promise of more jobs that we're no longer surprised if someone comes by and whispers:

Hello, little slave of work—shake your booty, make it twerk!

WHAT SHOULD PEOPLE SEE WHEN THEY LOOK AT YOUR FACE?

Me?

WITH WHOM DO YOU FIGHT YOUR BATTLES?

Myself?

HAVE YOU EVER BELONGED TO A TERRORIST ORGANIZATION?

No.

HAVE YOU EVER BELONGED TO A CRIMINAL ORGANIZATION?
No.
IS YOUR HOMELAND SAFE?
According to what criteria?
WHERE ARE YOU REGISTERED?
At home.
WHAT DOES THAT MEAN?
. . .
WHERE ARE YOU NOW?
A couple of days ago I was in New York. On election night I was sitting in a bar in Manhattan, a few blocks away from Trump and Clinton.
GO ON, GO ON.
I'm talking to some British managers from Shell. We're drunk and in good spirits.
Cheers!
I've decided to be tolerant, I don't want to judge them. Surprisingly pleasant, eloquent men; we get along well. One of them says he's a feminist, Angela Merkel's policies are destroying Syria, because no one is returning to rebuild their country, and Hillary Clinton has basically won. The other one, Kee-nic, is euphoric. He keeps saying, *This is amazing,* in a British accent. His deep voice and the melodious sound of the former colonial empire draw me in.
WHICH DETAIL ARE YOU LEAVING OUT?
. . .
WHICH DETAIL ARE YOU LEAVING OUT?
And his "ethnicity."
WHAT?
His "ethnicity" attracts me. But it makes me uncomfortable to say that. Or to think it.

WHY?

This is amazing, Kee-nic says, and with that he means the atmosphere of this New York night, the election, the anticipation, perhaps even the feeling we all have that we are witnessing a historic moment. Around midnight, I follow him to his hotel; we're convinced that in the morning the first ever female president of the U.S.A. will be confirmed. Around three a.m. we've drunkenly fucked ourselves to sleep. My cellphone vibrates. Text messages from my friends in Germany.

Nine eleven—eleven nine!

Be careful!

What the fuck?

I turn on the television; Trump has just started his speech. Kee-nic wakes up and snuggles up to me (he has such smooth skin and smells so good, is that coconut oil?). We sleep together again. While he pounds away with his meticulously trained manager physique, I can't take my eyes off the television. Kee-nic moans something, I can't understand it, so he says it again: *This is amazing. This is amazing.* I think, *Donald Trump's family actually looks shocked*, meanwhile I'm on the sixteenth floor of a luxury hotel in Manhattan getting fucked by a man whose company is systematically destroying the environment.

AND FOUR HOURS LATER, IN A PLANE TO DURHAM, THE NICE STEWARDESS SERVING COOKIES.

WHERE ARE YOU NOW?

Still in Durham.

On a wall someone has sprayed: *Black lives don't matter and neither does your votes.*

HAVE YOU EVER DESTROYED GOVERNMENT PROPERTY?

Black lives don't matter and neither does your votes. I don't think that's proper English. I think that will stay there for a while. I don't know if these things will ever end, or just get worse. In the U.S., I'm Blacker than in Germany.

This is amazing.

Excuse me?

This is amazing.

THE SLAVE TRADE IS THE MOST SUCCESSFUL BUSINESS MODEL IN HUMAN HISTORY. FORCED LABOR IS STILL A BREATHTAKING CONCEPT! TRADING WITH ENSLAVED BOD-IES: THE WHIPPING, THE RAPE, THE LYNCHING!

I love that idea!

In the English-speaking world there is a tendency toward exagger-ated language.

I would kill for the cookies they sell over there!

In Germany there's a tendency toward exaggerated violence.

I would kill them if I could.

People burn down asylum seekers' homes. Or they yell *Jump already!* to the refugees, until they plunge to the ground from the windows. Or an eighty-person lynch mob is chasing down random kids to stab them. I have to believe that these people live on the margins. I have to believe that the core of society condemns these attacks. Otherwise, the land in which I live distinguishes itself very little from the U.S. Otherwise, the land in which I live could soon vote the same way. Otherwise, the land in which I live would no longer be my home.

WHAT HAPPENS WHEN YOU FALL ASLEEP?

I fall.

WHAT HAPPENS WHEN YOU WAKE UP?

Sometimes there's just a melody, a giggle. Often just brief, cold fear.

WHERE DO YOU FEEL AT HOME?

When I'm asleep.

WHAT IS THE PURPOSE OF YOUR STAY?

Where, here on earth?

WHAT DO YOU DREAM OF?

...

WHAT DO YOU DREAM OF?

For a moment I see something flare up; an image from history class, but more current, somehow newer and with drones. Instead of men in steel helmets, the faces of my friends. My dear friends, how they're running, ducking, falling, as if they were being kicked and hit by bullets, whips, fists, and bombs—somewhere in Berlin, somewhere in New York, somewhere in Thuringia. My friends lying on the ground with severed limbs, covered in blood, with contorted faces, my friends between collapsed buildings. My friends with their eyes wide open, small flies circling them.

AND THEN?

And then:

My friends are a chapter in a history book that is slammed shut, unemotional, objective, because everything happened so long ago. My dead friends as something that doesn't concern anyone today. My dead friends as a memory, a memorial on paper about which people will say:

Don't be so sensitive, that was the zeitgeist back then.

I stare at the snack machine, the snack machine stares at me.

I can hear music coming from somewhere. In a fast-paced tempo, a rapper describes how she and her bitches hustle. Just fifteen more minutes, then the train will come. My stomach growls.

My face is reflected in the glass. I smile at myself and think, *It's nice to travel alone,* as I roll my curls between my thumb and forefinger. Just then, I notice a group of blond schoolkids, reflected in the glass as well. Without turning around, I see how they're standing there, swiping their smartphones. The song is playing on one of their phones; they don't speak to one another. Suddenly I feel like licking the reflection of their faces—really slowly, really thoroughly.

WHERE ARE YOU NOW?
In Berlin at the airport. After checking in, I'm sitting at the gate and looking through a floor-length window at the planes outside. I like people who wear garish vests and noise-canceling headphones.
YOU'RE SWEATING.
I had to hurry. I was running late.
WHY AREN'T YOU SMILING?
What?
AREN'T YOU HAPPY?
. . .
ARE YOU NERVOUS?
No.
ARE YOU NERVOUS?
Tired out, maybe a little excited. I haven't been on such a long trip in a while, especially alone.
WHY?
Why I'm traveling alone or why I haven't taken a long trip in a while?
WHY ARE YOU NERVOUS?
. . . There was an incident.
GO ON. GO ON.
I'm still sitting by the gate. Since I'm not sure whether there'll be food on the flight, I buy a Coke and Snickers from a snack machine near another empty gate. No one is there, except me and a man. He has a beard and a head covering that I can't categorize.
DID HE TOUCH YOU?
No. It's not that kind of story. He didn't even see me.
OKAY. GO ON.

As I leave to return to my gate, he puts on a plastic belt with a strange bulge at the waist. Then he throws a large garment over his shoulders, which covers him completely. I stop in place. The garment looks festive and he seems upset.

HE IS NERVOUS.

Explosives! Suicide bomber!

The words race through my head. I can't do anything about it. The man sits down and begins to rock his torso back and forth, making far-reaching, hectic movements as he mumbles something to himself. I think I see a look of fear on his face.

HIS LAST PRAYER?

. . .

DO YOU HAVE A WEAPON WITH YOU?

No.

PEPPER SPRAY?

No.

OTHER EXPLOSIVE DEVICES?

He has bands wrapped around his arm. I think: *Those are the cables or the wires.* I don't dare approach him.

Excuse me, sir, do you wanna murder me or is this just a regular prayer?

So I decide to do something else. I go back to the security screening area, where they're checking IDs and where people are chosen randomly for further screening.

WERE YOU CHOSEN RANDOMLY?

I'm always chosen randomly.

AND THEN?

I ask a policeman for help. He winks at me and—confusingly, in a thick Thuringian accent—explains something about how he and his colleagues certainly had done their job thoroughly, but that he will send someone over to check nonetheless.

No need t' vohry, okay.

I go back to the gate, sit down, and eat my Snickers. While I was gone, the man finished his prayer and changed clothes. His large garment has disappeared, he calmly walks over to three children playing and a woman with a colorful headscarf. As he sits down next to them, a policeman enters the room. He strolls around, surveys the other people waiting, and then he sees me. I want to lower my gaze, but instead I look at the man and his family again. The policeman's gaze follows mine, while one of the children climbs onto the man's lap.

WHERE ARE YOU NOW?

I'm getting on the plane.

No need t' vohry, okay.

Welcome aboard! How are you today?

Full of self-disgust, thanks.

Be a hero! Better safe than sorry!

If I'd been in New York, my paranoia would have made me into a heroine. There are posters in the subway that invite you to report every suspicion with a clear conscience—for the safety of the city, for the community. But I'm not in New York yet.

DO YOU THINK REAL HEROINES EXIST?

. . . This moment of mortal fear, this moment when I'm convinced that I'll soon be blown to pieces. And then the shame—of having thought someone capable of such an atrocity and denouncing them for that reason.

ARE YOU NERVOUS NOW?

I can't fly without at least three spectacular fantasies about a plane crash befalling me. And somehow I always imagine I would be the only one who survived. Does a plane crash as soon as a bird gets stuck in its engine?

Please fasten your seat belts now.

DEAD CHICKENS—THAT'S HOW THEY TEST THE ENGINES. Okay.

THE MORE CHICKENS CAN BE SHREDDED BY A JET WITH-OUT TROUBLE, THE BETTER.

Oxygen will flow.

A stewardess has applied her lipstick beyond the edges of her upper lip. When she tries to sell me perfume from her duty-free cart, I see a clown with a barrel organ.

In case of emergency, follow the following instructions!

I like the announcement that you should first help yourself and then children, in case anything happens.

Oxygen will flow!

PLEASE CONCENTRATE.

FEAR OF A PLANE CRASH, FEAR OF TERROR.

WHAT ELSE?

I don't want to be a person who is afraid of "terror." I mean, it's not like I'm always looking up when I walk by buildings to see whether a loose brick might kill me.

AND YET YOU ARE THE FIRST ONE TO GET OFF IF THE SUB-WAY SMELLS LIKE GAS.

Five other people got off with me. They were anxious too and decided to wait for the next train. I'll never forget how we looked at one another.

Do you want a cookie?

The armrest has four different channels with music; on the monitors, the same movie is playing for all the passengers. A turbulent romantic comedy set in New York, with a white female protagonist. A lot of scenes are shot on the streets of New York. I've never been to New York, but I still think: *All the people in this film are white, that must have been a huge hassle.*

CONCENTRATE.

YOU'RE NERVOUS, YOU DON'T FEEL SAFE. WHAT ELSE?

I'm annoyed about the movie.

And about the people who watch it, without noticing that something is missing.

WHAT ELSE?

I don't want to keep talking about these things.

WHAT ELSE?

I get distracted, look out the window, think about clouds and different kinds of terror, wonder how the toilet flushes. Wonder why I let this fabricated fear inside me. Wonder why I can't defend myself better against it. Wonder how all the excrement is disposed of. I suddenly think about a day at the lake.

WHICH DAY?

When I wanted to go swimming and there was only right-wing terror.

THAT SOUNDS TRITE.

You know, rural, neo-fascist no-go zones and the like.

HOW MANY SWIMMING BADGES DO YOU HAVE?

... Right-wing terror is when you're sitting at the lake and four Nazis come, two men and two women. They don't see us, we're sitting far off in the shade and are still afraid.

WHAT DO YOU MEAN BY "WE"?

My boyfriend and I, we're a couple, but not a happy one; we had a fight half an hour ago. Right-wing terror is: when the Nazis come, we belong together again. They undress, the way I imagine soldiers would, attentive and jagged. They fold their clothes together, are standing erect and stiff on a hot summer day, naked and self-assured, looking at one of the lakes in Strausberg as if it belonged to them. Right-wing terror is: not being able to laugh at their stiffness, for fear of being seen. The biggest and stoutest of the group has a swastika tattooed on his chest.

As the four of them stand there, two families start packing up their things. Right-wing terror is: when the atmosphere suddenly changes, the two families withdraw, and there are only a few people left at the beach. My boyfriend and I remain awkwardly in the shade. A white man sits at the shore, maybe in his mid-thirties, his small sons play in the shallow water. The Nazis don't see him right away either and go for a swim. When they come back to shore and dry themselves off—and stand there just as jagged as before, wooden even, no one is having any fun—they notice that only one of the little kids is white. One of them says loudly: *Ugh, there was a nigger in the water* and the word stabs me between the ribs. I say quietly: *We have to go sit next to them, next to the father.* My boyfriend replies: *No way. They'll think we're provoking them. Then we'll really be in trouble.* I say: *But we can't just leave those kids and their father alone with them.* My boyfriend says: *They won't do anything to the kids. But they'll do something to us. We're leaving.* We continue fighting in whispers. My boyfriend eventually wins out. Right-wing terror is: I can't risk the chance that he might get beaten up, I have no idea what the right thing to do is. Right-wing terror is: we, as well, withdraw silently. Back at the car, I call the police right away and learn that it's illegal to display a swastika in public. It's against the constitution. *Good thing that you called. We're really trying our best to catch people like that. Where's the lake again?* Right-wing terror is: after two hours of searching, the police still can't find it. When I get home, I have the feeling I've done something wrong. Or I've neglected to do something. Right-wing terror is: I still think about this day and the impossibility of knowing how I should behave. Right-wing terror is: I'm ashamed of my cowardice. Right-wing terror is: I was once that kid at the lake.

Excuse me, sir, do you wanna murder me or do you just wanna hate me while you're swimming?

What?

THE COMBINATION OF FEAR AND THE INABILITY TO SAY
SOMETHING, THIS POWERLESSNESS, THE INABILITY TO
ACT—I UNDERSTAND.

WHAT DO YOU DO TO FIGHT IT?

. . . try to be aware of it?

WHERE ARE YOU NOW?

Still on a plane.

Excuse me, may I see your boarding pass?

I changed seats. My seat is actually back there, but it was so cramped.

Unfortunately, that's not allowed.

But the whole row is empty. Oh, okay, is it because this is an exit row?

This seat is XL and costs eighty-three dollars extra, sorry.

Just because there's more room? But the other seats are way too small for me. I can't even stretch out my legs.

I'm sorry, you're going to have to return to your seat.

Yeah, okay.

WHERE ARE YOU SEATED?

. . .

WHERE IS YOUR SEAT?

. . .

WHERE DO YOU BELONG?

. . .

DO YOU HAVE A COMPASS WITH YOU?

Why?

DO YOU FEEL LIKE YOUR LIFE HAS A FOCUS?

Maybe.

DO YOU FEEL LIKE YOUR LIFE IS APPROACHING A GOAL?

No.

WHO ARE YOUR NEIGHBORS?

My neighbors?

WHAT IS YOUR PERMANENT ADDRESS?

In Berlin.

WHERE DO YOU COME FROM?

I come—

WHERE DO YOU COME FROM?

I come—

WHERE DO YOU COME FROM?

I come—

WHY DO YOU ALWAYS DELETE YOUR BROWSER HISTORY?

What?

ARE YOU IN LOVE WITH YOUR FREEDOM OF MOVEMENT?

WHY DO YOU CHEW YOUR NAILS?

Sometimes it's hard for me to notice—

WOULD YOU LIKE TO SEE A COLORFUL GRAPHIC OF YOUR
MOTION PROFILE FROM THE LAST THREE YEARS? IN THE
FORM OF A SURPRISE CAKE, OUT OF WHICH JUMPS—

—whatever is most important.

WHERE ARE YOU NOW?

. . . at home.

OKAY.

. . .

Two days before my departure, I made a stupid mistake. I had to cancel my flight with the American airline again. No one picks up at the
German service center. So I call the English number. Shortly there-
after, a woman slowly spells words to me in broken English that I can
barely understand but am supposed to type into a search engine. At
some point, while the cancellation is finally going through online and
the website is buffering, I ask her if she really is located in the U.S.

No, no, on Fiji. We talk about the weather; here in Berlin and there on the island, oh really, aha, yes, of course. We're very cordial with each other. Eventually she asks quietly: *In winter, where you live . . . does it snow?*

Yes, I say. She responds: *I have never touched the snow in my life.* It sounds like a secret and a little reverent.

So I try to describe to her what snow is like. How it feels to hold a melting snowflake in your hand. *It's like a very light raindrop, you know.* After we hang up, I feel like I actually met someone new.

SWEET. WHERE ARE YOU NOW?

I'm looking at the clouds again. I'm calmed by the thought that no matter how much rain and snow lies below me, the sun is always shining up above.

ARE YOU STILL NERVOUS?

I'm relaxed. The film is over and my anger has subsided. I often think I'm lucky to have been born into the life I lead. But maybe that's nonsense. When I close my eyes, I forget how vulnerable I am.

WOULD YOU LIKE TO FORGET WHO YOU ARE?

Why?

WOULD YOU LIKE TO FORGET WHO YOU ARE?

No.

WOULD YOU LIKE TO FORGET ME?

. . . No.

ARE YOU HAPPY?

About what?

ABOUT EVERYTHING TO COME.

. . . Yes. Strangely enough, yes.

It's like a very light raindrop, you know.

It's like a very light raindrop.

It's like rain.

I'll land soon and see new things, meet new people, speak a different language, and spend different money. I get to witness the election, which is likely to be an important historical moment—I have a good feeling.

I'm standing on the train platform with a few people waiting for the train. Four more minutes, my stomach growls.

For a moment, I have too many thoughts. I lose my grip on them. But I won't bend down to retrieve them; I'd rather watch myself in the glass pane of the snack machine. Just briefly, of course. I don't want anyone to think there's something wrong with me.

Suddenly I hear a long-forgotten melody coming from the snack machine.

I quietly begin to hum.
So quietly that no one on the platform can hear me, not even the small mice running between the tracks.

WHERE ARE YOU NOW?

I just landed. No one clapped . . . It looks cold outside.

DO YOU HAVE FOOD WITH YOU?

No.

ARE YOU TRAVELING WITH MORE THAN TEN THOUSAND
DOLLARS?

No.

AT WHICH ADDRESS CAN YOU BE REACHED?

I'm going to decide that spontaneously.

YOU CAN'T PROCEED WITHOUT AN ADDRESS.

Okay.

WHO SHOULD BE CONTACTED IN CASE SOMETHING HAP-
PENS TO YOU?

What's supposed to happen to me?

WHO'S YOUR CONTACT IN CASE OF AN EMERGENCY?

Should some pickup truck run me over tomorrow, my grandmother
would get a dramatic call from the U.S.—she'd get a heart attack
right away, too. So that's not a good option.

Intense heart attacks! Brought to you by: your grandchild!

Instead, I give them Kim's name and number. My grandmother
wouldn't be okay with that and neither would Kim. She hates the
fact that her information doesn't belong to her alone.

SMARTPHONES, FACEBOOK, GOOGLE MAPS—THOSE USED TO
BE THE MEGALOMANIACAL WET DREAMS OF THE STASI.

A sexy, sexy dream come true!

And maybe, I think, Kim hates me, too.

Sorry, miss, we have bad news. We've got your friend here in the hospital.

You were listed as the emergency contact. She's in very critical condition.
Could you please help us find—hello? Miss, are you still there?
But maybe Kim wouldn't just hang up if something happened to me.
Maybe she would pause, think about me, and start to worry. Or she
would pack her bag in a mad rush, leave her apartment, and come
after me. Maybe twenty-eight hours after that dramatic phone call
from the U.S., she'd be sitting by my hospital bed. I'd be lying in a
coma, completely battered from the reckless pickup truck, she'd hold
my hand. Then at some point she'd start to sob, a few tears would
wet my IV line, several empathetic nurses would gather at the door
and pray for me, for us, *Hallelujah*. After Kim had finally calmed
down and her tears had dried, she would stroke my cheeks encrusted
with blood and apologize to me in a whisper, very quietly, without a
sound, her warm breath tickling my ear. She would regret how we
hurt each other. And then finally I would awaken from my coma and
focus my sole remaining eye on her.

DOES IT BOTHER YOU THAT SO FEW MEN CRY IN MOVIES?
What?
ARE YOU RELIGIOUS?
WHICH FAITH DO YOU BELONG TO?
I don't belong to anyone.
WHAT DO YOU BELIEVE IN?
Social relations.
ARE YOU UNWED?
That sounds archaic.
DO YOU LIVE ALONE?
Yes.
WHERE ARE YOUR NEXT OF KIN?
I'm not sure.
ARE YOU VISITING RELATIVES ON THIS TRIP?

No.

WHERE DO YOUR RELATIVES LIVE?

I don't really have family, at least biologically.

The lone wolf, far away from its pack!

I didn't mean it like that.

Out in the open—the adventure begins!

I come from a family that's always unduly romanticized the idea of getting as far away from yourself as possible.

WHAT DOES THAT MEAN?

. . . I come from a family for whom travel was always an unfulfilled longing. But not really in the sense of a lone wolf, rather . . .

GO ON, GO ON.

Picture this:

My mother: a young woman with blue hair and a studded belt, a punk, stuck in East Germany. A young woman who gets involved with an Angolan in a small East German town where everyone knows one another. A young woman who wishes to get away, who longs excessively for her emigration permit to be approved, shortly after "the African" had to return to his country. A young woman who imagines them having a life together in Angola, a life under a different sun, with different mentalities, a life of freedom. But then, at age nineteen, a few months after giving birth to twins: an arrest, her emigration permit is revoked, her psyche crumbled like a cookie in a Stasi prison.

IS THIS A PITCH FOR THE NEXT CLICHÉ-FILLED EAST GER-MAN FILM ON PUBLIC TELEVISION?

The problem with clichés is not that they're not true.

RATHER?

They're often true. The problem is that they only ever describe the same, single perspective.

AND?

Picture this:

My mother: a woman who is raising me and my twin brother as best she can and as if we're to blame for her life, to blame for the reason she never got out of *this damned fucking country*, which is what she used to call East and then West Germany, whether before German reunification or after it—she always had to stay behind. Her man got himself a new family in Angola, since his old one didn't follow him back then. Besides this, always too little money, always alone.

BUT SHE HAD YOU KIDS.

My mother today: a fifty-three-year-old woman who's never been able to get over the many times she was imprisoned, or the violent death of her son. A woman who has herself institutionalized and pronounces me dead. A wounded animal who's been forced into a corner her entire life and bares her teeth.

RABIES?

What?

YOU CAN ALREADY DIE FIFTEEN DAYS AFTER BEING INFECTED.

HAVE YOU BEEN VACCINATED?

Against what?

EVERYTHING THAT COULD BE HARMFUL TO YOU.

This scar, this small, relief-like abrasion on my mother's upper arm, like so many of those who were born in East Germany. It fascinated me as a child. I thought it was a miniature map of a secret, wonderful land.

WEIRD.

DOES THAT MEAN YOU DON'T KEEP IN TOUCH?

She refuses to. The last time I saw her was at the funeral.

IN WHAT INSTITUTION IS SHE NOW?

I don't know.

AND YOUR BROTHER?

What about him?

HOW DID HE LOSE HIS LIFE?

Lost his life. Lost track of his life?

AND YOUR OTHER RELATIVES?

My father writes an email from Angola twice a year. One email always comes a day before our birthday, now it's just my birthday. He can't remember the correct date.

AND YOUR GRANDPARENTS?

My grandfather is dead, cancer, my grandmother is still alive.

WHERE IS SHE NOW?

Probably at home, in front of the television. Or at the doctor.

WHY SO DISMISSIVE?

Picture this:

My grandmother: a loyal supporter of the Socialist Unity Party and a proud mother of two daughters, proud in general and often, because of her good connections (she always got nylon pantyhose and jeans, chocolate from West Germany, and a beach rental on the Baltic), proud because of her pretty blond hair, teased high, proud of her striking beauty, her above-average intelligence, proud of the beauty and intelligence of her daughters. My grandmother: a vain teenager who longs for nothing more than to be a stewardess. To combine business with pleasure. To travel all over the world, to get away, without really being gone. *Because of course, East Germany is great. The GDR is my home, I don't really want to leave.* Become a stewardess, to escape her abusive father. Become a stewardess, to see and to be more than the dumb people in her small town. Become a stewardess, to experience what flying feels like. But then, she never became a stewardess, but became pregnant instead and later on a secretary. At age forty: disabled with back pain, and unemployable ever since.

SO MUCH FAILURE ON YOUR MATERNAL LINE.

Excuse me, is your family A) cursed, B) just very unlucky, C) mentally ill, or D) pretty solid regarding the circumstances?

My grandmother today: a cute, plump woman about age seventy, who has a fear of flying and can't even get on an elevator. A woman who loves the warmth of her heating pad. A woman who still dreams now and then of flying and who can't speak openly with me, her easily irritable granddaughter, certainly not about the other grandchild, the boy, who took his own life.

WHY CAN'T SHE TALK TO YOU ABOUT IT?

IS THERE SOMETHING YOU'RE AFRAID TO DIVULGE?

Nothing.

DID YOU KNOW THAT *DIVULGE* ORIGINALLY DIDN'T JUST MEAN TO MAKE PUBLIC BUT ALSO TO SCATTER ABROAD?

No.

AND DID YOU KNOW THE ROOT WORD OF *DIVULGE* IS *VUL-GAS*, THE SAME ROOT AS FOR *VULGAR*?

No.

DO YOU TRAVEL SO MUCH SO YOU WON'T DIVULGE YOUR SECRETS?

OR ARE YOU AFRAID YOU'LL SAY SOMETHING VULGAR?

All the men in my family are either dead or long gone. And the women left behind are damaged. Each in their own way. But I can travel as often and as far as I want. Even though it was never important to me. Even though I never had to work for it, I was just born in the right place at the right time. I can even think about traveling for vacation. And as I travel, I can think about the self-determined, pleasant experience I'm having, while thousands of other people are forced to travel. People for whom words like *crisis*, *wave*, and *influx* are used.

STOP, STOP, STOP. THAT'S A DIFFERENT TOPIC ALTOGETHER.

CONCENTRATE. TRAVELING IS THE SUBJECT, LONELINESS A
SIDE EFFECT. WHAT ELSE?

Why loneliness?

WHY ARE YOU CHEWING YOUR NAILS?

When we were kids, our mother sometimes went on vacation without us. Once she went to French Guiana and Suriname for two whole months. My grandfather was in the hospital at the time, as a consequence my grandmother's life fell apart. That's why Melanie, a friend of our mother's, looked after us. Sometimes Melanie's partner, a moderate neo-Nazi, was there too. When it was time for dinner, he liked to call my brother and me to the table, loudly: he'd yell through the apartment that us *coffee beans* should finally come to the kitchen. When our mother came back from vacation, for the first time ever her nails weren't chewed off, the cuticles weren't damaged, that's how great her time abroad was.

SO SHE DID TRAVEL AFTER ALL.

WHERE TO EXACTLY?

Afterward she was always sad for days that she had to return to Germany.

AND YOU?

I have more privileges than anyone in my family ever had. And I'm still fucked. I'm hated by more people than my grandmother could ever imagine. So, with this in mind, I try to convince her for twenty minutes not to vote for a right-wing party on election day.

Intense heartaches! Brought to you by: your grandmother!

WHAT ARE YOU DOING NOW?

As I pack a carry-on for my trip to the U.S., I'm having all the feels. Maybe because for just a moment, I can put down the baggage in which my mother, my grandmother, and my brother have stuffed their shadows. Maybe because I'll soon be traveling with a different kind of baggage. I think there's nothing more liberating than being anonymous.

THERE'S NOTHING LONELIER THAN BEING ANONYMOUS.

DO YOU REALLY THINK THAT TRAVEL HAS ANYTHING TO DO WITH FREEDOM?

Maybe. Or maybe the nostalgia I feel ahead of traveling is exactly the same nonsense that my grandmother and my mother bought into.

WHY IS THAT IMPORTANT?

My family?

HERITAGE. WHY IS THAT SO IMPORTANT?

At the end of the day, it's like this: I'm standing on a rooftop terrace in New York, I've had two glasses of wine, and I feel free and grown up. And then at the end of the day I think:

In New York I can walk along Fifth Avenue and eat a banana without any inhibition.

Suddenly my heart starts racing, I swallow a few times and look around the city. No wind, no barking dogs, I'm alone. My face is cool, the lights of the skyscrapers blink in the distance as if they were trying to tell me something via Morse code. *What is it?* I ask out loud, as I feel my heart beating too quickly. *Well, what is it?* For weeks now, this rapid heartbeat, especially at night. I've become accustomed to listening to it obsessively when I go to sleep. Years ago, a doctor said a rapid heartbeat was caused by mental health issues, fear. Fear of what? The skyscrapers won't tell me. I think, *Something is coming my way, I know it,* and I burp quietly.

YOU'RE STANDING IN THE MIDDLE OF A PULSING METROPOLIS AND YOU BURP QUIETLY.

Do people pulsate more intensively in a city of 30 million than in the Thuringian Forest? Do I have more in common with the people of New York than I do with those in the Thuringian Forest? Why do

I feel so good here? At the laundromat, on the street, at the Mexican takeout place. The only place I dare not go to is church. I'm worried people would be able to smell my atheism from miles away upwind.

FROM MILES AWAY UPWIND, GIVE ME A BREAK.

A few years ago, Kim said she saw a graphic that showed I'm from the least religious place in the world.

WHERE IS KIM NOW?

In Berlin.

AND WHY DO YOU FEEL SO GOOD HERE AND NOT WITH HER?

In New York I can walk along Fifth Avenue and eat a banana without any inhibition.

OUTSTANDING!

THE THREEFOLD PROBLEM WITH THE BANANA.

Let me explain:

1. If you're Black eating a banana in public: racist ape analogies, *ooga ooga ooga. Ouch.*

2. If you're East German eating a banana—the banana as a symbol for the inferiority of the beige East in contrast to the golden West. The banana as a bridge to prosperity, an exotic fruit symbolizing economic superiority. *Oh wow, and after the wall fell, the dumb Easterners waited in line for hours for that.*

3. If you're a woman eating a banana—blowjob this and that. The banana becomes an analogy for a penis and a tool of sexism. Insecure, pubescent teenagers traumatize other insecure, pubescent teenagers. *Act out* Deep Throat, *hahaha. Hahaha.*

In New York I can walk along Fifth Avenue and eat a banana without any inhibition.

And after that I realize: That was just a small taste of what others would call freedom. In New York, I stand around on a roof at night and stare nervously and cluelessly at a skyline that I know from films and postcards. And after that I realize: That was just a small taste of what others would call the future. In New York, I think about my brother and miss him a little less than usual. And after that I realize: That could be a good thing.

WHERE ARE YOU NOW?

Back in Berlin.

WHAT ARE YOU DOING?

I'm reorienting myself. I'm falling in love. I delete my online dating profile, work out, drink less alcohol, and sleep better.

REALLY?

No. I'm still in New York.

WHAT ARE YOU EXPERIENCING?

That I belong.

GO ON, GO ON.

That I go jogging and an older Black woman calls after me: *Keep up the good work, baby!* That I carry around this sentence with me for months afterward. That African Americans in the neighborhood greet me and affectionately wish me a nice day. Every day. That because of that my days are actually getting nicer. That African Americans say: *Darling, how are you today?* and it feels like: *Hey, darling, I like you, yeah yeah, and I really hope that you're doing well; let me stroke your cheek.* That I'm smiled at not less than five times a day. That I'm openly liked in public.

IS THAT ALL?

Everything that remains, yeah.

Black men in business suits, Black kids on skateboards, Black homeless seniors who squeeze themselves into the subway—I'm suddenly a part of that. I've never known that.

HM. AND WHAT ABOUT THE POLITICAL SITUATION?

That is the political situation.

. . .

. . .

DID YOU KNOW THAT ONLY 13 PERCENT OF THE ENTIRE
UNITED STATES IS BLACK?

Yeah. So?

DID YOU KNOW THAT ABOUT 40 PERCENT OF THE PRISON
POPULATION IN THE UNITED STATES IS BLACK?

This is amazing!

Excuse me?

DID YOU KNOW THAT OUT OF THE 2.5 MILLION PRISON-
ERS IN THE UNITED STATES, ABOUT 70 PERCENT OF THEM
AREN'T WHITE?

What's the question? Whether I also identify with criminal African
Americans?

DO YOU?

No idea.

HAVE YOU EVER BELONGED TO A CRIMINAL ORGANIZATION?

No.

HAVE YOU EVER BELONGED TO A TERRORIST ORGANIZATION?

No.

DID YOU EVER BELONG TO A GANG?

Yes.

EXCUSE ME?

I had a gang once, in grade school. During recess we would dig small
tunnels in the sandbox and hoped the resulting secret passageway
would lead us to even more secret places and treasures. Once, we
found a giant, mysterious bone and buried it again.

OKAY.

HAVE YOU EVER COMMITTED A CRIME?

No.

NO SHOPLIFTING, OR DRIVING WITHOUT A LICENSE, OR

GRAFFITI?

... Maybe.

Three strikes and you're out!

Excuse me?

If you're arrested three times and are convicted, you can get a life sentence—three strikes law.

For graffiti and stealing lipstick?

SOME STATES IN THE U.S. HAVE STRICTER LAWS.

All good things come in threes!

This is amazing, this is amazing, this is amazing!

THE SLAVE TRADE IS THE MOST SUCCESSFUL BUSINESS MODEL IN THE HISTORY OF HUMANITY. FORCED LABOR IS STILL A BREATHTAKING CONCEPT! TRADING WITH DEHUMANIZED BODIES: CRIMINALIZE, INCARCERATE, EXPLOIT!

I love that idea!

FOR EXAMPLE, I WOULD DISSUADE YOU FROM PURSUING YOUR CRIMINAL INTERESTS IN CALIFORNIA.

I'm in New York, not California.

Hey, young lady!

Hello.

Can you name ten body parts that consist of only three letters?

Excuse me?

Can you name ten body parts that consist of only three letters?

One time, I'm sitting at the laundromat. There's a TV set mounted in the corner, above the customers' heads, a Spanish telenovela is on. It depicts a muscular man breaking out of prison in order to marry his heavily made-up lover. I wait for my laundry, sit amid towering silver machines, beige linoleum, and the smell of fabric softener. An older Black man comes in, sits down next to me on the bench, and asks me the riddle about ten three-letter words for body parts. I give it a try. *Eye, ear, lip, toe . . . ?* In the end, he helps me solve the riddle and laughs with satisfaction.

SO?

Three days later I run into him again on the street. He looks battered.

SOMETHING CRIMINAL HAPPEN?

He beams at me, hugs me, and wishes me all the best. A harmless, warmhearted craziness flows out of him.

WOULD YOU HAVE LIKED TO HAVE A MAN LIKE THAT FOR A GRANDFATHER?

Why?

WHY ARE YOU TALKING ABOUT HIM?

WHAT'S YOUR POINT?

. . .

. . .

One time, for a whole hour, I look in vain for a copy shop and nearly fall into despair, because I have to print and mail something urgently. In a tax preparation office in Bushwick, I meet a young African American man. He offers me help:

I could give you a ride to Staples if you want?

I answer, *If you're not a creep.* He grins. During the car ride we have a nice conversation. He's a film director, overweight and absurdly funny, drives me around all day, to the copy shop, to the post office, to dinner. We get along, laugh together, and even today we still message each other sometimes.

DID YOU SLEEP TOGETHER?

No.

WHY NOT?

. . . One time, I go to an NBA game. Filled with exhilaration from the atmosphere, I let the armada of entertainment roll over me. Five different groups of dancing cheerleaders appear one after the other, with each subsequent appearance I am filled with excitement; loud, shrill sounds play during the entire game. A small zeppelin flies through the stadium and films the audience. On giant screens I can see people waving hysterically at the camera or getting out of their seats to dance in order to look cheerful. As soon as the zeppelin passes them by, they stop and take their seats again. People pass each other snacks constantly: hot dogs, pizza, nachos with cheese, the obligatory giant Coke. Everything is overpriced, tastes cheap and good. The cheering, the roaring, and the unmediated, rousing collective euphoria right before the start of the game is so intense that even I get swept up in it. Suddenly a young woman in a police uniform, a Latina, I think (is it important to mention that?), takes center court and sings the national anthem. When everyone stands up, I stay seated and get goose bumps: the quiet reverence that swiftly fills Madison Square Garden packs quite a punch. Thousands of Americans start singing simultaneously, a feeling like twenty senior proms and ten funerals at once. For a brief moment, all these people belong together. After the game, I can't speak for at least an hour, because I've been bowled over by the power of the event.

WHY ARE YOU BEING SO NEGATIVE? I THOUGHT YOU LIKED NEW YORK.

I do.

HOW LONG IS YOUR VISA GOOD FOR?

Ninety days.

ARE YOU PLANNING ON LEAVING AFTERWARD?

Of course.

YOU GIVE YOUR WORD?

Excuse me?

YOU'RE NOT GOING TO BE AN INDIAN GIVER, ARE YOU?

Do you think Native Americans aren't honest?

These people! With their casinos and their booze.

What?

They really know how to party!

A few years ago, I went dancing with Kim at a club in Kreuzberg: As we're leaving, a white guy, maybe mid-twenties, is standing in line, waiting to get in. He has bloodshot eyes, his shirt is unbuttoned, and he wears a cheap-looking contraption on his head made of plastic and feathers. Kim, who is just as drunk, sees him and marches up to him: *Have you even considered what kind of fucked-up statement you're making with that thing? Why it's problematic to wear a headdress like that? Where do you get off, thinking you can appropriate the culture from a marginalized minority? Do you even realize what kinds of privileges you have as a white cis man? Do you realize what a complete asshole you are?!* Before Kim can push the guy, I slide between them and tell him he should simply think about what he's wearing on his head and that we have to get going. The guy just looks at me and slurs something about not understanding what the problem is: *That chick is Chinese anyway, and Indians don't have anything to do with the Chinese, why is she getting so upset?* In that moment, I would've liked to throw a blanket over his shoulders.

WHAT KIND OF BLANKET?

One that's infested with a virus that I'm immune to. But unfortunately, I didn't have a blanket like that with me. So I pulled Kim away and let myself be berated about my lack of a backbone.

SO KIM IS CHINESE?

No.

BUT?

No but.

IS SHE GERMAN?

Kim was born in Germany and grew up there. She has a Vietnamese passport. Her parents come from a village south of Hanoi.

SO SHE'S NOT GERMAN?

Kim is ridiculously smart, but she's allowed to vote only in local elections in Germany, as long as she refuses to give up her Vietnamese citizenship. "Blood and soil" ideology, even today. At least the U.S. is better about that.

Born in the U.S.A.!

The land of limitless possibilities—that's actually a really uncanny slogan.

Born in the U.S.A.!

Is Germany the land of limited possibilities? Garden fences and bureaucracy versus going from dishwasher to millionaire and then a sweet life in Beverly Hills?

HOW ARE YOU PAYING FOR THIS TRIP TO THE U.S.?

I saved and borrowed some money. My grandmother also gave me some money as a gift.

WHAT DO YOU DO FOR WORK?

I work part-time at a call center, market research.

BUT WHAT IS YOUR MAIN PROFESSION?

Reflecting about myself and others?

SOUNDS BORING.

It's okay.

AND LONELY.

. . .

TELL ME MORE ABOUT IT.

I actually feel lonely only when I talk to my grandmother on the phone. Her sadness drips through the phone directly into me. And I allow it, because I love her. She's the only person in my family with whom I still have contact. Her monologues are just a list of doctor's visits, sicknesses, and TV shows.

MORE ABOUT THE U.S., I MEAN.

Oh.

DO YOU HAVE ANY INFECTIOUS DISEASES? DO YOU SUFFER FROM A PHYSICAL OR MENTAL ILLNESS?

Not that I know of.

DO YOU TAKE ANY DRUGS? ARE YOU ADDICTED TO DRUGS?

No.

WHY ARE YOU SO NERVOUS, THEN?

One time I get a panic attack in the U.S., in the middle of Times Square, because it is all just too much. Too much light, too much rushing, too many people, too many tall buildings, too many neon signs; totality hidden in a sheepskin of consumption and glamour. My heart is beating frantically, my legs are made of jelly, as I lean against the side of a building.

While I breathe intently, I notice a group of Latinos (is that important to mention?). They are wearing colorful outfits of famous film characters and posing on the sidewalk with passersby for money. Mickey Mouse stands next to Spider-Man, some white Disney princess stands next to the Hulk. I notice how a young man wearing an Elmo costume takes off the head, sticks it under his arm, hastily smokes a cigarette and stares at his phone. Maybe it's his break, maybe he's dealing with problems. He doesn't even glance at the kids who sneak past him.

THAT'S FUNNY. GO ON, GO ON!

One time, I'm sitting at the Comedy Cellar. I laugh myself to tears during some stand-up acts, and finally understand the magnitude of German humorlessness. What does it say about a country if it predominantly thinks slimey losers like Mario Barth are funny? What

I like best is the performance of a white comic who pretends to visit a water park with an imaginary child from the "Third World." She tells the thirsty child that people in the "First World" only use water to watch how it sputters out of fountains, apparently because people think it's so beautiful. But they don't use water for drinking. Then she shows the child a wishing well: *This is where people throw money, because they have too much of it and so they make a wish. And you know what they don't wish for?*

. . . No.

Water!

THAT'S FUNNY TOO. GO ON!

Since I arrived in New York, I've been texting with three people on a dating app. At some point the woman ghosts me. Once again, I have the feeling that I don't understand the rules of online dating. One of the two guys is interesting; we eventually plan to meet up. Two hours before the date, we both cancel; he won't have time until later and I'm already tired now. The next morning, he texts that he hurt his shoulder during a move, *Sorry, maybe another time, take care!* A little later, I travel through Manhattan, and in a pleasant way I lose track of where I am. At some point, a man sits down across from me. He looks similar to the guy from the dating app. We look at each other fleetingly; we find each other attractive. Finally, I think: *Why not?* I get up, go over to him, and with my phone I show him the dating profile from the guy who wrote *Sorry, maybe another time, take care!* I say: *Are you this guy?* His eyes grow wide. Then he nods, we stare at each other. He says: *I never met anyone I know in the subway before, this is crazy!* We laugh and talk for about five stops, then decide that we'll definitely meet up on Saturday, *Wow, what a coincidence!* We hug goodbye, feeling enthusiastic and emotional from the improbability of our encounter. After he gets off the train, beautiful feelings well up inside me; rom-com meets real life. On Saturday neither of us gets in touch with the other, we never see each other again.

WHY NOT?

A week later, I have tentative plans with another man to meet in the bookstore of the French embassy, there's supposed to be an exciting event there, *Feel free to drop by if you can. It'll be truly thought-provoking!*

At the entrance: a security check like at the airport. I walk up the stairs of the embassy and suddenly I'm standing in a room full of Black artists, writers, curators, publishers, and journalists. Everyone is extremely well educated, eloquent, laid-back, their presentations and panel discussions inspire me. *Black excellence at its best*, I later read in an article. *In Germany*, I think, *only white excellence shines— engineers, chemical companies, the auto industry, this and that. And Turks make kebabs.*

EXCUSE ME?

I mean, in the minds of most white people.

WHERE ARE YOU NOW?

No idea, back in Berlin?

May I see your passport, please?

I speak German.

Ach so.

The border police briefly nod at me as I walk past passport control. In Germany, no one says *Welcome back.*

WHAT ARE YOU DOING IN BERLIN?

Sorting myself out, falling in love. I deactivate my dating profile, work out, drink less alcohol, and sleep easier.

ARE YOU TELLING THE TRUTH THIS TIME?

I'm back, but not in spirit; everything went by too quickly. Or I'm back, but I feel different than before. Something is missing suddenly.

SOMETHING IS ALWAYS MISSING.

Three days after I get back, I call Kim. Over the phone, her voice sounds suspiciously normal. She's talking to me as if she had expected me to call; as if we hadn't ignored each other for an entire year. I can't tell if she's still hurt.

FROM WHAT?

Hello. I just wanted to check in.
    Hi.
You answered the phone really quickly.
    How are you?
I'm okay. You?
    Good. What are you up to?
I don't know. I'm just hanging around. You know, jet lag.
    Were you gone long?
Yeah, in the U.S. But I didn't really experience much.
Do you want to meet up?
    . . . Seriously?
Like tonight. I can also come to you.
    I've already got plans tonight.
Oh.
    It's a going-away party. But you could come along for a drink.
Wouldn't that be weird for the others and who is it for anyway?
    My girlfriend's sister.
Oh, okay.
Where's she going?
    My girlfriend's sister?
Yes.
    New Zealand.
To study?

Ask her yourself.
But when will you be there?
Nine.
Cool, then I'll come by at ten. If it's really okay. For your girlfriend too?
No big deal. I'll just tell her I only know you fleetingly. From a Tinder date.
Okay.
That was a joke.
. . .
They all know who you are; you probably know at least half of them.
Uh, sure. See you then.
You haven't even asked me where it is.
Well, where are you meeting?
At that bar the Blue Drum.
That's so far away.
Are you afraid of going now or something?
No. Well, see you then.
See you.

YOU TWO WERE SO CUTE BACK THEN.
What?
DURING YOUR VACATION TO MOROCCO, FOR INSTANCE,
THREE YEARS AGO.
I change my clothes four times before I leave.
AT FIRST YOU BOTH COULDN'T GET ENOUGH OF THE SIGHTS,
OF THE COLORS.
. . . Yeah.
WASHED-OUT TURQUOISE PAINTED ON THE WALLS OF
HOUSES, A WARM ROSÉ-AND-APRICOT SKY, THE CLEAR LIGHT
BLUE OF THE SEA, GOLDEN YELLOW AND TURQUOISE FABRICS

AT THE MARKETPLACE, BEIGE-RED CARPETS. AND IN THE
DISTANCE AN ETERNAL RED OCHER.

One time, while we are sitting down to eat and I look across the city,
I think: *If you're from here and you go to Germany, it must seem like a
hospital. Kim,* I say, *Germany is like a hospital, but as a country.* Kim
grins at me, astonished, with oil on her lips and a small silver fish
between her fingers.

SWEET.

WHY WOULD KIM STILL BE HURT?

I decide to wear white sneakers, black jeans, and a baggy gray sweater
with lipstick. My outfit says: *I'm easygoing, casual but not indifferent, I
gave this a little thought.*

YOU'RE NERVOUS.

We once witnessed a beautiful, wordless dialogue in Essaouira: A
wrinkled little man is standing at his stall in the marketplace. Two
white Americans come by, the thin old man nods at them. Then he
smiles and reveals blood-red teeth that perplex the Americans. He
waves them over with his hand, they go try some of the fruit he's
selling. Suddenly the Americans have blood-red teeth too and smile
enthusiastically—first at each other, then at the old man.

WHAT DO THE WRINKLED OLD MAN'S RED TEETH HAVE TO
DO WITH KIM AND YOUR COMING BACK TO BERLIN FROM
THE U.S.?

Morocco, the warmth, the two of us there together. We'll never
get back to that place. On the way to the bar, I press the palms of
my hands against the spot where I suspect is my troubled heart.
When I enter, I feel as if my body is walking right into something
dangerous.

IS KIM PRONE TO VIOLENCE?

No.

WHAT ABOUT HER SOCIAL CIRCLE—DOES SHE SURROUND HERSELF WITH DUBIOUS PEOPLE?
Nonsense.

HOW DOES SHE EARN HER MONEY?
She works as a project manager for some e-commerce stuff.

HAS KIM EVER BELONGED TO A TERRORIST ORGANIZATION?
No.

WAS SHE EVER A PART OF A CRIMINAL ORGANIZATION?
No.

DOES KIM HAVE ANY INFECTIOUS DISEASES? DOES SHE SUFFER FROM PHYSICAL OR MENTAL ILLNESS?
No.

WHAT TIME DID YOU GET TO THE BAR?
Maybe around ten thirty.

P.M.?
Approximately.

WHAT WERE YOUR INTENTIONS WHEN YOU ENTERED THE BAR?
I wanted to meet Kim.

WHAT WERE YOUR INTENTIONS WHEN YOU ENTERED THE BAR?
I wanted to be near Kim.

WHICH DETAIL ARE YOU LEAVING OUT NOW?
. . . Nothing.

WHAT DOES KIM DREAM ABOUT?
No idea.

WHAT IS SHE AFRAID OF?
Snakes and pigeons.

WHAT DOES SHE BELIEVE IN?
Justice?
I used to call her "my peace dove."

AND TODAY?

Today I think of Kim with the same feelings I have when I think of my brother.

OKAY . . . GO ON.

Picture this:

It's the beginning of the nineties, two Black kids are standing alone on a street corner of some small East German town.

My brother and I are six years old and we accidentally lock ourselves out of the house. He wants to show me something in the yard, we're home alone. So we each slip on a pair of our mother's shoes and run outside; the door shuts behind us immediately. After a few failed attempts to open it, we leave.

WHERE TO?

We don't know where our mother is during the day, or night, but our grandparents are always in the same place. So we approach a few strangers and ask them for some change. We're wearing white tennis socks that fill out two thirds of our mother's dark pumps. No one seems to wonder about that. When we've collected enough change, we call our grandparents' home from a phone booth. Their number is the only one that has ever changed since our childhood and the only one we know by heart. After twenty minutes, our grandfather drives up in his Honda. Without a word, he takes us to the new housing development, and to hot chocolate and Vienna sausages with ketchup.

WHERE EXACTLY WAS THIS NEW HOUSING DEVELOPMENT?

At the edge of town.

OF WHICH CITY?

. . . Sometimes when I think about Kim and me, a few years back—for example, in Morocco—then it's no longer my brother wearing my mother's high heels, but Kim. Together the two of us leave the telephone booth and walk to the beach. It's a hot day, no Honda is coming, no one is there but us. Slowly and quietly, we wade into the ocean, wearing giant pumps. Our shoes get heavier and heavier, we walk arm in arm, each of us holding a Vienna sausage in our free hand.

HAVE YOU BEEN DRINKING?

Yes.

HOW MUCH?

Not enough. Around four a.m., Kim and I are nearly alone in the bar. Most of the people have already left, including Kim's girlfriend. When they kissed each other goodbye, I had to look away. Now my glass is empty, so I order another gin and tonic and take a sip from Kim's beer while I wait. Kim waits until I have the bottle in my mouth and the alcohol pours into it. Then she whispers: *I'm sick,* and I have to laugh so hard that I spit beer all over my right arm. Later that evening she says: *It's always so nice when both of us are drunk, right?*

During our relationship, I had the feeling that she was sometimes sad on my behalf, almost as if I outsourced my emotions to her.

OUTSOURCED YOUR EMOTIONS?

And now it's just like that again.

YOU REALLY LIKE TO FLIRT WITH CAPITALISM, DON'T YOU?

DO YOU THINK COMPANIES THAT EXPLOIT PEOPLE ARE SEXY?

Why?

DO YOU GET TURNED ON BY SHELL COMPANY MANAGERS AND ENVIRONMENTAL DESTRUCTION?

Actually, I wanted to apologize to Kim.

Finally!

FOR WHAT?

. . .

THERE ARE SOME THINGS FOR WHICH YOU CAN APOLOGIZE
FOR YEARS AND YOU STILL WILL NEVER RID YOURSELF OF
THE GUILT.

What are you thinking about? Kim asks me suddenly, and I notice that
we haven't spoken in a while.

WHAT ARE YOU THINKING ABOUT?

She takes my hand in hers. With my free hand, I reach for my glass
and take a sip of my gin and tonic. *Can I tell you something funny?* I
nod. But Kim doesn't say anything. She just looks at me quietly; she
was always good at keeping eye contact. Her face slowly comes closer
and she kisses me on the mouth. With open, soft lips, no tongue. *Oh,
come on,* she says, takes my glass and finishes my drink, *we're going to
bed.* I stop myself from asking about her new girlfriend, Kim takes my
jacket off the hook below the bar and throws it over my shoulders. An
hour later, I'm lying in bed and can't sleep. Her back is turned toward
me, she's snoring almost silently, her butt against my hip, just like old
times, my insomnia is stronger than the alcohol.

WHAT ARE YOU THINKING ABOUT?

The boy who got stabbed.

WHICH BOY WHO GOT STABBED?

On our way home. But I don't want to think about that now.

WHAT HAPPENED?

. . .

WHAT KIND OF AN INCIDENT WAS THAT?

I would rather think about something else.

AND AT WHAT TIME DID THE INCIDENT OCCUR?

Something nicer.

DO YOU BELIEVE THINKING ABOUT SOMETHING NICE WILL
HELP CREATE NICE FEELINGS? DO YOU THINK YOUR HEART
AND YOUR HEAD WORK LIKE THAT?

Beauteeful feelings. My father always had difficulty pronouncing words with a short *i*. If he wanted to say: *You are twins*, then he would always say: *You are tweens*. At least that's what my grandmother told me.

CONCENTRATE. A BOY WAS STABBED.

PLEASE DESCRIBE THE CIRCUMSTANCES OF THE CRIME.

There are many days in a month that I don't think about my dad. I think about my mother several times a week. I always think about my brother. I don't think there's anyone who thinks about me every day.

WAS YOUR BROTHER STABBED?

No.

YOUR MOTHER?

She would never let that happen.

WHERE IS SHE NOW?

Unfortunately, I don't know for sure.

WHERE ARE YOU NOW?

On top of the Berlin TV Tower.

EXCUSE ME?

. . .

WHAT ARE YOU DOING THERE?

Drinking prosecco, looking down. The entry fee alone cost more than twenty euros.

WHAT ARE YOU DOING THERE?

It feels nice to slowly, half-drunkenly circle the city at this height.

WHERE'S KIM?

I haven't seen her since that night in the bar.

WHAT HAPPENED?

Nothing.

WHICH DETAIL ARE YOU LEAVING OUT NOW?

. . .

DID YOU TWO FIGHT?

No.

DID YOU HURT SOMEONE?

No.

DID YOU HURT KIM?

No.

WERE YOU AND KIM VICTIMS OF A CRIME?

No. At least not that night.

WHAT HAPPENED WITH THE BOY?

Two years ago, refugees occupied the TV Tower. They were protesting for their rights. I wonder how they managed that. I don't mean how they got up here, but how they stayed. In general, to want to stay in this country. Back then, my father left willingly, shortly after our birth. Even though his residence permit lasted a few more weeks.

LEFT FOR ANGOLA?

Yes.

THERE WAS A CIVIL WAR THERE AT THE END OF THE 1980S.

. . . That's what my mother told us.

AND YOU BELIEVE HER?

. . .

ARE YOU PLANNING ON OCCUPYING THE TV TOWER?

I don't think so.

ARE YOU PLANNING ANY OTHER UNLAWFUL DEEDS?

No.

IS KIM PLANNING ANY OTHER UNLAWFUL DEEDS?

Definitely not.

WHERE IS SHE NOW?

At work.

AND THE BOY WHO GOT STABBED?

Hopefully, he's still alive.

GO ON, GO ON.

. . . After Kim and I left the bar that evening, on our way home we came across the end of a knife fight. There we are, walking arm in arm, Kim's humming a melody. Then suddenly a boy runs into me from the side. Loud, incomprehensible shouting all around, a lot of people storming off in all directions. The boy who ran into me collapses to the ground. I let go of Kim and see that he has dark spots on his shirt. I take him into my arms to help him up, Kim is suddenly gone. She later tells me that the blood made her nauseated. I'm standing there, holding the unfamiliar boy, who's clutching his side. He can't stand up, so he sits down on the ground. His incensed friends are still running around aimlessly, talking on their phones with loud, hoarse voices, hysteria, testosterone, blackout, a disoriented swarm. They use their cell phones to call up more angry friends, so I use my free hand to call an ambulance myself while I crouch behind the boy. He leans his back against my knee. I can't think, my free hand on his shoulder. Suddenly one of the boys breaks away from the group, runs toward us, and yells: *Bro, show us your wound!*

With his left hand, he pushes up the injured boy's wet T-shirt. I keep holding the boy, while his friend takes a picture of the wound spitting out blood. Then the friend gets up, runs off, and yells something. The boy's body close to mine, he starts to whimper and press his hands against the wound, almost as if it became real to him only through the act of being photographed. I hold on to the boy until the paramedics come, until the police come. I hold on to the boy, as the police line his friends up with their faces to the wall:

Your friend's not going to die. He has two lungs, after all. Now be quiet, goddammit.

I hold him while the paramedics can't find the right bandages and curse under their breath. While a crowd gathers, staring at the boys, up against the wall, as they're being searched. While Kim is somewhere around the corner sitting on some steps with her eyes closed. I hold the boy the entire time, *But maybe*, I think now, *I've only been holding on to him for dear life.*

AND? WHAT'S THE OUTLOOK?

From the TV Tower?

FOR THE BOY. THE PROGNOSIS.

I don't know. After he's put in the ambulance, I go to find Kim.

IS THAT ALL?

What?

IS THAT EVERYTHING YOU DID?

The sun breaks through the clouds time and again; enamored couples look each other in the eyes, while they eat mini croissants, in love with Berlin. Dots build a circular pattern on the gray-brown carpet. Cheap lox with horseradish, overpriced champagne, muffled steps; up here it's almost like being in an airplane, almost like flying, but slower, with more room and without a destination.

HAVE YOU BEEN TO THAT RESTAURANT BEFORE?

No.

IS THE TOWER A MEETING PLACE FOR YOU AND KIM?

No.

DOES THE TOWER HAVE ANYTHING TO DO WITH THE BOY?

No one here is interested in me, but I can quietly take interest in everything. The waiters seem to be from East Berlin. As soon as I speak German: honest friendliness. When I allow a little of my Thuringian accent to come out: love.

Zee familiarity petveen us, it's . . . it's zimbly, vell, yu notice it, right, zat it's a different kind.

It feels good to look over the city from this high up. Flocks of birds fly by again and again. It's odd to look down on them.

DOESN'T THE STORY WITH THE BOY AFFECT YOU AT ALL?
As a waiter cleans up my 360 Degree Celebration breakfast, it occurs to me that I've been here before. In the early nineties, with my mother and my brother.
SO IT DOESN'T. WHY?
I think the interior looked exactly the same back then. Maybe there were already these chrome pedestals attached to the tables with digital numbers that lit up. Maybe back then we also sat at number eight: my mother is having a loud argument with a waitress, because she ordered the vegetarian lunch, but the cook, either out of generosity and/or out of ignorance, poured a hefty portion of meat gravy over the potatoes and the vegetables. The waitress and my mother are having a loud discussion about whether or not the food is still vegetarian. My mother says no, the waitress says yes; my brother and I are grinning at each other bashfully, sitting on comfortable, eggplant-colored leather chairs that don't creak. That was the first time I ever thought that other people also had a difficult time understanding my mother.
IN GERMANY IN 1998, AROUND 3 PERCENT OF THE POPULATION WERE VEGETARIANS. TODAY IT'S ABOUT 10 PERCENT.
Says who?
HOW DO YOU EXPLAIN THIS STRIKING INCREASE IN VEGETARIANS IN THE LAST TWENTY YEARS?
There's more education about the conditions of mass livestock farming?
ARE YOU A VEGETARIAN?
Sometimes.
SO YOU'RE A FLEXITARIAN. AND KIM?
Kim loves meat. When she cooks, there always has to be at least three different things served on the plate. Meat, vegetables, and a

third item. When there are only two things, as a matter of principle it doesn't taste good to her. And she's rather proud that she can cook so many Vietnamese dishes.

IF SOMEONE GETS STABBED, SHE LEAVES BECAUSE SHE CAN'T SEE ANY BLOOD. BUT SHE HAS NO PROBLEM CUTTING UP DEAD ANIMALS TO COOK AND EAT THEM?

At the time, my grandmother considered my mother's vegetarianism as evidence that there was something wrong with her. It was important to her to secretly shower my brother and me with Vienna sausages when we came to visit on the weekends. On the one hand, from her perspective, it was an attempt to prevent us from succumbing to the constant threat of malnutrition. On the other hand, it was an act of rebellion.

AGAINST WHAT?

Even today, my grandmother says that we all suffered a lot in Susanne's presence. But she says it increasingly less. I think she's slowly made peace with the fact that she's lost her daughter; that her daughter has turned away from her, from me, from everything related to her family and her past.

Excuse me, is your family A) dead, B) just very far away, C) invisible, or D) looking really pretty in these old pictures?

On holidays, when my friends go see their families or are visited by them, I sometimes walk around the city, look at my reflection in the windows of closed stores, and pretend I'm the only survivor of a zombie apocalypse.

WHY DID YOU SNEAK OUT OF YOUR APARTMENT SO EARLY THE OTHER DAY?

I'm not talking about that right now. I'm in a tower, looking down onto the city. I ate lox and drank champagne. The apocalypse can come; I'll have the best view of it from up here.

WHY DID YOU SNEAK OUT OF YOUR APARTMENT SO EARLY THE OTHER DAY? ON THE MORNING AFTER THE KNIFE FIGHT?

My grandmother has a terrible fear of elevators; under no circumstances could she ever make it up here, not even if her life depended on it.

Nobe, vild horzes couldn't drag me in zere, not for mein life.

Sometimes I think, *Maybe she's just afraid of anything that she can't control and anything unfamiliar to her, like Berlin, for example.* When we talk on the phone, from time to time she begs me not to leave the house after dark.

WHY DID YOU LEAVE THE HOUSE TWO WEEKS AGO AT SEVEN THIRTY IN THE MORNING *EVEN THOUGH* IT WAS STILL DARK?

. . .

WHY DID YOU SIT DOWN AT THE BAKERY ACROSS THE STREET, DRINK BITTER TEA, SMOKE FIVE CIGARETTES, AND SPY ON THE ENTRANCE TO YOUR APARTMENT BUILDING FOR TWO HOURS?

I was waiting for her to leave.

WHO?

Kim. After the night in the bar. I didn't want to see her wake up in my bed.

WHAT ELSE?

What?

WHAT ELSE ARE YOU STILL WAITING FOR?

. . . For someone to come visit me? Like a family member.

WHAT ELSE?

I'm waiting for myself to stop waiting.

HOW DO YOU MEAN?

The last time I visited my grandmother, after a few minutes a friend of hers came by unexpectedly: Rudi, an older gentleman who sometimes helps out with household repairs since my grandfather's death. When Rudi comes inside, he looks at me astonished. Then he starts laughing and blurts out in an all-encompassing Thuringian accent:

Nein! I don't pelieffe it. Arh! I zaw yu valking around hearlier, houtzide, vile I vas barking mein auto und I zought to myzelf . . . Put zat yu're Rita's granddaughter und not ein azylum zeeker, man, whaht luck!

Maybe I'm waiting for the day that my grandmother will finally realize what it's like to be me in the city she lives in. How much it takes for me to endure being in this place. If I told her about the school in Kreuzberg that refugees occupied a few years ago, if I told her about the desperate man who stood on the roof of the school and threatened to jump to his death if they were kicked out, because he'd rather die than be deported, if I told my grandmother about the white policeman who stood across from him on the roof and beckoned to this suicidal man, first with a banana and then with handcuffs, how would she respond? If I asked my grandma Rita whether she can see parallels between the hatred my father faced in the GDR—even from her friends and colleagues—and the hatred my brother and I faced from classmates, parents, and everyone who was generally a fan of Hitler's, if I asked her, if she could see the parallels between the hatred that Black people face in the U.S. systematically and the hatred that refugees face permanently, worldwide, what would she say?

Yeah, you're right. Thanks for these eye-opening reflections! From now on, I'm a completely different person and Rudi's opinions suddenly have nothing to do with my own, super-leftist, super-nice convictions anymore.

Cool!

How is she supposed to react if I ask her whether she could imagine that of course at first sight I have nothing to do with African Americans executed by white policemen or with refugees on some roof in Kreuzberg, but that at the end of the day, in my everyday life, I share more with these people than with her, my grandmother. Namely the fact that I am subjected to the same gaze that perceives us, if I can even speak of an "us," as the same, as marked in the same way, marked as the non-white one, as the Other, as evidence of the notion of race and difference?

THAT WHITE PEOPLE THINK THEY ARE WHITE AND BLACK PEOPLE THINK THEY ARE BLACK.

What?

THAT WHITE PEOPLE THINK THEY ARE WHITE AND BLACK PEOPLE THINK THEY ARE BLACK.

Yeah . . . exactly.

AS LONG AS YOU BELIEVE IN THESE CONSTRUCTS AND SUB-MIT TO THEM, YOU ONLY STRENGTHEN THEM FURTHER.

But they are more than just constructs. Those ideas are hundreds of years old; they are so effective, so all-encompassing—

RELAX. HAVE A DRINK FIRST.

Would you like another glass of chilled champagne?

How is my grandmother supposed to respond to the question of whether she knows what it means to know of no place where you are the norm?

YOU'RE SITTING IN A MEDIOCRE RESTAURANT WITH AN UNCONVENTIONAL ROTATING MECHANISM AND A SPEC-TACULAR VIEW. YOU CAN AFFORD THE ENTRY FEE, YOU CAN AFFORD THE FOOD, YOU CAN AFFORD YOUR LITTLE STUDIO APARTMENT IN A HIP PART OF BERLIN, CLOTHES, A VACA-TION WHEN YOU WANT, A HAIRCUT, THEATER TICKETS, LANGUAGE COURSES, THIS AND THAT. HOW MUCH MORE OF A NORM DO YOU NEED?

. . .

SO.

LET'S GET BACK TO KIM.

There is no going back.

WHY NOT?

. . .

DO YOU WANT TO GO BACK TO HER?

While I was sitting in a bakery the other day, I finally admitted that it's affected me. It was already complicated before. Since I screwed up a year ago, something has been missing, but now . . . Since then there's been too little trust.

WHAT HAPPENED?

WHAT DID YOU DO A YEAR AGO?

. . .

WHAT DID YOU DO?

Kim's birthday . . .

GO ON, GO ON.

Around midnight we were singing and drinking a toast to her— candlelight, chocolate cake, lots of friends, light-headed, flushed cheeks, a room filled with smoke.

Shortly after midnight I go to the bathroom with some guy. I sit up on the washing machine, pull down my pants and underwear, let him eat me out. All our friends could tell that we'd locked ourselves in the bathroom. Kim kicks against the door until it springs open. Then she just looks at me. Everyone just looks at me. Kim takes her coat and leaves her own party. I stay behind, drink even more, and spin around on the dance floor until I collapse.

WHY DID YOU DO THAT?

After the incident, Kim approached my mother about me. She wrote her an email and bcc'd me. I don't know if she did it out of revenge or because she was seriously worried about me.

WHAT DID THE EMAIL SAY?
I can't forgive her for that.
WHAT DID THE EMAIL SAY?
. . . That I'm self-destructing, stuff like that.
SELF-DESTRUCTING?
That Kim apparently wonders whether my destructive behavior is likely a result of her parenting. Or lack of parenting. That my mother should maybe give me a call, so that I don't end up like her other child.
AND?
My mother didn't respond.
The intense pain of rejection! Brought to you by: your mother.
I don't know if Kim took into account that even after all these years, my mother would still never be approachable. I don't know if Kim just wanted to mess with me. Maybe she really wanted to ask my mother for help.
HOW WOULD SHE HAVE HELPED YOU?
The last time she slept over at my place, I lay awake in bed all night. But not because of the wound between the boy's ribs; rather, because of the things she said to me.
YOUR MOTHER?
Kim. Maybe that night we would have slept together again, maybe we would have tried to start over. If it hadn't been for the knife fight.
NO ONE CAN START OVER.
WHEN DID YOU LAST SEE YOUR MOTHER?
Later in bed, after we had both calmed down, Kim told me that she'd always be there for me and would always love me. But that my life is too consumed with myself and my past. And she doesn't have a chance against those two.
I just don't have a chance against those two, you know.

What does that mean?

YES, WHAT DOES THAT MEAN?

That we should stop trying to get close to each other. Or rather, that we shouldn't start getting close again.

But don't get me wrong. I'd like to do something with you now and then, sober, in a public setting. But this, here, can't happen anymore.

DO SOMETHING SOBER, IN A PUBLIC SETTING.

FOR EXAMPLE?

Go to the theater. In a couple of months there's a play about the time before and after reunification. Would you be interested in that?

Hm, maybe. I dunno.

WHAT'S UP WITH YOUR EYES?

. . .

WHAT ARE YOU THINKING ABOUT?

From up here, as I'm looking out from the restaurant, it's easy to imagine how the entire city could be bombed. It relaxes me to imagine that. But not the clean-cut white couple at the next table, who have clearly come from the civil registry office beaming with joy. If I were to commit an act of terror up here, those two would be my first targets.

AN ACT OF TERROR?

I don't really mean that.

IS IT SAFE TO SAY THAT?

It's never safe.

In my case, it's more likely I'll get beaten to a pulp by three Nazis while walking along a lake in Brandenburg than become the victim of an Islamic terror attack in New York or Berlin, on the subway or in a cozy restaurant turning in circles.

OR BECOME A PERPETRATOR.

DO YOU OFTEN HAVE FANTASIES LIKE THAT?

Yes.

WHAT DO YOU DO ABOUT THEM?

Why should I do something about them?

DO YOU PLAY ANY SPORTS? DO YOU GO OUT INTO NATURE?
DO YOU GO CLIMBING OR JOGGING?

In Brandenburg?

HAVE YOU ACTUALLY EVER BEEN BEATEN TO A PULP BY
THREE NAZIS?

When I was seventeen I kept wishing it would happen, finally. The
fear of some realities can be worse than the realities themselves.
My brother had a baseball bat for protection from the age of fifteen.

SO IS THAT A NO?

Yes.

HOW OFTEN WAS YOUR BROTHER INVOLVED IN VIOLENT
ALTERCATIONS?

I'm still waiting for him to come back. For him to continue his life
where it stopped. I'm still waiting for this feeling to finally go away.

AND YOUR FATHER?

What about him?

DON'T YOU THINK HE'S STILL WAITING FOR YOU TO COME
BACK? FOR YOU TO CONTINUE YOUR LIFE FROM WHERE IT
STOPPED FOR HIM?

Why should that be important?

WHEN WAS THE LAST TIME YOU TWO HAD CONTACT?

That was in Morocco.

When I was there three years ago with Kim, we once took a taxi
from Sidi Kaouki to Essaouira, to the fish market. On the radio, a
Berber is singing a tune in a warm, husky voice. The taxi driver asks
where I am from. While I answer, I notice that, in contrast to when
I was in Germany, here I have become accustomed to mentioning

my Angolan father first and then my German mother. My African father is worth more in Morocco.

OKAY.

Kim doesn't say anything about it. But I'm sure she's noticed. Later on, there is a misunderstanding in the taxi. The driver refers me to a hotel where a lot of "sub-Saharan Africans" work. He suggests I could submit my résumé there if I wanted. *Do you know what a résumé is? It's a piece of paper where you itemize your life.* I say, *Yes, I know, but no no, I just meant: I can also work "from here," not: I can also work here.* The taxi driver seems disappointed. For a minute, I imagine what my daily life would be working as a housekeeper in a Moroccan hotel, with a small white bonnet on my head, bent over, groaning or humming . . . A different life, just a few kilometers away. Later that day, I write my father a message on Facebook. It's impulsive, the first message after years of sparse contact. *I just want to tell you that I'm in Africa and if you want, we can try to meet halfway between here and there.* After I send the message, I put the route into Google Maps. Each of us would need two days to travel to the midpoint of the distance between us, somewhere in the desert. The travel costs exceed my monthly income significantly.

WOULD YOU LIKE TO EMIGRATE TO MOROCCO?

No, why?

OR TO NEW YORK?

YOU REALLY LIKED BEING THERE.

Is everything all right?

What?

Would you still like to order dessert?

A boyish white waiter with an overbite scrutinizes me expressionlessly. I respond, *Would you like me to leave, so that the next affluent tourists can be serviced here every hour?* The waiter looks at me, shocked. And immediately I feel bad. I turn away and look out the window again, blushing dark red while the waiter and I keep turning without a sound.

SWEET.

Back then, when I was here with my mother and my brother, we fought about dessert. I ordered pudding, my brother cake. I wanted to trade, he didn't; my mother stayed out of it. Eventually I cried because I couldn't have my way.

HOW DID YOUR BROTHER DIE?

Why do people always want to know that?

WHERE IS HE NOW?

. . .

WHERE ARE YOU NOW?

. . .

WHERE ARE YOU NOW?

I close my eyes.

I take a deep breath.

I'm standing on the train platform of some small town, there's a snack machine behind me.

I open my eyes, blink, and look around.

Everyone is gone, I'm alone on the platform.

... No

NO WHAT?

I'm not here. I'm somewhere else.

WHERE?

Maybe Kim was right in that email she wrote my mother. Maybe there is really something wrong with me.

WHAT GIVES YOU THAT IDEA ALL OF A SUDDEN?

Kim had to leave earlier than me.

LEAVE MOROCCO?

Yes.

WHERE TO?

Hanoi. She wanted to check on her sick uncle and his paper factory. After she left, I sat on the beach all day long with pathetic thoughts and tried, without success, to distinguish the uniqueness of every wave with my naked eye.

WHY DO YOU CHEW YOUR NAILS?

This quiet, this powerful whirring, which is actually not a whirring at all, but a sound that I don't even have words for. It would be nice, to one day sit on the beach and die, and then be carried away by the waves, dissolve and become sea foam.

ARE YOU BECOMING SUICIDAL NOW?

No.

AND WITH A PEACEFUL SMILE THE TEST PATTERN OF THE EARTH TURNS INTO A QUIET WHIRRING.

Excuse me?

WHAT'S WRONG WITH KIM'S UNCLE?

He has lung cancer.

WHY DIDN'T YOU GO WITH HER?

. . .

WHY AREN'T YOU WITH HER?

I just needed a vacation.

YOU COULD'VE HAD THAT IN VIETNAM.

Kim can get by on her own. She's been to Hanoi a lot, speaks fluent Vietnamese. I would've just been a burden, Vietnam is her second home.

AND WHAT'S YOUR SECOND HOME?

. . . Myself?

COOL.

Yes.

Back then in Morocco, a few days after Kim left, I sat on the beach for a long time. At some point a man comes by, *I'm Hafik, hi, how are you?* He sits down next to me and tells me he is a fisherman. We hang around calmly and watch the ocean. Hafik has a gentle, pleasant manner. Eventually he offers me a mandarin. The fruit is still hanging on a branch with leaves. Hafik tells me about fish and fishing, about different techniques and animals, which taste the best and which squid are the healthiest, that alcohol will make you sick and he never drinks any. I offer him some of my water. He takes a tiny sip and thanks me profusely. He offers to take me out on the open sea, *inshallah,* and, naturally, only if I want to. Then he tells me about his other job, the one he does during peak season. He massages Spanish tourists at the beach using oils from the region. I ask him which job he likes better. He looks at me, irritated. When I get ready to ask him again, I realize what that question says about me. Hafik adds that he also has a horse. *If you want, you can ride it along the beach without cost.*

I gracefully decline and say: *I prefer to walk on my own two feet.* I think, *He's actually pretty good-looking, this small, wiry man,* and I guess he's about thirty-five. When he tells me he's twenty, I'm astounded. In the evening, he always walks home, beyond the mountains, eight miles away, that's where he lives, he says, smiling.

A few days later I go walking and at some point sit down in the sand. When I look between my ankles, I see mandarin peels. I sat down in the exact same spot.

AND ALL LIFE LEAVES THE DACHA.

What?

HAS YOUR GRANDMOTHER EVER BEEN TO FRANCE?

What does that have to do with Morocco?

HAS SHE EVER ONCE IN HER LIFE LEFT EUROPE?

I don't think so.

AND ALL LIFE LEAVES THE GARDEN COLONY.

Which life?

THE LIFE OF YOUR GRANDMOTHER, THE ONE IN THURINGIA.

BUT MAYBE SHE'LL MAKE IT.

Make what?

Bonsoir!

. . . Hello.

Quel honneur!

The night after Kim left, I went to the French restaurant where Kim and I had eaten: Without greeting me first, the owner calls out: *Hier, j'ai fait une bêtise!* And says he forgot to charge us for a bottle of wine. I gladly pay and he takes me to a spot at the last available table, the same table where we sat a few days ago. I order the same fish.

YOU SAT IN THE SAME SPOT.

Yes.

YOUR GRANDMOTHER ALWAYS SAT IN THE SAME SPOT, ALL HER LIFE.

Two guys, white men, come inside and look around, searching, but there are no seats available. I wave them over to me. I say, *Vous pouvez vous asseoir ici, c'est libre.*

They say *merci* and sit down. They speak Swiss German and "standard German," as they call it. After ten minutes, I reveal myself to be a "standard German" too. We have a friendly conversation. After an hour we realize that one of them, Jon, has relatives in my hometown. After an hour and a half we're astonished to find out that his uncle was my mother's best friend, before the reunification, when they were punks unsettling their East German province.

Quelle coïncidence!

What a coincidence!

These days, Jon's uncle is a pastor and my mother has disappeared.

YOUR MOTHER NEVER SAT IN ANY SPOT.

We're thrilled by the improbability that we happened to meet here, in a Moroccan coastal town with few inhabitants, the daughter and nephew of two once-close allies.

This is amazing!

C'est incroyable, n'est-ce pas, c'est fantastique!

We realize that when we were kids, we played in the same place at the same time: near the trailer that belonged to Jon's uncle. We recall a particular summer festival and that the water from the well didn't taste good because it had too much iron. After two hours, I'm still not sure which of the two men I find more attractive. After three hours, we're sitting by the ocean, in the dark, with even more red wine, and then in a bar. It's called Café sans Stress and the bar owner is pouring us some horrible-tasting rosé on the sly. A confused Moroccan Rastafarian keeps calling out *Konnichiwa!* to us and saying that he really understands Africa. Really. Understands. It. After five hours, I go with Jon and his Swiss friend to their hotel room. We have a threesome, a little tender, a little like in a mainstream porno for straight men. If one were to use industry terminology, one might label us an "interracial gang bang," along with listing other corresponding categories such as "bondage," "bukkake," "pussy licking," and "cosplay."

A THREESOME DOESN'T COUNT AS A GANG BANG, THERE HAVE TO BE AT LEAST FOUR PEOPLE INVOLVED.

After I get a few hours of sleep and return to my hostel, I lie down in bed, feeling excited. None of the other guests are awake. I smile into my pillow, which still smells a little like Kim's hair. *Hier, j'ai fait une bêtise.*

Yesterday, I . . .

Yesterday.

Suddenly, as I am lying down in my clammy room, I have an astonishing realization: Jon might have run into my brother back then. Maybe, years ago, they played together at the summer festival, in a small Thuringian village. Maybe all three of us played together; dressed as "cowboys and Indians," running around in a meadow, chasing one another, without a clue that the world is much bigger than this meadow and our city. Maybe Jon, my brother, and I drank water from the small well and said: *Yuck, that tastes like blood.* And then we laughed, kept on running, and shot at sparrows with a bow and arrow; that truly may have happened.

DON'T YOU HAVE A GUILTY CONSCIENCE?

I feel like I've dropped out of time. That's all.

DOES KIM KNOW WHAT YOU'RE DOING WHILE SHE'S VISITING HER DYING UNCLE?

No.

Bravo!

What?

Great show!

WHERE IS KIM NOW?

. . .

STILL IN HANOI?

I don't think so.

Now that's what I call great German theater!

WHERE ARE YOU NOW?

I close my eyes and take three deep breaths, breathing as deeply as possible.

Kim and I are sitting in a theater in Berlin. Morocco, the U.S., Vietnam, the boy who got stabbed, that's all behind us. Or somewhere inside us.

I open my eyes.

WHAT ARE YOU TWO WATCHING?

A play about reunification.

WHAT DO YOU FEEL?

During the entire play, I want to take Kim into my arms, put my hand on her leg.

WHAT ELSE?

As I look around the theater I notice that we're the only non-white people in a room of about a thousand.

WHEN DID YOU START PAYING ATTENTION TO THAT SORT OF THING?

Maybe during one of my visits to that strange hypnotherapist? That was a few weeks after my brother's death. Different people around me said things like: *You can't get through this alone* and *You need an intervention right away!* That's why I went to the first available therapist. When she told me, during the fifth session, how astonishing it is that I usually dream about myself as a white person, I lay there like a cold fish.

WHAT ARE YOU FEELING NOW?

The production is good, but the jokes are stressing me out. Again and again there are Hitler salutes and racial slurs, each time followed by the laughter of well-off white people. In a few weeks, I'll write a long email to the director, explaining to her what triggers me about the play. I'll kindly ask her to have a conversation with me. And again, weeks later she'll choose not to answer me and instead—directly following my email—she will perform her moral superiority in a theater magazine, garnering good publicity. I remain a cold fish.

DO YOU ENJOY PLAYING THE VICTIM?

Excuse me?

DO YOU FEEL GOOD WHEN YOU CAN YELL: THERE AND THERE AND THERE, THE OTHERS ARE THE PERPETRATORS, THE WORLD PAINS ME, OUCH!

DO YOU THINK POLITICAL CORRECTNESS IS SEXY?

Definitely, of course.

Bravo! Bravissimo!

Many audience members are highly enthusiastic after the play.

YOU'RE NOT?

Kim watches the show more calmly than I do. Each time, when someone gives the Hitler salute on the stage, she says loudly: *Boring.* We like some scenes, now and then an impressive choir takes the stage, the evening has a nice rhythm and beautiful costumes. Finally, a large projection of a punk girl's face is shown—an original photo, documentary material, filmed live and projected onto a giant screen. The girl's hair is dyed partly black and partly blond, molded into bold spikes shooting out of her head. With a melancholic, intense gaze, she stares directly into the camera from dark-framed eyes. She's maybe thirteen or sixteen, in the background a naked person darts around. My heart starts racing. I know that face, I feel dizzy. For a moment I'm convinced that I've truly and irrevocably gone crazy. But then I become increasingly certain: That's my mother's face. It's a photo of my mother as a teenager. Before I existed, before she knew me or I her.

Kim, I whisper, *I think that's my mother.*

Really?

Kim looks at me concerned, without reaching for my hand.

SENSATIONAL!

No, I really mean it.

Unbelievable!

WHAT HAPPENS THEN?

I hear a faint whistling in my ear.

I close my eyes.

I breathe deeply, open my eyes.

I'm standing on a train platform in a small town,
in my so-called hometown,
behind me the snack machine.

My eyes are burning, I look around me.

I'm standing on the train platform with lots of people, waiting for the train. Four more minutes, my stomach growls. I think: *There are so many people here.*

Two of them were a couple, years ago. They haven't seen each other yet, standing three feet apart. If they run into each other on the train, one of them will be delighted and the other won't be. I switch which leg I favor and lean back against the snack machine.

All of a sudden, I think of a pet turtle that a school friend had. When we were kids, we watched it often. Sometimes we would wrap it in string, tie it to a branch hanging in the water, and it would swim for hours in the same part of the lake without getting anywhere. I don't know exactly what kept me from just untying the string around its shell.

I'm standing on the platform with lots of people, waiting for the train. Four more minutes, my stomach growls. I think: *There are so many people here.*

Suddenly the loudspeaker crackles. But there's no announcement, no one speaks.

The loudspeaker crackles again, then I hear wheezing. Somewhere in the area, someone is struggling audibly to breathe.
The loud sound of this gasping for air and breathing painstakingly in and out can be heard through the loudspeaker, echoing across the platform. It seems as if this person either forgot what they wanted to say or is trying not to say something evil that they've always wanted to say.

Four more minutes, my stomach growls.

A giraffe with a too-short tie stands next to me. She wants to get a snack. After inserting two coins in the machine, she notices, glancing into her wallet, that she doesn't have enough change. When I see she has several fifty-euro bills in her pocketbook, I decide not to give her the twenty cents.

I'm sitting huddled in the snack machine.

The glass is fogged, the air is muggy. By now, I'm completely wrapped in cellophane, bits and pieces from a coconut-chocolate bar are sticking to my hair and back, shit and urine to my feet. I use my middle finger to draw a turtle on the milky glass. Maybe one of the people on the train platform can see it, from the outside?

A few people are standing on the platform and waiting for the train. Four more minutes, their stomachs growl. They think: *There are so many people here.*

Now I'm thinking of the turtle again, from way back when, in the lake. I wanted to know if it would eventually think of biting through the string on its own. That's why I didn't do anything and just observed it. But it never thought of that.

In the meantime, its former owner, my classmate, suffers from ALS and can't move anymore. He's on a respirator and has been waiting to die for two years. He weighs only half of what he did back then. I can never bring myself to visit him. I'd rather stay here in the snack machine and make little animals out of cellophane; swans, tigers, turtles, pigeons, snakes, and hedgehogs. They probably have a lot to say to one another.

I'm lying naked on the train tracks.

Everyone is gone, I'm alone.

It's quiet.

Recently someone crushed the snack machine like an oversized beer can. All of its contents, including me, spilled out onto the platform and the track bed, fizzling. My landing was hard. Since then a trail of snacks, excrement, and little cellophane animals runs between my battered body and the battered machine. A funny collection, untidily spread out between the tracks like the entrails of a steamrolled pigeon.

I'm alone on the tracks.

It's quiet.

Everyone is gone.

Grass shoots up between the tracks, the metal is rusted.
A swan flies backward past me. My gaze follows it until it's out of view. Slowly I get up and walk step by step across the overgrown track bed, along a train path overgrown with moss in some spots.

There's something lying off in the distance, a mountain of plastic film, a giant bundle; I get closer. Someone's under there; a person shrink-wrapped in cellophane. I feel hot. My brother, my twin brother is lying there. He's nineteen years old and dead. His eyes are glazed over, he's smiling at me through the transparent plastic film. I work up the courage to carefully go over to him.
Hello, I whisper gently.

His eyes are wide open, his milky pupils follow my movements. I say, *Come on, let's go into the sun,* and I grab him through the plastic film, under his armpits. Groaning, I drag him a few paces, rustling and crinkling, away from the track bed, away from the platform, back behind the tracks, into a meadow.

From here we have a decent view of everything.
My brother is lying there all twisted. I sit down next to him. As I rip open the cellophane around his head, the leaves in the trees rustle in the wind.

what am i doing here?
I don't know the answer to that question.
It's quiet.

where am i?
Once again, I don't know what to say.
Minutes go by.
An ant is walking backward down my arm.

with me, I finally say, and don't know what that means.
    where exactly?
I hesitate. Eventually I mumble:
it doesn't matter.

    okay. so what am i doing here?
you've been dead for twelve years.
    really?
yes.
    why?
because you wanted it that way.
    why?
because you weren't doing well.
    why?
. . .
    what are you doing?
i'm kissing you on the cheek.
    nice.
oh well.
    jump already.
what?
    that's what they yelled the other day, right?

that doesn't have anything to do with you.

    then why is it coming up here?

the sentence has been burned in.

    jump already.

it hasn't been confirmed . . . that's a completely different story.

    what are you doing now?

i'm exhaling laboriously.

    what am i doing?

you're letting everything happen. you're letting yourself fall.

    usually you lose consciousness when you jump to your death, right?

    before you die. your brain does that for you.

only if you jump from high enough.

in your case, i think the distance was too short.

    that's too bad.

    what are you doing now?

i'm imagining that i'm hugging you. i'm extending our last hug from twelve years ago for a few seconds. we were at our grandparents', just did a toast with champagne, shortly after our birthday.

    for the first time ever i didn't wish for anything.

there were four kinds of square cake: plum, russian zupfkuchen, bee sting cake, and i forgot the fourth.

    zupfkuchen is my favorite cake.

we greeted each other chummy with a hug, and jokingly patted each other too long on the back, "how you doin', my friend?"

    but there was one more, final hug.

later that day i carried you up the stairs. you're drunk and telling nonsensi- cal riddles, your arm around my shoulders, something about a monkey in a cage. you're joyful, annoying, adolescent. when we finally get upstairs to your kitchen, we make sandwiches with cheese, cucumber slices, and remoulade.

    remoulade?

i say to you, "don't make the slices so thick." but the green chunk with bread already disappears in your mouth. your small drunken eyes, as you're grinning. i think, you look happy with a mouthful. and the next day you disappear from my life.

    why?

. . .

    why?

just fifteen more minutes, then the train will come. that's enough time to buy one more snack. you're watching my luggage.

    i feel warm.

and then you decide to stop watching my luggage, and you jump in front of the train.

    i jump from the edge of the platform . . . how quickly do the police come?

very fast. while two policemen run through the station together with an emergency doctor and a paramedic, at first i just follow them with my gaze. when they climb the stairs to our platform, i start running too, rushing up the stairs as if in a dream.

    do you often dream of that?

no, never. while two policemen jump down onto the track bed, the conductor steps down from the freight train, and stares in the direction of the emergency doctor. she, on the other hand, is already crouching above your body, staring at your face, then at mine, then back at you.

    take him to the hospital!

i yell without thinking. then i jump onto the tracks and kneel next to you. my pants slip down below my butt crack.

    you need to take him to the hospital!

i yell again, the emergency doctor doesn't look at me. a policeman, who's squatting by your feet, says: well, he's dead, one can clearly see that. as if i was too dumb to understand the situation or was responsible for it.

whew.

would you still be alive if i hadn't gone downstairs to buy two apples?

   no.

   what am i doing now?

you're three years old, running barefoot across a meadow, in your left hand you're holding a long stick that you drag behind you.

   cool. and now?

you're seven and you have a crush on a girl on our street.

   and now?

you're eight, you're sitting in school and you need to fart.

   and now?

you're twelve, you're sitting in school and you wait for the nazis to leave the schoolyard.

   and now?

you're sixteen and you're getting the spot between your lip and your chin pierced.

   what am i doing now?

you're nine and you're climbing so high up in your favorite tree that you forget how to come back down.

   and now?

you're fourteen and you're having sex for the first time. your girlfriend wonders why the light has to stay off.

   what am i doing now?

you're beating someone up with a baseball bat. black power is written on your notebooks. you're fifteen.

   i have a monkey and a box!

what?

   i have a monkey and a box.

. . . okay.

   i put the monkey inside the box.

why?

   . . .

is that a magic trick?

   i can't do magic tricks, can i?

   can you do magic?

no.

   if i could do magic, i'd conjure up a new hairdo for you!

what's wrong with my hair?

   i thought you don't like it.

meanwhile, i'm okay with myself, with my body and my hair.

   since when?

. . .

   since when?

*since i know more black people . . . do you remember when your girlfriend
toni drove us home that night?*

   what night?

*you were in the back seat and drunkenly grabbed my hair and babbled:
"have you ever really, thoroughly rooted through this afro?" then we went
upstairs together, ate, slept, got up early together, and went to the train
station.*

   please take this pill.

   that's what the emergency doctor said, right?

and that i should say goodbye. and meanwhile i shouldn't move you.

   so that my brain doesn't get spread across the tracks.

*when she said "take this pill," i understood that i would soon be suffering
from shock. that everything really happened.*

   well, he's dead, one can clearly see that.

maybe i am a little responsible for the situation?

   nope.

please wake up!

what?
i can't stop reciting that.
what am i doing now?
you're four and you're wearing our grandmother's jewelry: pearl necklaces, rhinestone brooches, clip-on earrings. you're standing in front of the mirror and think you look beautiful.
and now?
you're eleven and playing soccer with my friends. i'm refereeing the game without a whistle, just using my fingers, no one is listening to me, you get fouled. when you foul them back, a tussle ensues, you get your first black eye. you're secretly a little proud of that.
what am i doing now?
you're a year old and you're being fed with a bottle. a mosquito stings you on the nose.
and now?
you're seven and with me and our grandparents at the zoo.
two meerkats appeal to you.
what am i doing now?
you're thirteen and you're trying to rap for the first time.
and now?
you're twelve and you ejaculate for the first time. you're not embarrassed at all.
and now?
your friends organize a surprise birthday party for you. there are eighteen muffins on the floor of your room with eighteen burning candles sticking out of them. it's important for you that you celebrate with your friends and i celebrate with mine. as you enter your room, you cry from joy. then you start to tremble and you run out. no one knows what to do, everyone's looking at me.
do i have tattoos on my arms?

i don't think so. when i dream about you, though that hardly ever happens, we hug and hold each other tight, tighter than we ever did in real life.

  deep.

  do you remember my voice?

no.

  do people still talk about me?

no.

  do you still know how i smell?

yes, how your t-shirts smelled. i mean, you were barely out of puberty, that was stronger than any deodorant. and your morning breath was terrible.

  take him to the hospital!

after you woke up, you always had such thick yellow crust in the corners of your eyes. was that because of the weed you smoked? did you somehow sweat that from your eyes?

  what?

sorry, that was nonsense.

  i have a monkey and a box. i put the monkey in the box. where is the
  monkey?

huh?

  i have a monkey and a box. i put the monkey in the box.
  where is the monkey?

. . . in the box?

  where is the monkey?

. . . in my imagination?

  i have "one" monkey and "one" box. i put the monkey in the box.
  where is the monkey?

i have no idea.

  i "put" the monkey in the box.

where "is" the monkey?

  i put the monkey "in" the box.

dude.

> *i put the monkey in the "box."*

dude, where is the fucking monkey?

well, he's dead, one can clearly see that.

> *what are you doing now?*

i'm breathing heavily.

> *and now?*

i press a pillow into my face and hold my breath until i can't anymore. yet i don't stop, i keep going, i keep going up the stairs with you, we teeter, i hold on to you tightly, i'm there for you, you're drunk.

> *what am i doing now?*

by now, you look so grown up that people who see us together think you're much older than me.

> *i have a job at a bank!*

. . . it's a little boring, but still okay, because you like to wear suits. i pick you up after closing time. tonight we're going to a party. we'll drink, dance, and watch people drink and dance.

> *i never went dancing with you.*

i get us some schnapps; the first round is on me.

> *. . . this feels funny.*

what?

> *well, what you're doing here.*

sometimes your death seems like a trip to me. i imagine that you—if you still exist—

> *but i'm here, clearly i still exist.*

you know what i mean.

> *what?*

you know, spiritually. in case you really still exist somewhere.

hey!

in any case, i imagine that you are passing by many different stations and that your life with me was only one of them.

that sounds dumb . . . what am i doing now?

you close your eyes.

what are you doing?

i stroke your cheek . . . you're dreaming.

of what?

that you're still alive.

haha.

sometimes your number pops into my head, all of a sudden. twelve years later and i still have the feeling that we'll talk on the phone soon. we'll tell each other what happened during the week. i hear you say "so, alfred" while i pick up the phone. i have no idea how you came up with that nickname for your sister.

so, alfred.

when i write your name down a lot, i get a spaced-out feeling . . . i was always so worried about you, i had so many nightmares that they'd do something to you. do even more than what they'd already done. i think of how you came home one day, with a knife in your leg, and how you were ashamed. you were so small, and they already hated you so much.

jump already.

now no one else can hurt you.

jump already.

now nothing else can happen to you.

what are you doing?

i'm smiling.

what am i doing?

you're smiling back.

and now?

you bite a piece out of something. maybe it's zupfkuchen, maybe a piece of
bread with a thick slice of cucumber.

maybe an apple. what are you doing?
i'm still smiling.

nice.
it's the only thing that helps.

with what?
against what.

lol!
hahaha.

sometimes when you're in a good mood, to the point that you can
hardly believe it, such a good mood that you have a laughing fit because for a brief moment everything is fine, everything is okay and
nothing is hurting you, then you miss me the most, right?
hahaha!

should i laugh too?
go ahead.

. . . and?
you have the best, warmest laugh in the world.

again?
yes.

what's happening now?
we've grown up together, we're drinking coffee.

am i eating zupfkuchen?
naturally.

would you kill someone in order to see me again?
what?

would you kill someone in order to see me again?
. . . yes?

 a good friend?
maybe.
 someone young, who's my age?
maybe. unless he looks like you.
 haha. are you afraid of death?
no.
 are you angry at me?
i could never be.
 am i more important to you, now that i'm gone?
yes.
 what am i doing now?
you're ashes. we spread you around.
 what are you doing?
i'm letting you go.
 is it working?
sometimes, sometimes not . . . it's good that i stopped asking why.
 why?
because i would never find the answer.
 why?
because i can't ask you anymore.
 why?
. . . why did you jump?
 . . .
why did you jump?
 the trick is: i never say no.
what?
 the riddle is always just repeated, so much that you think that your
 answer is wrong. but i never say that it was wrong.
i can't follow you.

the monkey in the box.

the purpose of the riddle is to annoy you, to confuse you, that's all.
you're supposed to think that there's an answer and that drives you
crazy. that's the point. but there is no right answer.

okay. and why is that?

II

(picture this)

A friend came to see me in a dream. From far away. And I asked in the dream: "Did you come by photograph or train?" All photographs are a form of transport and an expression of absence.

JOHN BERGER
A Seventh Man

The picture is in black and white. Four eyes stare back at me. The two gazes are very different, ambiguous. An initial, impulsive title could be: *Like Night and Day*. Or: *Opposites That Don't Attract*. Or: *The Beauty and the Punk*. But the photo is called: *Susanne's Dream*.

In the photo there are two women positioned in the center. Susanne's on the left and to the right next to her is a delicate, naked girl. In the background there's a wide field in different shades of gray. It appears as if both women are sitting; they're photographed from their head to the end of their torso. The naked girl's bent right elbow is resting easily on Susanne's shoulder. A white flower is stuck behind the girl's ear, in her presumably light blond hair. She looks self-confident, coy, maybe with a touch of a smile at the camera, her eyelids are nearly completely covered by the hair of her light blond ponytail, her nipples are erect. Although neither of the young women is positioned in the middle of the photo, Susanne is the somber center. She's wearing a wide, cascading, dark sleeveless shirt; underneath one can see the peaks of her breasts, likely she's not wearing a bra, her arms hang loosely at her sides. Susanne's neck is bent toward the left, she's holding her head slightly askew, away from the other girl. Her hair is sticking up in jagged spikes from her head, if not for the hair spray they would hang down at chin length. One-third of her hair is dyed in bright colors, the other two-thirds are dyed in dark colors. Her eyebrows and eyes are contoured with thick black lines that almost reach her temples. Susanne's gaze at the camera is melancholy, emphatically bored; her face is made up with broad vertical lines and triangular dark surfaces. Her makeup reminds me of Maori tattoos. I have no idea what it referred to back then.

Hello, are you still there?

Yes.

So, my dear friend Burhan says, *anxiety is one of the most common mental illnesses and the easiest to treat with therapy.* He's been working as a psychoanalyst of late. *For now, for the moment, it's still important to take some medication in order to get out of it.*
We've been talking on the phone for ten minutes and he repeats himself several times to reassure me; it doesn't work. I'm wide awake for the fourth night in a row. During the day I slept only a few hours. It's eight in the morning.

When we were kids my brother and I used to watch a cartoon about a monster who collected discarded fingernails from people, an abundance of wealth. He would boast about this treasure to his monster friends. But the other monsters discovered that the monster had been collecting toenails all those years. The entire time he had been swiping the wrong nails from different human children. When that was discovered, his wealth disappeared from one moment to the next; a magnificent currency became counterfeit money. In the same cartoon, a different monster always carried his own eyes in his hands, with his hands held up high; that impressed us. Later we wondered whether the monster grew fingernails himself and, if so, for whom those might count as a treasure like gold.

My brother had been dead only half a day when my mother arrived in our so-called hometown to see him. We had talked on the phone beforehand, I told her about the incident a few minutes after it happened. Her cry through the telephone into my ear was inhuman, an archaic animal sound. Then she got into a taxi and hit the road. For six hours on the highway, she knew about the death of her son and couldn't believe it. It was only two days later when she could finally touch my brother's stiff corpse in the crematorium that she could understand his death, and his death took hold of her and her body. I didn't want to be there; I had already said goodbye to him earlier, at the scene. Afterward my mother told me, offhand, that it felt good to see him. *He was already gone, a hard shell, like he was made of wax. And he had long nails, such long nails.*

A lot of people think that your hair, fingernails, and toenails continue to grow after death. It's not true, it's an optical illusion. The flesh, and the skin along with it, the fingers under the nails, the skin under the hair just retreats faster, it collapses, diminishes. And that creates the impression that your fingernails turn into claws and your hair looks visibly longer after death. What is true is that your fingernails grow faster and stronger during pregnancies. When life is created inside a body, the processes in the cells that contain keratin accelerate. When life leaves a body, these cells disappear more slowly than all the others. In the time in between, which we call a life span, fingernails are cut, lovingly manicured, or ignored, hair is dyed, extended, curled, and straightened, or ripped out. And we always trust that everything will grow back. Until the day it doesn't.

In the photo essay *Let's Talk About Race* by Chris Buck, there's a photo that depicts an elegant nail salon. In the photo one can see eight women. Five of them are, in part, sitting and laughing, talking on the phone, looking at their phones, or reading a magazine in large light brown chairs. They have smooth dark hair and appear relaxed and happy, wearing colorful casual city outfits. At their feet are three white women sitting on low beige stools. They are wearing red smocks, black blouses, and light brown pants. The frontmost blond woman massages a customer's naked feet; the other white workers are doing similar activities, they appear focused and polite. All the clients in the expansive chairs are of Asian descent, the photo is staged, must be staged, not because of its glossy advertising aesthetic, but rather because it's an image that never occurs in reality.

Two blond women cut kebab meat from a skewer and bake pita bread; behind the transparent plastic counter, there are four female customers in headscarves waiting for their food. Three pale, strawberry blond German women enter a law firm after hours to clean; all the Senegalese German employees have already left. Several Vietnamese German actors are performing one of Bertolt Brecht's plays on stage at a theater in Rostock; in the audience the spectators are predominantly of Asian descent, they look bored as usual. In college seminars for philosophy or art history, the children of Turkish manual laborers are called on exclusively and they ask long-winded questions that are actually lectures. At a taxi stand, five white German women are waiting next to their cars, smoking and drinking coffee; it's so cold one can see their breath. At some random Berlin airport, elegantly dressed Afghan German managers leave the terminal and call a taxi.

In Buck's series there is also a photo of a girl who's standing in front of a store shelf full of dolls. The white girl is photographed from behind; she's wearing a pink, horizontally striped dress and has a pink tie in her light-colored hair. The shelf she's staring at reaches from the top to the bottom and from the left to the right of the frame. There are three rows of shrink-wrapped Black dolls staring back at the girl. The photo reminds me of an experiment that was run during the 1940s for the first time: white and Black American schoolchildren, aged three to seven years old, were given two dolls that were differentiated only by their skin color (one was black, the other white) and otherwise were completely identical. The children were asked several questions. Which doll is the pretty doll? *This one.* Which doll is the ugly doll? *This one.* Which doll is good, which is evil, etc. The majority of the kids chose the white dolls as the nice ones, the pretty ones, the smart and good ones; the Black dolls were the mean, dumb, ugly, and evil dolls.

See! His nails are never cut / They are grimed and black as soot / And the sloven, I declare / Never once has combed his hair.

From a very early age I was taught what counted as beautiful and what didn't. My grandmother liked to read children's books to me, including *Struwwelpeter*. Even with an arsenal of combs and brushes, my hair couldn't be tamed. That's how she put it too, to subdue, to tame, as if she were trying to temper something wild.

In the original *Struwwelpeter*, there is a story about two boys who make fun of a Black man, and as punishment they are colored black, when St. Nicholas dips them in a pot of ink. As children, my brother and I never questioned that looking like us was enough of a reason for taunting and malice, or even considered as a punishment from a moral authority.

My grandmother made sure that I always looked neat—that my clothes, my manners, and especially my hair appeared proper. She tried out countless expensive cosmetic products on my hair: mousse, hair cures, sprays, and gels. And I was happy that she took up the task. She even bought me and my brother tons of new, pristine clothing. And countless times she asked me to let her clean my nails, to finally let them grow. *After all, you'll soon be a young woman.* My grandmother grew up at the end of the 1940s and the beginning of the 1950s in a small village where, even though there was no Catholicism or any other religion, morality counted as one of the most important virtues. The fact that she became pregnant out of wedlock was a massive blow to her reputation, and it was even worse that she would later become the first woman in the village to get a divorce (shortly after her father forced her to marry the child's father). Maybe since then, she had always tried to rehabilitate her reputation by putting outward appearances to the test. Or maybe she was just a little shallow. It's not surprising that this impulse only grew stronger when in the 1980s she unexpectedly and frequently had to care for two children whose skin color was considered a stigma by society.

I thought my grandmother's shimmering nails, which were always manicured and, as I recall, always colored in different mother-of-pearl shades, were very beautiful. Since she can't see that well anymore, she often gets manicures at the nail salon. When she talks about the people who do her nails, she never refers to them as nail cosmeticians or nail designers, rather she talks about them as if they all came from Fiji and as if it were okay to reduce them to this alleged affiliation. I rarely talk to my grandmother about it. She says my political beliefs always cause us to argue. Maybe I have to respect her wishes, just like she respects my wish not to talk about my brother.

Dr. Wünschel, a small, endearing psychiatrist in a much-too-large blazer, prescribes me psychotropic drugs: he's the only one with whom I can get an appointment on short notice. His long sleeves cover his hands up to the tips of his fingers. The chairs in his office in Kreuzberg are worn out, the hallways smell like dog.

There's fear now all the time, the psychiatrist can't take it away from me.
How could he, it is intangible.

A man, maybe in his early sixties, is sitting in his living room across from me on a dark-colored leather couch. (Kim says that for inexplicable reasons, these white men of the baby boomer generation are really into leather couches. I suspect that my friend Burhan also has a couch like that at his practice.) The man's light-colored eyes remind me of those of reptiles, although there's something warm in them. His gaze is unyielding, inquiring; he speaks to me in short sentences without filler words, without pauses for thought. The man is used to speaking with others about himself, his work, and his ideas. He cooks a delicious curry with chicken, raisins, and basmati rice. Behind his leather couch, there's a surprise for me. It's a large print of a photograph that he shot over three decades ago. He has a lot of plants in flowerpots in his living room. The traffic noise from outside penetrates the room. When the photographer later hands me the photo, he'll tell me that it's one of his most successful photos and it shows one of his favorite models. And then:

With my signature it's worth a thousand euros.

He'll say it in such a way that it doesn't even sound vain, just matter-of-fact. Before that, while we eat, he'll fulfill my request for a few anecdotes. He'll talk about a young girl who had just transformed herself into a punk, *at a time, mind you, when something like that had never existed before.* He will fondly and warmly remember a girl who in actual fact was respectable and happy. And especially social. For example, back then, when he took the fifteen-year-old girl with him to Czechoslovakia to take pictures, there were some professional models who would have never thought it necessary to clean up their dishes after eating. But the young girl and her friend had indeed paid attention to such things. Many times, they'd even wash the dirty dishes of the other models. Moreover, it was especially amusing how one of the photographers who worked for the fashion magazine *Pramo* had begun to cry when the girl first came on set. He just didn't know how he was supposed to work with her and her unconventional look. He was horrified and seriously started crying as soon as he saw her. But the young girl wasn't even bothered by that. She was just interested in taking photos. Although she didn't want to be photographed nude, she was very clear about that.

No, his relationship with her was in no way sexual. At the time, the beginning of the eighties, the girl was half as old as he was. It was more like a paternal relationship. For example, when the girl repeatedly had problems with her parents and got kicked out of her house, he offered up his apartment to her. No, of course they didn't live together; he had been traveling for two weeks at the time. When he got back, he was dumbfounded. He had expected all kinds of disorder and chaos. Drinking, screaming teenagers who partied in his apartment all day long. But it was the complete opposite. The young woman had cleaned everything up so nicely that his apartment looked neater than it had when he left. *Everything was immaculate, perfectly immaculate.* She had even labeled some of the glass jars in the pantry with "flour," "sugar," etc. On top of that, the silverware had been polished, sorted, and put away. When he came back, the girl even cooked him noodles as a thank-you. He still doesn't know how she dyed the noodles black. He just had to laugh when she served them to him. That was the kind of rebellion she liked. But the noodles still tasted totally normal.

After dinner, an unexpected discussion about Islam arises between me and the photographer. We talk about the power of images today and the power of images back then. The photographer can't understand my position that Islam in itself is not dangerous. Shaking his head, he tells me that women who wear burkas aren't free, and that many Muslim refugees will commit crimes. He says that this ideology has no place in Germany, and he rejects my idea that every religion only becomes an ideology based on its interpretation. He doesn't want to see that most of the images circulating in the media about Muslims are undeserving and one-sided. He doesn't suspect how tired this conversation is making me, droning on and on. In the middle of it, he gets up to have a smoke by the window. He's polite to me the entire time, and repeatedly offers me a cigarette. I decline it with thanks, even though I would really like one. *Oh, come on,* the photographer finally says, not patronizing, but rather charming, *when you're my age, you'll see.*

The surprise that is leaning against the back of the sofa is a large print of the young girl, labeled *Susanne's Dream.* The photographer will tell me that the title was inspired by Arno Schmidt's novel *Bottom's Dream.* Then he'll ask how Susanne is doing these days. Where does she live now. I won't have any answers to these questions.

In his practice, while he breathes heavily and keeps getting interrupted by a barking cough, Dr. Wünschel tells me that only death is free. *Ha, not even that, because someone has to pay for that, too! You know, for the funeral, get it! Haha.*

His laughter sounds rehearsed, morbid chatter is his way of telling me that the psychotropic drugs have side effects. And one of them, he continues, is a dry mouth. But in case that might bother me, these days you can buy synthetic spit at the pharmacy.

The psychiatrist doesn't laugh when he says this, he just observes me attentively.

After I've picked up the medication, I read the package insert over and over. At night, I call Burhan and ask him to find out everything about the side effects. Half an hour later he claims that a Swiss female colleague of his, who is also a psychiatrist, confirmed that everything is fine with this medicine and it is totally appropriate for my situation.

I doubt he was able to reach her so quickly.

One of the first CDs I bought myself, during the late nineties in the music section of Müller's drugstore, was from the band the Roots. The album was called *Things Fall Apart*. There was a black-and-white photo on the cover, maybe it came from the 1960s:

In the foreground is a young African American woman in a white dress, behind her an African American man in a white shirt, dark pants, and leather shoes—both of them are running from something. The woman's face is contorted, perhaps there are screams coming out of her wide-open mouth, or maybe she is crying. When you look at the photo, your eyes are drawn to her first. Then to the young man, who's running about two feet behind her. While he's running, he turns his head to watch his pursuers; you can't see his face. In the direction where he's looking, several white policemen, wearing even whiter helmets and dark clothing, emerge from the dark, blurry background of the photograph. They're running too, but they look much more relaxed. Their faces reveal no clear emotions. It's indistinct how many of them there are—their numbers seem to both end in the background and simultaneously not at all. A row of threatening, neutral, almost identical-looking men, coming feasibly from nowhere, and ending nowhere. Some of them have a hand on their belt, next to where a nightstick or a pistol could be.

A few years ago, for a short period of time, I worked as a substitute teacher at a few elementary schools in the neighborhood of Neukölln. In Berlin, all you need to get this job is to have a college degree, any subject will do, and to fill out a form online. Sometimes I was hired without anyone having met me, seen me, or spoken with me.

In many of the classes, more than half of the children weren't of German descent, some only spoke broken German, their future plans consisted of becoming *a taxi driver like my dad, a stay-at-home mom, a YouTube star,* or *a female gangster rapper.* I felt like a real-life version of Michelle Pfeiffer in *Dangerous Minds*: a woman who would finally give these kids the right education in the right way and awaken their ambitions in the process. During German class with the sixth graders, I read and analyzed German-language fairy tales from Africa and the Middle East, sang songs by Michael Jackson and the Black German pop singer Joy Denalane with them, discussed the lyrics, and let them introduce their favorite songs to the class. They all admired Michael Jackson; I was surprised that every child knew him, while to them Joy Denalane sounded old-fashioned and uninteresting. And some kids were puzzled that I wore my hair in an afro, *because that's so eighties.*

Back then, I couldn't have said what attracted me to the dramatic album cover of the Roots. I also couldn't have asked the salesman in the drugstore what the label "Black Music" on the shelf was supposed to mean. Or to put it differently, I couldn't have asked on which shelf I would find the category "White Music" and what kinds of things were included there. The Beatles, Madonna, Vivaldi, Nena, and Rammstein?

In my first week in one of the schools, I found out that a boy was being abused by his mother. After I informed the school social workers, the homeroom teacher, who was out on sick leave, suddenly announced that she was well and returning immediately; I never found out what happened with the boy. At another school, I always sat in on a class before I taught, and I saw how a teacher made the students who did poorly in math stand in a corner of the classroom for the entire period as a form of punishment. During the breaks, some teachers spoke so snidely about nine-year-olds that I had to leave the teachers' lounge.

From the mid to late 1990s, hip-hop was my music, my musical canon. This youth culture, imported from the U.S.A., constructed an image of a cool kind of Blackness that had never before existed in Germany. A new narrative about Black people emerged, their artistic expressions and identities inspired me. So when I was a teenager, eagerly and without thinking, I wore baggy pants, just like many of my white classmates and friends. We listened first to American, then eventually also German-language hip-hop. We pathetically tried to rap, sometimes even spray graffiti. Since I already had a tendency toward nervousness in my youth, I never managed to squeeze out more than a letter. But I felt cool first and foremost: I thought I was a little cooler than my white friends, I'd convinced myself that because of its origins, hip-hop had more to do with me, and belonged to me more so than to them. It was the same with TV. Steve Urkel on *Family Matters*, Mr. T on *The A-Team*, the Huxtables, and the Fresh Prince of Bel-Air all had more in common with me than soap opera characters like Derrick, the outrageous, scheming, immortal Jo Gerner, or the doctors from the series *Lindenstraße*. It wasn't because the actors in German shows were white, but rather because they were white and not cool.

Once, during my time as a substitute teacher, I met a "world studies" teacher during my lunch break who taught at a neighboring high school. He was in his mid-fifties, short, charismatic, and cared about social issues. At first, the man told me how great it must be for the kids that someone like me could finally teach them. After some small talk, I gave him some photocopies, and he thanked me, confused. I had read about Anton Wilhelm Amo, "the African philosopher of the Enlightenment," in a magazine and copied some of the pages. Now I asked the world studies teacher if he could discuss people like Amo with his students for a change, so that they didn't learn only about the achievements of white men. He scrutinized me at length; maybe he was thinking. Then he asked me if I could suggest some material for his art class, since I was apparently such an expert. Because, for instance, he often wonders whether there is also contemporary African art that doesn't just consist of thrown-together junk. *Could you recommend something to me?* He insisted he didn't mean any harm and that personally he thought very highly of Africans. For example, the women who took the subway with him in the mornings were always very put together.

When I visited my father in Angola for the first time back in 2005, I was surprised that for most of the male youth there, 50 Cent functioned as a kind of identification figure and role model. Not a day would pass without me seeing a 50 Cent T-shirt in some suburb of Luanda or hearing his music play on the radio. Only then did I realize how absurd the dominance of American pop culture is, and how problematic that is. I was blind to that in Germany.

There's a photo online of the all-female Black German hip-hop group Tic Tac Toe, together with Michael Jackson. The caption of the photo is: *Three little stars and a mega star: Every now and then, Michael Jackson shows how down-to-earth he is—here he is before his concert on June 3rd 1997 in Cologne, greeting the singers from Tic Tac Toe, who performed as the opening act for three of his concerts.* Michael

Jackson is wearing a silver-gold outfit and neither sunglasses nor a mask. Tic Tac Toe's Lee and Ricky wear black outfits with a bare midriff; Jazzy has a black shoulder-free body suit with a sweater tied around her waist. The smiles of these four standing together, and their gazes at the camera, seem honest, restrained, nice, maybe even proud. Michael Jackson looks white, in terms of the color. His pale hand cautiously touches Jazzy's upper arm.

When I was a kid, there was nothing I wanted more than a cream. A wondrous ointment that I could put on before going to bed that would make me white overnight. Remembering this wish as an adult fills me with shame and sadness. Throughout my childhood, at age ten, at age twelve, I heard rumors that Michael Jackson suffered from a mysterious illness. An illness that did exactly what I wished for: his skin turned white, he couldn't do anything to stop it. In one final, painful operation, he let himself be completely transformed. A lot of people joked that his music could no longer be considered Black Music. As a child, I was envious of this sensational illness beyond measure; envious of him and everyone who suffered from this illness. I wouldn't have thought of being envious of white people.

Too many intense feelings that I don't recognize, that run me over, too much of everything. Fear of falling asleep, obsessive thoughts before I fall sleep, a racing heart, sleeplessness, brooding, circulatory problems, fear of fear, less and less sleep, finally fear of falling asleep, increasing fear, in all possible situations, increasingly more during the day, increasing fear of people. Their faces want to approach me while the subway jerks around, their grimaces invade me and simultaneously remain in front of my eyes, even when I look away or close my eyes. While I'm experiencing this, I know I won't be able to capture it in words, and the ugly, colorful patterns on the subway seats can't save me. The whole time, I expect the unexpected, I'm on high alert, I try to avoid the faces of others, I sweat, too many gazes. After I exit the train I have the feeling that they're following me, all the hovering faces of the others, their evil, fucked-up, big-city souls stick to my heels, their eyes in my eyes, from behind me their gazes penetrate the back of my head and penetrate me, even though I'm walking away. I know this can't be real, just like the voices I hear before and after falling asleep, when I finally do fall asleep, I know for sure all of this can't be real but am still fascinated by it, I know I can go even deeper, a door is open and behind it I can think in a way I've never thought before. My hands shake, I'm sweating, I observe myself, run away from myself, from falling asleep, from others. Time and again, I wait for the voice that doesn't sound like mine but is mine nevertheless. I'm frightened of it, notice how I'm waiting for the voice, I observe my thoughts from the outside; there's something inside me, am I thinking or am I thought, something that could obliterate me, I think or see or observe; everything's a threat.

When I get to Burhan's, I lock myself in the bathroom, still shaking, crying, distraught. For inexplicable reasons I keep hitting myself on the neck, I can't stop. Burhan is knocking on the door from the outside, I don't say anything. For a few seconds I'm convinced that he wants to hurt me; that his evil little face will also float toward me in the air, just as with all the people on the subway. Burhan knocks again, I still don't say anything, then he goes away. If I start screaming now, I don't think I could ever stop.

Duane, a good friend of Burhan's from England, is visiting him in Berlin. We go for a bite together, show him the Korean take-out spot Ixthys. This fast-food restaurant confuses you with a mixture of good food, uncomfortable stools next to small wooden tables, and a flood of Christian sayings printed in the menus and on handwritten banners hanging on the walls. If Duane is confused by all this, he doesn't show it. I, on the other hand, am confused by Duane and try not to show it. Burhan didn't tell me much about him. He said only that he and Duane played soccer together in Luton for a while, and that some friends call Duane "Snow." I assumed that was a reference to either cocaine or *Game of Thrones*. On the way to Ixthys, in the subway, on the street, and finally when we enter the restaurant, Duane is constantly being stared at—secretly, blatantly, even by me. It's been a long time since I've felt the weight of such scrutinizing gazes so thoroughly. After we've ordered different types of bibimbap and some fish soup, and Burhan has been eloquently holding a conversation in English with a British accent, Duane addresses the elephant in the room. Maybe it's because I'm a friend of Burhan's, maybe because Duane has no problem with constantly having to discuss his appearance, constantly having to explain his existence, he tells us about his skin. He says he was born this way, it didn't start later like with most people. When he was still little, his mother had taken him to all kinds of doctors. Once, when he was seventeen, one of the doctors said to him:

Why don't you just go all white?

At this point, Burhan shakes his head while grinning. I think that back in the day the two of them gave each other a lot of high fives. Duane continues: there are many pictures of him online, especially on social media, I can see him in all kinds of outfits. Giving me a wink, he adds that I could even see him shirtless in some pictures.

Great, I say.

But if he were to show us photos from a while back, we would be surprised. In most photos from his childhood, you can't even see the white spots. We might think that he's just messing with us. *It was all makeup, it's all makeup,* he says, and takes a sip of tea. Apparently, it was normal for him that his mother usually put makeup on him. He doesn't know if she did it for his or her benefit. Anyway, she just did it. He says it's no wonder, then, that he constantly felt ashamed, inferior, etc. But at some point, he decided he couldn't continue like that. And then he started posting photos of himself. He was overwhelmed by the many positive reactions he got. And he was driven to keep going. He adds that by now he can live off it.

Really? I ask, and I notice that a few other customers are listening in.

Yeah, he basically made his appearance into his unique selling point, and thus in an industry where everything revolves around appearance, *best thing that ever happened to me.*

But actually, Burhan says with rice in his mouth, *Duane only now started being in charge of photos of his body. And through that, for the first time, he was able to influence what kind of idea people had about him as a person.*

Yeah, Duane says, but in the meantime, he adds, and that's the strangest thing, his skin disease has started to normalize itself. Some of the light spots are becoming darker, his cells are suddenly doing the thing they should have always done.

That sucks, mate, Burhan says.
Yeah, I don't want it to fucking leave, you know.

Then they change subjects, talk about soccer. I google "vitiligo." Online a colorful painting appears. It's called *Madeleine de la Martinique,* was created around 1782, and shows a naked black-and-white-spotted toddler in the foreground and in the background a Black woman who appears to be holding the girl and handing her an apple. I read something about Le Masurier, the Frenchman who painted the piece and produced many similar works at the end of the eighteenth century. Paintings that showed people enslaved by France on the island of Martinique, in cheerful tumult, in a pleasant mood heading to delightful bazaars—a wonderful market bustle, a rich selection of wares and foods, people in expensive clothing—the lighter the skin color, the higher their status and the more splendid the material around them. Beautiful images of a romanticized view of colonizers.

On the way back I tell Duane that the first time I was in Angola, I was shocked that women bleach their skin. At the same time, I tell him, these yellow unhealthy-looking women who had tried to lighten their skin using pills and chemical creams fascinated me. But I still found it horrifying what some people do to their skin and impressive how he, Duane, handles this whole thing.
Well, Burhan interjects, *isn't lightening your skin with a little cream the same thing as when white people use self-tanning lotion to turn themselves into carrots?*
Nope, I don't think so, I say, before I've had time to think about it.
Why not?
. . . Because self-tanning lotion and tanning beds aren't as unhealthy as using chemicals to bleach the melanin out of your skin?

Burhan squints his eyes: *That's not an especially convincing argument.*

I try again:

Because white people don't try to look like Black people, am I right? Rather, they want to look like they just came back from vacationing in the Seychelles. They're trying to imitate a natural process. But Black people or people from South Korea or from Jamaica or wherever the fuck they do this shit are trying to look like white people. That's just not natural.

So what about Duane, says Burhan. *Is he also not natural?*

I sigh. Burhan, who used to go by Benny in school and who always acts as if his life has not at all been affected by the fact that his mother fled to Germany under extraordinary hardships, lives among three different languages here and doesn't speak any of them fluently. Burhan, the eternal bachelor, relationship-phobic to the core, helpful and vain, my best friend. I just wish he weren't so self-confident and couldn't always con me with his psychoanalytic drivel—

Duane starts to laugh.

You Germans, you take everything so seriously! I think the key to everything is keeping a sense of humor, innit?

He adds that he refuses to answer. When the tenth stranger in a week approaches him with *Oh my gosh, what happened to you?* he just says: *I was bitten by a radioactive chameleon,* and keeps walking.

Cheers to that! Burhan says, and switches the subject.

Later that night, we talk about trips that we're planning. I say that at some point I'd like to go back to the U.S., probably to Detroit, since I've never been there. The U.S. never interested me before, but lately that's changed. Burhan says he just wants to go to the North Sea, like in the lyrics from this popular German song—"Westerland." He says, during his downtime, he wants to escape the commotion of the city. But of course, professionally big cities mean guaranteed jobs for him as a therapist, *knock on wood*. Duane's thinking about going to South Africa. He wants to see Jo'burg and Cape Town with his own eyes, experience the people there, the food. I'm lying next to Burhan in bed, Duane on an air-filled mattress. *Such a good, silly item*, I think, *that has made it possible for me to sleep for weeks.* Burhan needed peace and quiet in his bed again, he gets up at six thirty a.m. on weekdays; he got the guest mattress without comment. Burhan and Duane drink whiskey and share a joint. I drink tea and share a bar of chocolate with myself; alcohol is taboo since I started taking medication. We talk reticently while we watch *The Voice* using Burhan's projector. Sometimes Duane laughs during moments when I'm moved to tears, then the mattress makes squeaking noises beneath him. The light and dark spots in his face are like an echo of my mother's painted face in *Susanne's Dream*.

While hopeful people sing as well as they can, I look at my fingernails. For weeks now I've stopped biting them. It's as if they now grow faster than before. They're sturdier, have more sheen and strength, and those white spots that are apparently caused by a lack of calcium or magnesium have disappeared. I wonder where they've gone to, thinking: *My nails have outpaced me, my grandmother would be proud of me.*

When I leave the bathroom and enter Burhan's room, he sits relaxed at his desk in front of his laptop, watching the sports report. I sit down on the sofa and cry a little quieter; Burhan turns to me.

While he speaks, I can't bear to look him in the eyes.

Cautiously, he urges me to take the medication. The obscure side effects listed on the package insert, the dubious little Dr. Wünschel in his much-too-big blazer, Burhan's sighing pleas, the fear that I might go even further off the rails—I've been carrying the pills around with me for weeks instead of just taking them, I don't trust them.

Burhan says my condition is acute.

And then, calmly, finally: *So.*

There are three people in the photo, a tall one and two little ones, a grown woman and two children, from a distance of about six feet. The colors are dull, there's a light sepia filter more than anything else. It's unclear whether that's a result of the age of the photo or if color film looked that way back then or if the world it depicted just looked like that in reality. The three people are in mid-stride, they're walking next to one another along a lightly cracked path, perhaps the sidewalk on a quiet street. Based on their clothing, it could be fall or winter. The woman has short, dark, wavy hair; she holds her head turned to the side and is looking back at the children. You can't really see her face, her expression could be worried or concentrated, attentive, or maybe she is speaking. There's a white spot near her earlobe, probably an earring. She's wearing a bright-colored jacket with several buttons, her hands are shoved into the pockets in front of her stomach. The jacket's hem borders her waist-high dark blue skirt, which reaches below her knee. From the side, the skirt has long, straight pleats. She's wearing black boots that cover half of her calves; beneath those she's likely wearing thick woolen stockings. The children she's looking down at are walking next to each other and gazing straight ahead. They're about half as tall as the woman and wearing heavy anoraks and pants made of a sturdy material, maybe jeans, along with light-colored shoes that could be sneakers. One child is wearing a pink anorak and a pastel-colored striped wool hat, along with white earmuffs on the sides of their head. They're holding a stiff-looking plush rabbit under the arm, which one can tell is a rabbit by the bunny ears sticking straight up to the child's chin. The other child is walking

slightly behind the two people but also appears to be walking in between them. Their body is partially covered by the woman and partially covered by the child in front. This child is wearing a blue anorak
and otherwise the exact same pants, same shoes, and the same head
covering as the other child, but no earmuffs. They seem to be the only
person looking at the camera, or just past it, with a tinge of a smile
perhaps. The children's faces are too blurry to recognize any clear facial expressions. The child in front seems serious, strained, their eyes
are in the shadow of the small peak of their hat. The other child appears to be holding on to the woman's skirt. Their right arm is reaching up and immediately covered by dark blue material. One can't tell
whether this child is holding a stuffed animal too. The woman's body
is creating an angular shadow on the ground, the children's feet are
standing in it like a puddle. The photo seems empty, even though it's
full of objects. Perhaps at the exact second when the photo was shot,
everything was momentarily still.

There are newly constructed apartment buildings in the background
of the photo.

When they were built, the description "newly constructed buildings" was fitting, it stood for great possibilities. Brand-new living
modules, modern and towering over one another, with radiators
in the rooms instead of coal ovens, with warm running water from
pipes instead of cold water in washbasins. And along with that, the
promise of a big, caring community, dry, spacious cellars, courtyards divided by picket fences; cellars through which one could go
from housing unit to housing unit, people felt connected. That's
why there were also courtyards with jungle gyms, where children
could play alone and simultaneously always be in sight of the entire
neighborhood.

Maybe the children are mumbling a nursery rhyme to themselves or the woman is telling them a story. Maybe one of the three people depicted was just loudly yelling something, and now hears an echo of their voice.

In front of a high-rise, a bare, thin tree towers in the sky. From the distance, it looks like the highest branches are growing on the roof of the high-rise. The sky behind the branches, above the high-rise and above the woman's turned head, is made of an impenetrable texture. It's unclear whether this photo shows a good moment or a bad one. Whether or not the three people photographed are enjoying walking through these newly constructed buildings, or which memories this photo might awaken. When people talk about the dreariness of East Germany, it's possible they think of photos like this. But maybe they're precisely wrong about that.

Next to the child in the pink anorak is a patch of grass running parallel to the flagstone path, with some coniferous bushes. To the left of the woman, however, the street is cut off by the photo. One can see the rear end of a light blue Trabant, its front end appears to be facing toward the high-rises. Right next to the woman (who is wearing shimmering mother-of-pearl nail polish), below the curb, the car reflects the sunshine, its paint job shining brightly. Maybe this truncated part of the car belongs to a Lada or a Wartburg—other brands often found in the GDR. Trabi, Lada, Wartburg—these cars today are all either derided or worshiped as a part of nostalgia for the East. Some say disparagingly that you had to wait ten years for these cars made of cardboard, what a godawful country.
Why is it that after the wall fell, nothing the GDR had achieved was acknowledged in West Germany?

When I was ten years old, without warning, my mother told me a story. We were standing in the kitchen and she showed me how to prepare a TV dinner. Noodles in cheese sauce, so I could cook something for me and my brother after school.

Grandma probably told you about the time I went to prison, right? We had an especially sadistic female warden. Sometimes she would rip up women's photos. Those were pictures of their husbands, families, friends. Luckily, when I was arrested, I didn't even have a chance to grab a photo. Only today do I realize: *She probably meant a photo of us.*

This attempt to destroy tangible, positive memories—maybe this is akin to what the West did to the East after reunification. And to believe exactly that is probably what it means to really be an Easterner.

I sleep for fourteen hours and on the next day, sixteen. A large, friendly slug snuggles up into the upper back of my head. These days, it actually seems as if I can feel my brain, it tingles. The racing of my heart, the restlessness, the brooding, the fear—with each week everything becomes plainer. In the afternoon, Burhan and I go shoot some baskets, I mostly make them, but don't get excited about it; everything is moderate.

On the way back to his apartment we pass a wall. On it, the following is sprayed:

What are photos of us when they lock us inside ourselves?

Maybe I should ask the photographer what this sentence means. I'll see him soon. The first conversation was cordial, but it was difficult to find a time to meet. He's usually busy, and I was hindered by myself.

The dryness in my mouth is unfamiliar, I notice it most when I pronounce words that start with *F*. But it doesn't bother me otherwise. I suggest to Burhan that we go get some soup. He says he'd rather cook, maybe a mushroom risotto; fine with me.

What are photos of us when they lock us inside ourselves?

It's possible that the photographer will tell me things from my mother's past that I couldn't have anticipated, things that have been hidden until now and that affect me indirectly. Things that will disturb me or pacify me. I have high expectations.

Two years after Kim and I first met, I slept at her place sometimes. After our first, drunken getting-to-know-each-other in Cologne, we had lost sight of each other. Two years later, we ran into each other one Sunday in the Grunewald. After that we'd meet and write to each other with increasing frequency. At some point, for weeks, we started to pretend we were just good friends and maybe one of us had missed the last train at night or was just too lazy to go home. I acted inhibited, I was shy and confused. After several exciting months, we sometimes took each other in our arms, slept closer together, and caressed each other a little. I had an absurd fear of our first looming sexual experience, I kept convincing myself that we were just good friends and that I wasn't really into women; that I didn't really belong to yet another marginalized fringe group. At the time, Luise just said: *You're crazy, sex with women is the best. You're such a late bloomer.*

John Henry is the subject of many stories, plays, and novels. But mostly he was sung about in folk songs that circulated throughout the U.S. in the late nineteenth century. They were meant to make hard physical labor more bearable. According to the legend, at that time in the U.S., John Henry worked with a hammer. He rammed steel drill bits into stone—together with a zillion other African American workers who shortly before had been slaves. He used those steel bits to drill holes in the stone. In turn, explosives were put into the holes to blast as many boulders as possible to enable the building of railroad tunnels. Thousands of African Americans died from the dangerous working conditions, even today there are trains traveling daily past their nameless mass graves, through tunnels and vast, impressive landscapes. According to the legend, one day John Henry's power and ability as a hammering steel-driving man was tested in a competition against a steam-powered stone-drilling machine. He was stronger and won the competition. But the price was high: Directly following his victory, he died, with a hammer in his hand. His heart failed from sheer exhaustion. Today, John Henryism is a syndrome that can affect people who are repeatedly faced with emotional and physical stress caused by racial discrimination.

In Kim's building, a family of four lived on the ground floor, they appeared to almost always be at home. The oldest male, maybe in his early fifties, often sat on the terrace and chain-smoked. During or after, about every fifteen to twenty minutes, he was befallen by a long, intense coughing fit. Usually he ended his wet death rattle with a loud, scratchy spitting sound. Kim and I called him the Polish sack of mucus, because we often heard him talking loudly on the phone in Polish, and when he did, he'd always sit alone on the terrace. His phlegm accompanied us for a year and a half, while we cooked, while we conversed, fought, slept together, or read each other books; we even heard him when the window was closed. Mornings at seven a.m., nights at one a.m., Sunday morning. Sometimes it seemed as if he never slept and just sat down there around the clock, with his ass in jogging pants glued to his white plastic chair. Even in the early days of our timid flirtations it occurred to me that it was stupid that we called him the Polish sack of mucus. His alleged nationality didn't have anything to do with his coughing. *Hm, you're right*, Kim said. Since then, we continued to find him disgusting, but when we talked about him, we referred to him only as the sack of mucus on the ground floor. Back then, we wanted to be politically correct in every detail of our private lives.

Once while I was at a lecture about African literatures, at the end, a woman with a Saxon accent raised her hand to ask a question. She wanted to know if there are parallels between African postcolonial narratives and the literature of the former East German states after reunification. Because, in principle, both places were colonized, Africa and the GDR, both came under the hammer, so to speak. Her equivocation made a lot of people in the room angry, suddenly the atmosphere became tense, many smirked while shaking their heads. The moderator played down the question and tried to generalize the woman's comment; she didn't receive an answer, at least not verbally.

A few months after I had slept in my own apartment alone for the first time, Luise convinced me to go on a bike trip through Masuria in Poland with her and two of her girlfriends. It's not really my kind of vacation, but Luise was persistent. She kept sending me screenshots of expensive trekking bikes, tight biking shorts for women with sewn-in cushions for your butt and matching seamless underwear, as well as a lot of euphoric voice messages where she sketched out how intense and wonderful everything would be. Besides, she added, then we could finally have a real conversation again, without interruptions, without Milli. Later, by the time we'd been biking for two weeks, it had rained almost every day. We still got along well, but we often had to clarify the dynamic within our group—one of us was usually annoyed. When the day didn't go as planned, when biking was more demanding, when the food didn't taste good, or our bodies were freezing cold. After a week, we came upon a clearing in the middle of the forest. One could camp there, even if there was only a porta-potty and a small lake. In the early evening, a nice lean woman came and collected our złotys. In addition to us, two long-term Polish campers also spent the night in the clearing—a beautiful fat woman with her small husband. They had built themselves an elaborate camp, with a lot of colorful tarps and long, thick sticks; they even had a kind of outdoor kitchen. He served and spoiled his wife around the clock, brought her coffee, cake, and scrambled eggs while she was fishing. Massaged her back when she wasn't fishing. His T-shirt said: *Polygamy rocks*. The next day, for the first time since our trip started, the sun shone; we were lying about—in hammocks, on towels on the ground, on the wide dock that led to the water. We went swimming, ate ravioli from the can or oatmeal with fruit. Early in the evening, a group of young men came with a canoe and set up their tents. Friendly teacher's aides from Bayreuth, one of them had been born in Poland. We later sat together around the campfire in the dark, politely talking about all sorts of things. Luise made a lot of jokes and laughed, often very loud. She seldom let us get a word in edgewise; maybe she thought one of the students was attractive. Luise's girlfriends were even more reserved than me, but for that reason they took even bigger sips from the bottle of vodka that we passed around the circle. At first, I just pretended to drink whenever the bottle reached me, because of the pills I was on. After a few rounds I gave up and enjoyed the warmth that crept down my throat into my stomach. Around midnight, a jeep suddenly tore through the forest at top speed. It slowed down just before our campfire and braked suddenly, its lights blinding us. Two men got out of the five-seater jeep, both with shaved heads. Five more, all clean shaven as well, stayed in the crowded jeep, staring at us through the windows. As the Polish German teacher's aide translated for us, they claimed to be from the forest patrol and wanted to see our IDs; he seemed tense, fearful, and stood up straight. The men in the jeep grinned at us or looked serious. Of the two who had gotten out, the smaller, more petite one suddenly approached me with something in his hand that

I couldn't recognize. He asked me questions in Polish and looked me over carefully. I responded now and again that I didn't understand, *Niemką, Niemką.* The other, feistier one pointed at the fire and hissed something; the teacher's aide nodded. I knew right away that these guys were right-wing, I could sense that they had no problem with violence. Luise tried briefly to protest, they should first show us their IDs. The teacher's aide resolutely silenced her. Suddenly, the thin one asked me questions in English—where I was from, what I was doing there.

I'm on a holiday trip with my friends, we are here with our bicycles.

After they had finally seen our IDs, they advised us to thoroughly put out the fire later, then climbed back into their jeep and drove away. But pulled off downhill, only ten yards away. Then they all got out and sat around on the dock for several hours, in the glow of the headlights, conversing loudly. The later it got, the hoarser their voices became, sometimes one of them screamed something into the night. I was sure that as soon as they were drunk enough, they'd return and beat us up and/or rape us. Luise rejected my suggestion to flee into the forest. *After all,* she said, *we outnumber them and in the worst case we have to fight. But scattered throughout the forest, with them in the jeep, our chances are even worse.* I think Luise has never seen a fight between violent, drunken men and nonviolent men.

The teacher's aides decided at some point to stand guard in shifts. They told us that one of them would always remain at the fire. If something happened, they'd raise the alarm. Thankfully, with heads heavy from vodka and with a strange feeling of indifference, we accepted their suggestion. Whatever happened would happen. Shortly before I fell asleep, I wrote a pathetic farewell letter to Burhan, just in case.

Then nothing happened.

By morning, the men and their jeep were gone, and there were crushed beer cans lying everywhere. The fat woman, who was fishing again and drinking coffee, had just thrown a fish back into the lake. On the previous evening, her partner and she had said nothing during the alleged ID check; they had just stared into the fire. Now the teacher's aide was translating for me what they said: that those guys definitely couldn't have been from the forest patrol, because fishing is forbidden here, but they did so anyway all night. *And they took the fish with them!* Moreover, she apologized to me on behalf of her countrymen: They're not all like that, even if something like this happens with increasing frequency; it's also the fault of the government. I wanted to know what exactly the smaller Pole had said to me; what exactly was she apologizing for. The teacher's aide skated around my question, embarrassed; the man just wanted to find out if I was a refugee by testing my accent, that's why he had so many questions. Refugees are a problem in Poland, he finished, even if there actually aren't any.

Even though I know it can't be true, sometimes I imagine that Poland, Hungary, and Romania sounded as promising to my grandparents in GDR times as the following places did during my childhood: swimming in Lake Maggiore, hiking in the Rocky Mountains, eating snails in the south of France. But it's not true, these promises didn't exist, neither for my grandparents nor for my mother, and maybe that evades my imagination. No Lake Maggiore, no Rocky Mountains, no snails, only that which is already there and already known, or somewhere that is similar to home.

When my brother and I were about four or five years old, together with my mother we moved into a small rented house that needed to be refurbished and renovated from the ground up. Today I know that previously she had tried everything to emigrate, either with or without us. She even tried to sign over custody of us to someone else, but nothing worked. Maybe that's why she decided to invest an enormous amount of energy into a derelict building, so she could achieve something at least. For months, many of her friends helped out—back then she still had friends—and we lived on a chaotic, exciting construction site. Once, my brother and I played in one of the empty rooms and found a hammer lying on the floor. We thought we could help the adults out by imitating their work, so we hammered little holes into an unsound wall. We were proud of what we achieved, and we didn't understand why our mother was so upset. When she later recalled this anecdote, she jokingly called us little "Heroes of Labor." She never mentioned that at the time we had been locked inside an empty room.

When I talk to my grandmother about the olden days when we are both sitting down for coffee and Russian zupfkuchen, admiring the photos on her walls that belong to two young people who do not yet know that they will soon lose each other, I never know if she curses the GDR or longs to have it back. But maybe those aren't contradictions, maybe both things are possible. For example, she once said that Gorbachev did so much for the GDR and that he was a really good man: He even allowed Poland to become more democratic in the late 1980s. Only then did the place become truly interesting as a vacation spot for most citizens of the GDR. Never mind that during the seventies, the Poles still bought the stools right out from under them. But that didn't matter to the young people of the GDR at the end of the eighties who were hell-bent on democracy. For a long time, everything in Poland had been much less developed than in the GDR. But when they were all allowed to come over in the seventies and stood in line to buy our goods, well, one noticed something backward even in their mentality. *Nein, nein, zey veren't impolite or anyzing, but . . .* In any case, the Poles were a totally different kind of people, my grandmother said, a very different culture, one could see that immediately in their consumption, and also when their country became more progressive.

When she talks like that, I don't know whether she thinks of democracy as inherently good or bad.

During school breaks, my mother, my brother, and I usually stayed in Thuringia. My brother and I sometimes played near the trailers of our mother's friends, outside of the city, in the countryside. During the day, we climbed trees, spit in wells, hammered nails into random planks, or fought each other on straw bales. In the evening, we sat by the campfire and ate dough that we pulled off heated sticks, with glowing faces and beautiful, uncanny stories in our heads. At night, we slept in a tent and imagined that it was sitting on the summit of the highest mountain in the world. It didn't matter that most of our classmates weren't in the city at this time. It didn't matter what they had experienced, snails, Lake Maggiore, etc. We had experienced enough.

Sometimes I think that during these times, my mother felt even more trapped in her life than she did in GDR times.

Kim ultimately wanted to take action against the sack of mucus on the ground floor. On the computer, she wrote an honest letter. Bilingual, in case the man didn't understand German; she let a Polish-speaking friend check the translation she got from online, printed out the error-free letter, and laminated it. The letter stated, among other things, that having to constantly listen to mucus-filled coughing is unfortunately quite disgusting. It continued, perhaps the dear neighbor can go to the doctor or spit within his own four walls, in the bathroom, for example, into the toilet. Kim and I discussed at length whether we should leave the letter anonymous or sign it and place it in his mailbox. We decided to let it be anonymous, since we couldn't judge how the family would react or what they were capable of. A few days later, I asked Kim if anything had happened. She answered that she didn't put the note in his mailbox after all, she no longer thought it was the right thing to do. She had spoken with a neighbor about it. The woman had told Kim that she understood Polish and sometimes listened in when the man and his wife fought drunkenly. Apparently, a few years ago, the pair had lost their adult son in a car accident and they blamed each other for it and continued to live unhappily in their ground-floor apartment with their two remaining children, because they didn't have enough money to do anything else. Besides, apparently the husband had suffered a stroke not long ago and had trouble getting around. The neighbor had said, *He gave up long ago.* Ever since then, it was no longer easy to become annoyed with him. Empathy mixed in with our disgust; it suddenly seemed tactless to deliver the letter.

The idea of another sexuality and my fear of it disappear, as soon as I experience this sexuality. The idea that the Poles have a different, backward mentality compared with East Germans disappears as soon as Poland appears to be more democratic than the GDR. The suspicion that I could be a refugee, the utmost subaltern, can no longer be maintained, as soon as I produce my German passport. The fact that African Americans are still suffering the aftermath of slavery, during which they were degraded most inhumanly, may never be resolved. Not as long as African Americans count as the other Americans, as Americans who must be labeled with the prefix African. The idea that my mother is a distinct part of the family, and that she pursued completely different, almost contrary interests than I did, could be self-righteous. Maybe this idea can be resolved only if I get closer to my mother again, so I can look behind the wall that I created out of one-sided, filtered childhood memories. The idea that my brother is a person who differed from me only slightly, who basically resembled me in every respect, could also be self-righteous. I didn't lose myself, I didn't lose a part of myself; rather, I lost another person.

I wonder whether the coughing man is still sitting on the terrace beneath Kim's apartment and whether Kim is listening to him together with her new girlfriend, just as we did back then. Which new nicknames they have thought up for him, which activities his coughing is disrupting. Maybe the man has managed to free himself from that life. Maybe he used a hammer to smash through the ominous walls of his existence.

Probably not.

Burhan's couch is the place of refuge I seek out the most, the wine-red leather against my cheek is comforting. While he's at work, I take a break from myself there. Distance, pills, sleep, and quiet enter me, my so-called soul is finally dangling, but somehow gone at the same time. I start reading the various books on Burhan's shelves, again and again, between the lines, I get confused, I can't retain anything. Sometimes I stare out the window for half an hour without thinking, sometimes I watch one movie trailer after the other with his projector, but don't watch a single film.

I really enjoy all of that.

When I close my eyes, I see darkness and a few spots of light, sometimes a face from my childhood, sometimes a tornado over a dark gray foaming ocean.

I think, I now know what it's like to feel like my mother. What it's like to be untenably at the mercy of yourself.

The photo is in black and white and shows a well-traveled wintry street. In the middle of the photo there's a young man, who's leaning forward while riding a bike. He appears to be going uphill. The young man is either sitting at the very front of the saddle or he's standing up with his legs bent, riding toward the person taking the photo. The handle-bars, which he grips with both hands, are reminiscent of a racing bike, you can't tell what brand of bicycle it is, perhaps Diamant. The young man is wearing dark gloves, dark gray pants, and a light gray jacket. In hindsight it's impossible to say whether his outfit is colorful or not. His pants reach just above his ankles, his feet are on the pedals wearing light-colored socks and likewise dark gray-looking shoes. He seems so focused, happy, smiling slightly or maybe not. With big eyes, he's look-ing at the road stretching before him, not at the camera. He's wearing a keffiyeh around his neck, casually wrapped, falling in broad folds on his left shoulder. Even today, many refer to this scarf as a Palestinian scarf. When the photo was shot, the young man probably wore it as a symbol of leftist, anti-imperialist convictions, or maybe he wore it merely to shield himself from the cold. A gray cap, similar to a baseball cap, sits on top of his curly black hair that's sticking straight up. One can see a blurry, light-colored imprint on it. Today, the young man wouldn't stand out in any Berlin bar or on the subway trains of New York. Back then, his outfit may have been too light for the all-encompassing winter.

According to my grandmother, my grandparents and my father got along exceptionally well in the short time they were acquainted. When one looks at the letters he wrote to them during the 1980s (my brother and I were a little over a year old at the time), one notices a socialist character to his words; maybe that's what united them. At age nineteen, he writes indignantly about how *uncivilized* Angola seems to him shortly after his return, how slowly everything progresses there, how much capitalism continues to exploit everything, especially the valuable natural resources. In these letters, my father repeatedly expresses admiration for my grandparents, and all the help that they bestowed upon him and Susanne. Nearly all of it is written in flawless German, with a clean, beautiful signature.

In the photo, three cars in a row drive behind the young man, they're probably all Ladas, status symbols of the time. Three hazy heads hover in the windshield of the foremost car, which is about five feet behind the young man. The second Lada appears behind the first but farther to the left; only half of it is visible, one of the headlights shines brightly. One can see only the dark gray angular outer edge of the third car. The entire left side is taken up by a pile of snow that has been shoveled to the side, it's white-gray. The dirty piles line the street like pointy low walls running from the foreground to the background. Bare silhouettes of trees tower over the snow on both the left and right sides. On the opposite side of the road, there are four or five massive vehicles, the same height as the Ladas, about six feet. I see them from behind, on the right side, they seem robust, bulky. Even though they're not in the center of the photo, they dominate the atmosphere as they drive downhill toward the foggy background. There's a spare tire perched on the back of the last vehicle. Under that, two small brake lights are shining. Back then, these vehicles were called Russki convoys; Soviet soldiers sat inside them.

To this day, my grandmother speaks disparagingly about Russians. After reunification, her younger brother married a Russian woman.

If you believe my grandmother, this *tart* was cunning, devious, and interested only in expensive fur coats, always wearing cheap Russki perfume. She says that, in general, there was a deep hostility between Russian and German women. For example, the *Russian tarts* used to cut to the front of the line at the bus stop. Even if there was already a long line of people waiting, they would occupy the best spots. As "second-class citizens," the German women had to get on the bus later and sit in the back. I don't tell my grandmother that that reminds me of a more bearable variant of Rosa Parks, instead I try to listen without judgment. I don't know what it's like to spend your youth in the presence of Soviet soldiers, what kinds of traces that can leave behind, what kinds of injustices happened, how many rapes there actually were. I also don't know if my grandparents would have become staunch Nazis after reunification had my mother and father not met beforehand. I know only that there were a lot of violations, on all sides. Of dignity, of pride, and of the body.

Even today, my grandmother only speaks about my father with great respect and affection. She says that back then, he had convinced Susanne to leave the punk scene, they never forgot that about him. On Facebook he once wrote to me that back then, it was as if Susanne had broken some kind of oath. After she gave birth to the kids and after her first attempt to become bourgeois again, a lot of her friends seemed disappointed. No more dyed hair, no more safety pins in her ears, no more upholding attitudes that departed from the mainstream, no more alleged stirrings of freedom. In another letter to my grandparents, my father wrote that Susanne had recently sent him twenty packs of cigarettes. He was very happy about that, but also sad; the smell of the brands Cabinet and f6 had reminded him of the GDR. Moreover, he reported with great anticipation that he will likely soon be able to pick up the documents that are necessary for the marriage and that have been translated into Portuguese, from the embassy.

Once, when I asked my grandmother if she'd like to have my father's current email address or telephone number, she said no. I suspect she wants everything to stay sealed. Even my father asks how they're doing every now and then, but after more than thirty years, it doesn't seem to be an option to just contact them himself. It was also never an option for my mother and father after her arrest. And even I feel closer to the young man in the photo than to the man who sporadically and impulsively shares his feelings with me online once or twice a year and doesn't respond to my answers. I would've liked to have known these two people: this hopeful eighteen-year-old who's riding his bike to his girlfriend's, and this girlfriend, a respectable, happy girl who recently caused a stir in the Czech Republic with her outlandish look.

After six weeks, finally I can sleep alone in my apartment again. I no longer wake up if I have less than ten hours of sleep.

Burhan is relentless. He says I can't avoid going to therapy.

Okay, then.

I make three attempts.

The first one goes like this:

The psychologist—white, tall, and lean—greets me at his practice, grinning mischievously. Black leather sofas and an armchair, beige aluminum blinds ornament the windows, no plants, a lot of books. Everything is a little sparse, but still cozy. I tell him as much as I can, reveal myself quickly and purposefully. The psychologist doesn't ask me any questions, he takes only a few notes on his pad. I speak for a long time, with pauses, eventually about the stabbing in Neukölln, as I was walking with Kim, a good friend. He looks at me, still no questions. I remember more, start into a monologue, speculate that shortly after the incident I started holding on to the spot with my hand when strangers walked past me. *You know, the spot where the boy held himself after he was stabbed. And recently, I say, I have been dreaming frequently about white men who chase black men with harpoons, maybe there's a connection there?* The psychologist is silent. *Maybe there's a connection between my fear and the increase in right-wing violence and sentiment among the public that's been worrying me, it reminds me of the past, more specifically the past reminds of today, I grew up with explicit racism, in eastern Germany, in the nineties, smashed windows in our childhood bedrooms, the gas pistol my mother hid under her mattress; I want to say, I understand the fears of people who live in asylum seekers' homes and that might trigger something in me, and when my brother died, he had been roughly the same age as the boy who was stabbed, I was too when I died, um, I mean he.*

The psychologist clears his throat. My chatter makes me feel like I am shuffling across increasingly thin ice wearing platform shoes made of steel, deliberately but without knowing where else to go. Suddenly a movement goes through his torso, as if he flinched while falling asleep and woke himself up. He asks me whether I have any other siblings. Yes, in Angola; I've known them fleetingly. He adds, do I have friends? *Yes, a lot, they're my safety net, I couldn't do anything without them; I mean, I've been sleeping on their couches and in their beds for over six weeks, I already said that.* He continues, what kind of apartment do I live in, where I can't sleep? I talk about my studio apartment, where an alcoholic drummer lived before me and died. I tell him about the spooky energy that I attribute to the apartment. I don't say *spooky energy* but rather *strange vibes* and I immediately wonder if the psychologist even knows what I mean. I lose control, can already feel the cold, endless water through the ice. But I keep speaking, nonetheless, about the drum kit that stood in the hallway and was gradually covered in dust, months after I had moved in. I talk about the name of the dead drummer, whose name is still next to my doorbell a year after I moved in. I tell him that I've been a bit scared in this building for a while already, long before this overwhelming fear came on. *The only people who live there are strange folks in small studio apartments. A guy you never see or hear lives beneath me, there's never a light on in his place, every day at five p.m. his alarm goes off, otherwise it's quiet. Beneath him, there's an alcoholic who once called to me on the staircase with big eyes and a toothless grin: If you get too loud, I'm gonna come knock on your door, you hear me, I'm gonna come knock! Beneath him, on the ground floor, there's a woman who has inflamed* vocal cords and a dog named Sunny. When she calls after Sunny in the courtyard, which she does often, it sounds like the clichéd incarnation of an evil villain. Sunny stinks and looks like an older, gaunt version of the girl from the horror movie The Ring. And all these people live in the same kind of studio apartment as I do, just with different furniture and smells. That makes me feel uncomfortable somehow, that must have an influence on me, especially because the drummer died here, well, sometimes I have the feeling that death is insistently attached to my life.

The psychologist sits up straight.

After a pause, followed by a sigh, he says:

Well, yes.

I think you did everything right.

But you are indeed a minority in this country.

My mouth is dry; there's nothing that I can swallow.

He continues:

You feel torn between cultures. I think those are problems that exist in the here and now, with the external world. My therapy is directed more toward people who are burdened by the past . . . therefore, I don't think I can offer you any help. And in principle, your questions can't be answered with therapy.

I wake up, I'm drunk, even though I don't want to be drunk anymore. My brain feels like it's been preserved in schnapps. I'm disgusted by the smell of alcohol on my breath, everything is dull. There's a white man with long hair lying next to me. I have vague memories running around my head of how we kiss, bite, and lick each other's face in the back seat of a moving taxi. How he takes off a leather glove and slips his hand into my underwear. I see us standing at a bar, how he's sitting down next to me and placing his hand on the back of my neck without saying a word. I see myself dancing with my eyes closed, and everything's spinning. I get up, slowly climb down from my loft bed, my head aches throbbingly, I open the window, outside it's a pigeon-gray day, nearly past. When I turn around, there's a bulldog sitting across from me. The dog is looking at me attentively, silently he wags the little knob on his butt. I walk past him, into the bathroom, my butthole feels sore. I see myself standing in a dilapidated building, some guy fucks me from behind, another one is watching and jerks off, both of them look pretty young, there's no dog in sight, no glass in the windows, just square-shaped dark holes. It smells rotten in the bathroom. When I stand under the shower, I first make the water too hot, then too cold, I puke bile onto my toes. Two hours later, the guy and the dog have disappeared, we didn't talk or cuddle, I am lying alone in the darkness that penetrates my room and me, in the filthy bedsheets. I wish I had a close-fitting wooden helmet to keep my thoughts together, there is no order anywhere. I see myself standing on a table in a club, trying to dance and drink simultaneously, and spilling whiskey cola all over my chest. I see myself standing in front of a club and screaming at a bouncer. I see myself in the bathroom, twice turning down some speed, then taking a line after all. I see myself in a bar talking to someone and then abruptly throwing my schnapps glass against his head. I don't know how long I was on the go, maybe twenty hours, out of the corner of my eye I see nervous, flickering shadows. My heart has been racing for hours, I watch TV shows, eat chips, cocoa powder with a spoon; the idea of going to the gas station to buy something to eat is out of the question. I can't order food either, no one can see me like this. In case I do allow myself to be lulled to sleep, at night, the shadows could get me. Every now and then I read suicide notes from strangers on the internet who succeeded in committing suicide. They are apparently real notes. Every thirty minutes I turn on my phone to see if someone couldn't reach me. I stream children's shows and rom-coms, harmless input for a haggard body. On the way to the bathroom, I tie the terry-cloth belt of my bathrobe around the transverse beams of my loft bed, as a test. At six a.m. there's actually a message on my phone. Luise's three-year-old daughter, Milli, tells me excitedly that she has brown skin now, *I have brown skin, too, just like you.* After that Luise says, a little embarrassed, that Milli absolutely wanted to make this call and both of them would love it if we could see each other after their vacation. All night I have the feeling that the bulldog is sitting under my loft bed, with glowing eyes and a thin, red, erect dog penis; when I close my eyes, I'm afraid this animal could come up my ladder. As it gets light outside and the first birds start to sing, I fall asleep. Actually, I've known for weeks that I need help. I decide to call Burhan the next day, but it takes three more days and nights of sleep deprivation for me to call. Then I write a message in the morning, around seven thirty.

hey, i'm not doing so well.

could we maybe talk on the phone if you're free?

After twenty minutes, he calls me back. When I hear his voice, I immediately start to cry and put down the phone so I can blow my nose and give myself a slap in the face. At some point, I hear Burhan's voice call out from the phone into my pillow, asking:

Hello, are you still there?

Burhan is relentless.

The second attempt goes like this:
The therapist sounds likable over the phone, her voice is a little weird and whiny, during the intake interview I think she's funny. Sometimes she makes irritating noises with her closed mouth; they remind me of a cow, I can't make sense of them. She dresses a little like a child—colorful, baggy wool sweaters with animal prints, loose-fitting jeans. *She could be sharp*, I think. Often people who don't look so consistent or elegant on the outside place more value on what's inside.

During our fourth meeting, for the second time she tells me a story that made an impression on her. It's about children who were fathered during National Socialism in concentration camps. She says the newborns were smuggled out of the camps in secret and were allowed to grow up freely. Nonetheless, she adds, studies have shown that their stress levels are permanently higher than those of other children, *you know, normal children who weren't fathered in concentration camps.* And later in life, in the case of the nervous, anxious camp children, even just a little stress was enough to put them in an absolute state of emergency.
Once again, the therapist compares these kids with me.

During the fifth meeting, she tells me something she already told me during the first but with a lengthier conclusion. She says I may not know this, but she treated a Black child once and the sessions dealt with racism, too, among other things. Unfortunately, she adds, back then the child lived in East Berlin and there the racism was naturally impossible to avoid in some places. That's why she always picked the child up and traveled with them to West Berlin by train. And that had clearly helped them a lot. But then she concluded the story differently than before. Once, an African man was on the train too; he saw her with the child. And then he flirted with her, that was obvious, *He wanted to have sex with me!* When she got off the train with the child, the African man got off too. So she told a man from the security service that the African had harassed her and that security should please detain him until she and the child could get out of sight. As a result, the man became verbally abusive. When he was detained, he screamed the most unbelievable things at her from across the platform; he even called her a racist.

Ever since I can remember, white people have repeatedly asked me if I've been burned recently.

During puberty, I told the most racist jokes. Their punch lines revolved around comparing my skin to chocolate, dirt, or shit. I thought I was clever, because on the one hand I already knew all these jokes and on the other hand I was the best at telling them, so I could control them.

Ever since I can remember, white people have repeatedly asked me if I have drunk too much cocoa—sometimes maliciously, sometimes ironically, once flirtatiously.

When we were kids, Grandma Rita used to lovingly call us her chocolate crumbs. Even today, she sometimes says that. I've often tried to explain to her that besides showing affection, comparing my skin to chocolate first and foremost suggests that she views her own skin color as normal and my skin is a deviation from normal. Otherwise, she wouldn't always have to remark upon it. Otherwise, she would have gotten the idea to call my grandpa, when he was still alive, *my sweet marshmallow* or to call her daughters *my dear, hard-boiled, orderly peeled eggs*. Nevertheless, she insists that she calls me chocolate crumb, because she thinks my skin is so especially beautiful.

When I was fifteen, I wanted nothing more than a tattoo above my ass. The following would have been written in ornate cursive: *Black Sugar*. Luckily, that never happened.

Once, when I ran my hand over the freshly shaved head of my first boyfriend, the one who used a remarkable amount of violence in order to keep the local Nazis off my back for good, I was astonished: he had such soft skin, I didn't expect that. When I was a kid I heard the word *skinhead* fairly often. I knew that skinheads were evil people without any hair who hated me. That might be why I assumed that the shaved heads of skinheads must be rock-hard, that their skin was less human than mine.

For a long time I thought that the former Black German MTV vee-jay Milka's real name was definitely something else.

Kim once told me that ever since her big sister was sixteen, she'd been saving up for plastic surgery. Kim's sister was convinced that she absolutely had to have eyelid surgery. *And why not? We take it for granted that other people have surgery so their ears don't stick out.* Kim said that back then she couldn't talk her sister out of it; Kim's sister didn't understand what Kim's problem was.

In first grade, my friend Marcel was disappointed when we were on the school playground and it began to rain and my skin color didn't wash off.

Today, skin and hair care products like cocoa or shea butter and coconut oil have moved into the German mainstream and, with that, are now available in drug stores. Beforehand, they could be found mostly in so-called Afroshops. In my early twenties, in a small West German town, I walked by one of these stores where I had never been before. A woman stood in the doorway, came out onto the street, and called to me reproachfully: *Girl, your hair looks dry! Come here.* Obediently I went to her and bought a few different products that she recommended to me. I assumed that she understood my hair better than I did. After a few days, I got a rash from one of the creams.

Burhan remains relentless.

The third attempt goes like this:
First, I change my online search. This time I enter:
"Berlin, therapists of Color." The search results show equipment for
therapists (colorpuncture) and results from Craigslist (*urgently looking for a trainee position as a therapist*). Additionally, there's a list of
websites that appear to competently advise how to find the most suitable therapist. Under every search result, there is a note in light gray
with the words crossed out:
Missing: ~~*of Color*~~

Feeling the warmth that can naturally be found in the touch of two children holding hands. Or when Milli reaches for mine as we walk through the streets together.

Being able to feel, in my body, how my brother and I scuffle as children, how he fidgets and squeals while I'm sitting on his chest with my knees on his arms, giving him a wet willy.

Remembering Kim's kisses on my skin, on my throat, in the nape of my neck, and elsewhere.

The weird handshake that Burhan and I give each other, shortly after we first met at a flea market in East Berlin:
We're both interested in a teapot and bid the price inappropriately higher. Ultimately, neither of us buys the kitschy thing, but we go to get tea together, talk, laugh sometimes. Afterward, it's unclear what the appropriate form of farewell would be. We don't know each other well enough to hug, but we know each other too well to not have any physical contact; our handshake is silly and binding.

My fist landing dully in the face of a drunken man who's grabbed Kim's crotch in a club.

The wonderful game that my brother and I would sometimes play in the bathtub as kids: naked and wet, we sit in the bubbles, and again and again, with outstretched hands, we chop off each other's body parts and yell: *Meat market, meat market!*

The weird moment when I wipe three-year-old Milli's narrow little butt while she bends over in the public restroom and calls out to me: *I'm done.* As if my forefinger and middle finger were made for the crack between her butt cheeks.

My grandmother's calming caress in the crook of my arm when I was a child, which could put me to sleep within minutes.

Sometimes I think it would be nice to remember not just narratives and images, but also touches.

To carry an archive within yourself that has saved all the touches your skin has felt, and that can be recalled at any moment. So that you can access them when you're sitting together with someone on the couch drinking tea and eating cookies, reminiscing about the past.

Several more months pass before I can find a suitable therapist. Then at some point, Luise recommends a female psychologist to me. A charismatic blond woman with warm eyes. Her practice is in the basement. There, we sit across from each other at a large round marble table. Every week there are fresh flowers on it, sometimes kitschy bouquets in an otherwise soberly decorated environment. Now Luise and I are effectively sharing a therapist, which is weird; we intentionally don't speak about her to each other or about when our sessions take place.

One day, while I'm walking to the subway crying and relieved after an intense session, I realize that I know more people who go to therapy, have gone to therapy, or want to go to therapy than people who would find this kind of self-reflection strange. Then I think of my grandmother, how years ago I urged her on the telephone to finally start therapy, since most of her suffering is clearly psychosomatic. She reacted harshly. What gives me the right? She's an old woman and therapy costs a strength that she no longer has. If she were to now discuss everything, to chew over everything that happened to her, she would probably have a breakdown, she could no longer manage all of that in the short time she has left.

After our phone call, I was ashamed and regained more respect for her.

My desire to trace the contours of the light and dark spots of Duane's face with my fingertips.

Imagining how the broad terry-cloth belt of my bathrobe feels around my neck. How it keeps me from plummeting into an unknown nothingness, how it allows me to feel: Something is holding on to me and breaks my neck, something holds me tightly, and in this grasp, this final touch, I will die and will no longer be let go.

The endless, often repeated joke in elementary school: holding out my hand to my friend Marcel for a high five and, when he's about to slap it, pulling my hand away abruptly.

How much I enjoy sleeping next to Burhan, even though he snores. We don't touch each other; while I dream, I barely register his presence. This kind of closeness without touching is possible with only a few friends.

The unrecognizable object in the hand of a petite Polish man who believes he's allowed to interrogate me, and me feeling like he might literally bash my skull in at any moment.

The ritualized, departing handshake between me and diverse therapists would be a better, different handshake if it were accompanied by an apology.

My hand, which grabs my brother's arm and pulls it back shortly before he jumps in front of the train.

That time I wanted to go to Köpenick with Kim to buy a used cabinet I found in a classified ad: a man opens the door and is annoyed, refuses to greet me with a handshake, my hand remains stretched out, without a purpose, in the space between us. He stammers, the cabinet is no longer for sale. In the background, in his living room, I see an Imperial War Flag.

My hands and teeth, which shred apart an Imperial War Flag.

The many times I neglect to stroke Milli's head, in order to not encroach on her personal space, in order to not appear too desperate for love.

My feet, which destroy a cabinet from Köpenick or a man from Köpenick.

The hug that I should have given my mother, half a day after my brother's death, when she arrived in a taxi.

Maybe it would be good if we also carried a negative archive of touches. A compassionate collection of physical encounters that never happened, but rather maybe could have happened or should have happened.

When I visit my grandmother, I don't tell her anything about my therapy or the time before, instead I show her different photos. Copies of prints from the photographer. Photos that he never developed, photos of her teenage daughter that she doesn't know: one shows my mother running across a barren field, accompanied by a boy and girl of the same age. How she stands still and appears to bend one of her large round earrings into shape. How she's a respectable girl.

As we look at *Susanne's Dream* together, it suddenly occurs to me that the face of the naked Czech model resembles that of my grandmother when she was young.

You're right! my grandmother yells, laughing, and she immediately places her hand over the naked breasts in the photo.

The pictures make my grandmother nostalgic. Unlike our previous conversations, she tells me about her youth. How she was pregnant and had to run out of the meat market to throw up. How she started puberty and there was only one sink in the house, in the dining room. How for that reason, she sometimes dared to go downstairs and wash her private parts only at night when everyone else was asleep. How she always had to accept the most beatings when her brothers had done something wrong. How she had been afraid of the Soviet soldiers, especially at night when she was walking home. How painful the birth of her first daughter was, how easy the birth of the second one was in comparison, she virtually slipped right out of her in the hospital corridor. How much she loves all her children, including me.

What I wouldn't give to meet my grandmother and my mother at an impossible moment in time when we're all fifteen years old.

What would we want to tell each other, what would we trust each other with?

Would we be friends?

When I leave my grandmother's house with *Susanne's Dream* in a plastic shipping tube, I think: *This is the most expensive piece of paper that I own.* On the way to the train station it starts to rain. I can't stop imagining that the rain is getting into the tube, onto the photo, and the makeup on Susanne's face will be smeared: my mother, soaked, looking like a killer clown.

On the first evening that I sleep in my apartment alone, Luise, Milli, and Burhan pay me a visit. I've just put new sheets on my bed and I'm clipping the ends of a bouquet of flowers when my doorbell rings. Luise and Milli arrive first. I hear Milli on the staircase, she's singing as she counts the stairs. Then she runs into the apartment grinning, holds a giant helium balloon in front of my face, and yells: *Gesundheit, Gesundheit!*

Thanks, I say. I take the ribbon at the end of the balloon and pat her on the head.

It's nice that you're both here.

Luise steps into the doorway, gasping:

We didn't know if you'd prefer a dinosaur or a dolphin; it was a long discussion.

She has vegetarian lasagna with her. Burhan, who comes fifteen minutes later, brings tiramisu. *Nice balloon*, he says as he sits down at the table with us. I serve carrot-and-coconut soup as an appetizer. It's the only recipe that I know by heart; every friend of mine has eaten it at least three times.

That night, as I lie in my loft bed, the rustling balloon keeps me company. It's silver and pink, and from time to time it scrapes the ceiling gingerly. Maybe it's the air from the heater, maybe the dead drummer is tickling it. My sleep is thin like rice paper, but it's still sleep. The next morning, I get up unusually early, try to do yoga for about ten minutes, then I go take a shower. When I come back to my room, the balloon is gone. I go to the open window. The sky is an immaculate, wondrous light blue plane, across from me there is a chimney sweep on the roof.

I call to him, *Have you seen my dolphin?* and point to the horizon. The chimney sweep looks at me confused, so I yell again:

My dolphin is gone!

Now the man in black turns around, with an outstretched hand he brushes his thumb and forefinger across his eyebrows and perhaps recognizes what I mean in the distance. Then he turns back around, looks at me earnestly, and shrugs his shoulders.

III

(vanishing points)

It is far easier to talk about loss than it is to talk about love. It is easier to articulate the pain of love's absence than to describe its presence and meaning in our lives.

bell hooks
all about love

WHERE AM I NOW?

You're sitting on a plane, in a window seat. The sky is blue, eight hours up in the air, soon you'll be on another earth. Your seat is comfortable, you don't feel bad, the airline is screening infomercials encouraging donations for humanitarian projects.

WHERE AM I FLYING TO?

Vietnam.

WHY AM I GRINNING LIKE THAT?

You just thought of something:

When you were kids, for a while you and your brother thought you could make wings out of cardboard with which you could actually fly up into the sky. Wings with handles made of rope that you would thread through small holes in the cardboard and tie into knots. You were possessed with the idea; again and again you painted these wings on paper and knew that with them, if you gained enough momentum by running downhill on a slope, you would lift up from the ground and fly. The slope—a concrete surface, a kind of driveway without a garage, but way too long and wide for a driveway anyway—had been built in Erfurt, long before your mother moved there with you. You and your brother never actually tried to build the wings or run down the slope, you always just fantasized about it.

MAYBE I SHOULD TURN BACK AND DO IT BELATEDLY?

Presumably you would crash while doing it and break at least one bone, maybe even your lower jaw. And maybe that would be good; after all, you never broke anything, that's where you and your brother were different. Or maybe you should find a quiet spot in Vietnam and make these wings, strap them to your shoulders, and, flapping nervously, run into the ocean.

IF I'M EVEN ALLOWED TO ENTER THE COUNTRY.

DO I HAVE AN ID?

You can go wherever you want and other people can't go anywhere. It's as natural for you as going to the theater.

SOMETIMES I CAN'T STAND THIS PRIVILEGE.

And sometimes you enjoy it without hesitation.

I KNOW.

In this respect, you're white.

THANKS FOR THE TIP.

Because of your ID.

UNDERSTOOD.

In Poland, during the bike trip with Luise and her friends, it might have saved you from a brawl, or rape.

SO WHAT?

You should be grateful for your passport. This document protects you more than any queer BIPOC-karate-self-defense course ever could.

I AM THANKFUL.

Right before you started the bike tour to Poland, you wanted to break in your new bike, test out the absurdly expensive equipment. For that reason, you rode your bike adventurously through Brandenburg for an entire day. Maybe your pills had made you courageous: When you take a break two hours later in a small village at the parking lot of a supermarket and eat your granola bar, a young man addresses you, Jacob. You both strike up a conversation. He tells you about his passion for martial arts and shows you a few moves. Later, you walk along a stretch of country road together, share a granola bar, and you don't ask him about his ancestry. In the end, you stop

in front of a large iron gate. Behind it, you see a multistory building
that reminds you of a barn and a hospital simultaneously. Jacob says:
I must go here now, and looks sad. At exactly this moment, a blue
Trabant drives down the street. The white driver rolls down his window, stretches out his arm, turns his hand into a gun, points at you
both, and pulls the trigger. Jacob doesn't see it, his back is to the man
as he drives by. Confusedly, you suggest that Jacob should come to
visit you in Berlin sometime and you exchange cell phone numbers.
In the coming weeks, every time he writes to you, you don't know
how you should answer.
Hey, girl, have you forgotten about me?
. . .
Hello?
If you had given Jacob your brother's passport, maybe he could have
now lived on a street without Trabants driven around by pantomime-
friendly passengers.
MY BROTHER'S PASSPORT, WHY?
Sometimes you imagine that back then the police didn't immediately
ask for his passport while he was still warm, lying on the train tracks.
That you didn't have to take a taxi to his roommate's immediately after his death in order to get the document, and hand it to the policewoman with an awkward, robotic arm, only to get it back a few days
later riddled with holes, voided. You imagine that instead, due to
clever foresight, fifteen minutes after your brother's death, you keep
his passport and hide it. You call to the policewoman, who is now
exhausted from climbing the stairs: *I can't find anything, I'm sorry*,
and shrug your wingless shoulders. After she disappointedly tips her
hat to you and shuffles back down the stairs, you giggle into your
brother's pillow, whose wrinkles remember the back of his head as
whole: *Heehee, I tricked them.*

Hey, girl, why don't you answer my—

SORRY, BUT I CAN GO WHEREVER I WANT TO AND YOU CAN GO NOWHERE, BYEEE.

At some point you block Jacob's number.

HOW LONG WILL I BE IN VIETNAM?

As long as it feels good.

AM I NOT AFRAID?

Of what?

DO I HAVE A GUN WITH ME?

Sometimes, when you're nervous, you make a gun with your hand while it's in your pocket. For example, when the pilot begins the landing process.

SO I AM AFRAID.

No, you feel astonishingly confident.

During the three weeks you'll be in Vietnam, not once do you see or sense aggression, neither do you think anyone is a terrorist, and you don't ever see anyone who openly scratches his balls.

BUT I JUST GOT HERE.

When you leave the airport, you think you can taste the hot air that weighs heavier than the fine rain. A woman who is balancing a large tablet with sliced pieces of melon climbs onto a moped. It occurs to you that Kim once said that in Vietnam there is no comprehensive feeling of nationalism. The light drizzle moistens your face. In the parking lot of the airport a man is wearing a knapsack with a tube sticking out. Water is spraying out of it; the man is watering flowers while it rains. He wears a gray motorcycle helmet on his head.

The first few days you're walking through the city, you see that a lot of young people, including adolescents, are wearing glasses, but old people never are. And older people, especially in the rural parts, but sometimes also in the city, are actually wearing conical rice hats.

Hats that in Europe belong to a cliché image of Chinese people, hats that by the end of your trip you no longer notice.

DOES THE CHILDREN'S SONG "MY HAT HAS THREE CORNERS" HAVE ANYTHING TO DO WITH THAT?

No, why?

IS THE CHILDREN'S SONG "THREE CHINESE WITH A CONTRA-BASS" ABOUT RACIAL PROFILING?

A week before last, you visited your grandmother in Thuringia for a day. She was proud that she could more or less walk again, she wanted to go into "the city" to eat with you: Enthusiastically she describes the all-you-can-eat-buffet in a Chinese restaurant on the top floor of a shopping center. Grinning and limping, she wants to get on the glass elevator on the ground floor with you, because these elevators are the only ones she can still use and therefore enjoy. A young woman with a shaved head wearing a bomber jacket is already in the elevator— your grandmother is puzzled that you'd rather take the escalator; you don't answer her when she asks why. At the restaurant, you immediately notice that everyone working there is speaking Vietnamese with one another, but the food has nothing to do with China or Vietnam, rather it conforms to German eating habits. This place is one of countless "Chinese restaurants" in eastern Germany that no Chinese person has ever entered. When you try to explain that to your grandmother, she looks at you disappointed.

You always have something to complain about, don't you?

HOW AM I PAYING FOR THE TRIP TO VIETNAM?

You lived frugally during the last two and a half years. Additionally, alongside your therapy every now and then you organized workshops with children and teens, sometimes you worked as a substitute teacher in schools to balance things out. And you worked at the call center again, twice a week.

OLIVIA WENZEL

I THINK MARKET RESEARCH IS PERFIDIOUS.

Still, you sometimes have nice conversations. A senior citizen once told you in detail about how her husband shot himself with a hunting rifle at the Wannsee. The worst of it was he had taken the dog with him.

Why couldn't he have let the dog live? It was still in good health.

And a man, possibly in his fifties, told you that he's tried twice to hang himself in his apartment, but each time the awful music coming from his neighbor's apartment stopped him. He didn't want to die angry. You said that dying angry isn't a bad way to die. Even though at the end of the conversation you had to tease out how much money the interviewee had and what products they spent the most on, you listened to them sincerely. On the telephone, people can sense if the person talking to them is open to hearing their stories. That's why you are supposedly one of the best interviewers in your department.

WEIRD.

Your colleagues with Turkish names usually call themselves Müller and Schmidt on the phone. The interviewees are quicker to trust someone with a German-sounding name.

AND?

Sometimes you're worried that one of your colleagues from the call center will call your grandmother, and then she'll pathetically tell her life story to strange ears that are paid to listen strategically. With details that she would never tell you. But she'll tell this friendly Mr. Müller, *such a nice young man, we had a great conversation.*

ARE MY WORK AT THE CALL CENTER AND MY SUBSTITUTE TEACHING JOBS ENOUGH TO FINANCE THIS TRIP?

No, not really.

AHA.

. . .

178

1,000 COILS OF FEAR

WHICH DETAIL AM I LEAVING OUT?

. . .

WHAT AM I NOT SAYING?

In Angola, your father has become a rather well-off man by now. At
an early stage he invested in oil pipelines. Once a month he wires you
money. That's why you can afford the things you afford.

WHY DOES HE DO THAT?

He started doing that after his son's death. You interpret it as compensation for pain and suffering.

BUT I NEVER THINK OF VISITING MY FATHER WITH THIS
MONEY?

He doesn't visit you either.

AND WHY AM I IN VIETNAM?

When you head into downtown Hanoi from the airport in the shuttle bus, a pompously staged Vietnamese revue show is playing on the
large monitor that's hanging behind the driver. On the screen, there's
always a heterosexual pair that performs romantic songs and is mu-
sically accompanied by an orchestra. It's always a beautiful man and
a beautiful woman, the woman's skin is always much lighter than
those of the other Vietnamese around you. Every pair sings a duet,
he wears a suit, she wears a floor-length dress. Singing, they pine after each other, come together, part, hold each other's hands, then let
themselves go again, full of feelings, as if tormented. Now and then
the camera shows the orchestra, some of the musicians are white; you
don't know why this surprises you. During the trip from the airport
to downtown Hanoi, about ten different pairs perform, seamlessly,
without any moderation in between. Your hands massage themselves, relaxed; you see more and more new suits and dresses, always
worn by new, beautiful bodies, always staging new, painful romance.
Every song sounds honest and kitschy to your ears, the singing lulls

you to sleep. You doze off briefly, dreaming of Burhan. A ladybug crawls into his eye in order to live there.

Later, when you get off the shuttle and take your backpack from the luggage room and the tumult of the city penetrates your body, you don't feel as if you belong, but you still feel like you've arrived. A delivery driver's green backup motorcycle helmet fits only begrudgingly over your curls, it looks like it's sitting decoratively on top of your hair. When the driver drops you off in front of your accommodations, you think you see relief in her eyes. Her clientele is normally smaller than you.

You are my greatest adventure!

What?

The world is a book and those who do not travel read only one page.

Notes with English phrases are pinned to the wall of your accommodations.

Life at its essence boils down to one day at a time. Today is the day!

Otherwise everything seems pleasant and the maybe twenty-five-year-old Winnie, your hostess, warmhearted. In the evening, you both go for a walk; Winnie is approachable and is very interested in getting a top rating from you, but she's also silly and spiritual. She has a large gap in her teeth and says she wants to show you a few good snack stalls. It's already dark, the city is lit, nowhere is quiet. After fifteen minutes you pass a group of Vietnamese senior citizens who are dancing in the yellow-orange light of lanterns or doing aerobics, it's not clear. At a snack stand, the two of you eat some kind of wafer with sticky coconut flakes. The snack reminds you of cotton candy and a fruit that you know from back in the day. Then you keep walking. Winnie tells you she secretly started her business two years ago, her parents live a half mile away and don't know anything about it. Winnie says, when they leave their apartment, she always gets a text message from her sister. By now, her mother has been let in on the secret, because for eight months it's been going really well, and the investment will soon be paid off, it has to be, because she, Winnie, has put a large part of her savings into this venture, *haha, wish me luck*. Then she changes the subject, she tells you lately she's been reading the book by Sadhguru, his *New York Times* bestseller about joy. *Have you heard of it?*

NO, I HAVEN'T.

When you ask her what she likes to do for fun, Winnie answers, laughing: *Tinder! To learn better English*, and she tells you that she sometimes sends white men, who write to her in droves, on dates with each other.

These men come to Hanoi and text me stuff like "Do you wanna be my lotus flower?" So I set them up on dates where they think they will meet me, but instead they meet each other.

Even though the city is full of vehicles, oppressive heat, and people, later on, in your memory, it will first and foremost be green: Hanoi's palm trees, which line the broad streets together with well-lit stores selling "Western" products. Gnarly trees winding up toward the sky. The many thick power cables that are often hanging freely and that remind you of vines, the heavy rain—by far these are the things you will miss.

BUT I JUST ARRIVED.

Yes.

HOW WILL I RECOGNIZE THE COMMUNISM THAT APPAR-ENTLY PREVAILS HERE?

You won't notice anything.

WILL WINNIE AND I KEEP IN TOUCH?

No.

At night, in bed, you leave a voice message for Kim. After three minutes, your thumb lets go of the button it's been holding down for the recording. You send the message, because you can't do any differently. Then you tag and erase it.

hey, thanks for all the photos the other day, they really made things more bearable for me. i especially liked the photo with the girl in the inner tube. but send me some photos of you too, not just from instagram. i'd like to see how everything looks down there, what you're up to. well, more specifically, i actually have a very good idea, because . . . so please don't feel blindsided or anything, but i'm here now too, i just landed in hanoi. no worries, i don't want to stalk you or anything, i'm good and i just wanted to get out of berlin, have an imperialistic vacation, this and that. until now everything's been really okay. for example, ever since i arrived, i haven't been afraid. i already sensed that, but now everything here is so . . . so easy somehow, well at least on the surface, i mean you can probably describe that better than i can: in any case, i will be here for a few weeks now and have already had my first encounters . . . i'm sure i'll have a good time. just now i was out walking with the girl who owns the place i'm staying at; she calls herself winnie, i think it's to make it easier for the tourists. anyhow, we were just walking around, and there was a girl sitting on a moped between two adults, and she was staring at me with her mouth wide open and pointing at me. so i did the same thing back to her. then she suddenly looked at me so sadly, and by then they had already rode past me, and i felt a little bad. children in general. before i flew yesterday, i sat in berlin waiting at the gate and i turned around to face a kid playing behind me, who was toddling over the seats. the child was maybe two or three, now and then running back and forth without any shoes on, knocking on the chair backs, at some point against mine. and then they look at me, we smile at each other, and i say: hey, little zombie. but while i'm saying this, the child sneezes suddenly and a few of the drops land in my mouth. i look confused at the parents and say in german: 'scuse me, your kid just sneezed in my mouth. but they don't seem to hear me. so i try again in english, sitting there like some peeved british lord: excuse me, your child just sneezed into my mouth, lol, disgusting. but neither of them turns around; maybe they're embarrassed or they think i'm weird. so i turn back around and then i start thinking about all kinds of childhood illnesses. which childhood illnesses i had and whether the kid could have infected me with something, mumps measels rubella, but then again we folks from the gdr allegedly are the most vaccinated people in the whole world, ah . . . okay, in any case, i'm here now and i would be glad if you called me back. that's all for now. ciao.

Instead, you write Kim a message: *This may come as a surprise, but I just wanted to tell you that I'm also in Vietnam. I'll soon be traveling south from Hanoi and I'd be happy if you felt like meeting me somewhere. But no pressure, only if you happen to be free; I know that you have to spend a lot of time with your family. And anyhow, I already have a full schedule planned. So in case it's not possible to meet, it wouldn't be so bad. Take care.*

WHAT KIND OF SCHEDULE DO I HAVE PLANNED?

Nothing.

WHY AM I HERE?

Shortly before your departure, you spend an afternoon in Berlin with Luise and Milli.

WHY AM I IN VIETNAM?

When you enter a greenhouse at the Botanical Garden, Milli can barely contain herself.

BUT I'M IN VIETNAM NOW.

Again and again, she looks enthusiastically at the wonderful flowers and tall plants in the different sections, she stares at the glass ceiling and yells: *I'm the pricklieth plant in the world!* then runs out of your sight. You and Luise run after her, Luise is annoyed by her screams, you think it's cute. *I'm the pricklieth plant in the world!* Milli yells again, and you're both not sure where her voice is coming from. When you find her again, she's standing in front of a pond, astonished. A narrow path of slippery stones leads over the water. The three of you walk along it, one after the other. You hold Milli's hand, orange and silver koi swim at your feet. After a few steps, she pulls herself away to walk on the last few stones by herself, but she starts to stumble and lands with one foot in the pond. Immediately she starts crying loudly, for several minutes. In a neighboring greenhouse, Luise unpacks a second pair of pants, changes Milli on a bench, and begins to peel a pear. When you tell her about your travel plans, she holds the knife still.

Vietnam? But what are you planning to do there for so long all by yourself?
   Travel around. See where Kim's family is from. Relax.
Mhm. What does our therapist say about that?
   I think I don't really have a choice right now, you know. If I stay here, somehow I won't get any further.
What do you mean?
   Get my life in order and stuff.
I thought you've been doing better in the meantime.
   Yes, sure. But visiting my mother . . . that was too much somehow.
Hm. You are also welcome to sleep at our place for a few nights again. Then Milli will at least be quiet in the morning.
   Naw, I've already booked my flight. But thanks.
Escapism, that's good too.
I really hope that this helps you.
   Me too.
   . . . What's wrong?
   . . .

Why are you looking like that? . . . Are you having trouble sleeping again?
  I'm just going to tell you.
What?
  I'm pregnant.

Milli, who is trying hard to tie your hairband around an information sign, turns toward you. Unexpectedly, before the sentence you just hurled into the greenhouse can touch the ground, she asks you:
Are you thad?
Those magnificent speech impediments of hers.
No no, Milli, you answer tensely, *but I might be having a baby.*
Then she starts to smile, climbs onto your lap, and discloses to you with big eyes: *And I'm getting a new desk soon.*

WHERE ARE YOU NOW?

The day before yesterday I was out to eat with Henning around the corner from my place, Chinese. I mean, real Chinese.

WHO'S HENNING?

After we eat, we get our obligatory fortune cookies. When I take the cookie out of the crinkly golden foil, I think that there's probably no one else in the world who likes fortune cookies for the cookie, I mean for the taste.

THAT'S THE MOST MISERABLE SNACK THAT WAS EVER IN-VENTED. BESIDES RICE CAKES.

My fortune reads: *He who digs a pit for others will fall in himself.*

DO YOU BELIEVE IN THIS KIND OF JUSTICE?

No. Nevertheless, the phrase strikes a chord.

My grandmother fell into a hole seven years ago, while I was in Morocco. She was raking leaves in autumn, in her plot at the community garden. My grandfather had already been dead for two years, since then the garden was her everything. In her meticulousness, she also raked leaves from the adjacent plot and while doing so set foot on the neighbor's property. There was a spot of rotten wood hidden under the leaves, and beneath it there was a shaft about five, maybe six feet deep. She says she can neither remember the wood breaking nor falling into the hole. She only knows that she screamed like she'd never screamed in her life, as if she were on a skewer, as long as she could, again and again, and at some point she became hoarse, and one of her legs was totally twisted and smashed. But she couldn't feel the pain yet, that only came later. She also fell unconscious repeatedly. Now and then, upon regaining consciousness, she thought to herself: *No, Rita, you can't die down here in a ditch!* And then she started screaming again. That was as if . . . *That was as if I had been saving up my entire lifetime for those screams. My voice no longer sounded like my own. And then at some point I thought: Oh boy, Rita, now you really are going to die down here.*

DID HER SCREAMS SOUND LIKE YOUR MOTHER'S SCREAMS ON THE PHONE?

Shortly before night fell, a neighbor, who had forgotten something in her garden shed and came back for it in the evening, found my grandmother. Even now, my grandmother calls her a guardian angel. A helicopter brought my grandmother to the hospital; in the following years she had five operations. Compound fracture, very complicated, time and again they put new wires and rods in her leg, it had to be broken again and again.

WHY IS IT THAT YOU'VE NEVER BROKEN ANYTHING?

. . . Luck?

WHEN WAS THE LAST TIME YOU WERE IN THE HOSPITAL?

Last week, right after I visited my grandmother for an entire day. In the middle of the night, I was suddenly convinced that I wasn't really pregnant, that it was an ectopic pregnancy or a false pregnancy: when I go to the emergency room, the female receptionist scrutinizes me sympathetically. An hour later, a thirty-year-old man is grinning at me:

The pregnancy is clearly in your uterus.

But the staff here is pretty young, I say. He nods.

Where are the older doctors?

All lost! Good luck in any case.

Do you want a picture to take with you?

I can't recognize anything on the ultrasound, just a spot in a dim cave. If I didn't know better, I would have thought there was a hole in my womb.

IS THIS HENNING THE FATHER?

Is that important?

SINCE WHEN HAVE YOU BEEN EXPECTING?

Are you really expecting me to answer that?

HOW DOES THE WORD *ABORTION* SOUND TO YOU?

. . .

HOW DOES THE WORD *ABORTION* SOUND TO YOU?

. . . Like a conditional invitation? From a person who I always thought couldn't stand me and I couldn't stand them either.

DO YOU WANT TO ACCEPT IT?

The day before yesterday while we were eating, Henning said he feels that people who make art and don't have any ideas almost always work with holes. He has to admit that he's done that too. His last initiative, however, went wrong. In the middle of the night before his solo exhibit, he broke into the gallery, or more specifically the office above it. There he prepared everything carefully. Then, when his exhibit opened, a friend, whom he had previously let in on his secret, filmed the opening. How people stood in front of his video art, interested and orderly, while they poured free wine down their throats. The following could be read on a large screen: *Please wait until!* And some of the visitors actually did that, placed themselves in front of the screen and waited. Finally, his moment had come. With a loud crash, he fell through the ceiling into the gallery. The night before, he had sawed a hole, or more specifically the outline of a hole. On the screen, his fall, which was filmed, was playing on a loop, as well as the moment the terrified guests jumped out of the way. One man was so frightened, he even spilled his red wine all over his expensive Acne jacket. But, according to Henning, because this man was a rich, powerful, prominent art collector, Henning couldn't sell anything that night.

YOU'RE SPACING OUT.

True.

I'm spacing out in the forest.

I no longer know how I got here and I'm thinking about holes.

WHAT FOREST ARE YOU IN?

In a perfectly normal forest.

In the meantime, it's warm enough to walk around in a sweatshirt. The light looks clean, clear, and optimistic. Unfortunately, I can't give you my exact whereabouts.

WHY NOT?

Because I promised not to.

YOU'RE NOT GOOD AT KEEPING PROMISES, ARE YOU?

Yes. I mean, no.

DOES IT ANNOY YOU THAT COMPARED WITH ESSAYS ABOUT GERMAN COLONIALISM, THERE ARE THREE HUNDRED TIMES THE NUMBER OF ESSAYS ABOUT THE GERMAN FOREST?

I'm trying to open a map on my phone, but my internet isn't working. I tell myself, *You have to stay calm, you can manage it even without the internet.* While I walk around and hear the branches breaking quietly under my feet, I think: *My grandma, my mother, and I, we are really three stubborn old dogs.*

DOGS THAT BARK *AND* BITE!

What?

WHERE EXACTLY IS THIS FOREST?

I'm not allowed to say.

I suddenly notice how alone I am and take a deep breath. If my breath had a specific color, it would be neon green.

WHAT ARE YOU DOING IN THE FOREST?

My mother wanted me to meet her here.

I DON'T BELIEVE YOU.

It's true. She asked me to visit her, or more specifically she invited me. A few months ago, I contacted her for the first time in years. That was part of my therapy.

DR. WÜNSCHEL'S ADVICE.

No, the therapist in the basement, with the marble table.

Are you really listening?

. . .

If I understood my mother correctly, the place she's staying at is just temporary. We spoke briefly, she gave me her address while she was using a telephone booth. Until then, I had thought telephone booths no longer existed. My mother didn't want me to write down the address. That's why I know it by heart, those were the conditions. The apartment is here in the forest, that has to be enough.

IS THERE SOMETHING IN YOUR EYE?

No.

THEN WHY ARE YOU BLINKING LIKE THAT?

I'm not blinking.

NOW YOU ARE.

A few years ago, while I was working as a substitute teacher, I gave the students the task of imagining that they were trees.

PLEASE STAY ON TOPIC.

A ten-year-old created a short story about white birch trees that tried to expel a black oak tree from the forest. They were upset, because they discovered that the black oak got too much sun and they no longer wanted to be in its shadow. When the student told his story to his class, which aside from him was exclusively white, he thought it was extremely funny. I had to fight back tears.

ARE THERE BLACK OAK TREES WHERE YOU ARE?

No. I don't think there are any black oak trees in Germany.

WHERE'S YOUR MOTHER NOW?

I already met up with her. That was two hours ago.
Now I need a break.

I crouch down and squat above the ground, eventually sitting. Cold moss, everything is peaceful here. My salmon-colored sneakers contrast radiantly with the green ground. When I sit here like this, my existence, my worries up until now, and my life in and between cities all seem grotesque. Concrete, nicotine, and discos. Drinking, self-fulfillment, and the internet.

At some point I stretch, stand up, brush off my wet bottom, and start walking. I feel bad for my grandmother, because she no longer has the opportunity to come to spots like this. By now, she is plagued by so many fears and pains that her only movement is back and forth between her apartment and various doctors.
DID YOUR MOTHER INVITE YOUR GRANDMOTHER TOO?
I can't imagine that. Most likely, they aren't in touch anymore. My mother can't bear my grandmother.
AND YOU?
I'm not sure now; in the past I could bear both of them.
WHEN DID THEIR FALLING-OUT BEGIN?
When my mother started puberty?
My grandmother used to tell me often that before puberty, my mother was a really great girl. So well-behaved, so clever, so organized, so pretty. She said that Susanne even excelled in the Free German Youth and gave the best speeches. She was so good at it, because prior to that she had always been class president. I think for a few years, before my grandmother started to be ashamed of her daughter's behavior and had to justify it to the Stasi, she was actually quite proud of her.
They just picked me up, and then I was sitting there. I had no idea how

I should explain it to them. Why she suddenly ran around with these freaks. Why she didn't want to be in the Free German Youth anymore. Naturally, Grandpa and I were afraid for our jobs. And afraid for Susanne anyhow. They said that if that continues, they'll have to put her in a girls' home. In order to reeducate her. So then, of course, we promised them that we would try everything to turn her around, to get her back to her old self, her socialist self, well, you know what I mean.

While my mother cooked something, I asked her why the Stasi had arrested her back then. That was probably a mistake—too fast, too direct. She actually wanted to show me something, but never got around to it. Instead, she said: *I've had enough,* placed my cell phone in my hand, led me to the door, and complained that I should come back in a few hours, after I'd got my shit together.

LOSING YOUR SHIT SEEMS TO BE EASIER FOR YOU.

Now I remember which way to go. I noticed this tree stump on my way there. The closer I get to the small clearing with the bungalow, the slower I go.

YOU LOOK DIFFERENT THAN USUAL.

I've gained a little weight.

OUTSTANDING IDEA.

WHAT WAS THE CAUSE?

One time, when I was eleven, my mother drastically lost a lot of weight:

My brother and I are playing a board game in which you have to build barricades; she comes home and tells us, laughing, that a friend of hers didn't recognize her at first from a distance. But when he got closer, he said to her: *Man, Susanne, your knee . . . you look like a concentration camp prisoner.* Something about that made her very content.

I realized how much her weight changed from year to year only when

I was at my grandmother's house the other day and looked at photos. What bothered me most was that it had never occurred to me before. At every Christmas celebration a new body, at every birthday a new hair color. When I was a kid, I didn't think it was strange that we'd sometimes eat so much with our mother that we'd get stomachaches and even threw up now and then.

WHAT DOES YOUR MOTHER DO HERE . . . BESIDES EAT?

I don't know what she's hiding from.

DOES SHE LIVE NEAR A WELL?

What kind of well?

ONE THAT CONTAINS CHAMPAGNE.

LIKE IN THE LAND OF MILK AND HONEY.

My mother doesn't drink alcohol.

There are rivers great and fine
Of oil, milk, honey, and wine.
Water there serves no purpose
Except to be looked at and to wash with.

On the phone she indicated that the police were looking for her. She said they wanted to force her to testify in court, which she is willing to do under no circumstances. That's why they wanted to imprison her, for being in contempt of court. She added that I didn't need to know any more. Because I didn't need any more trouble.

WHAT COULD TROUBLE YOU?

At the moment, nothing is troubling me.

I just thought of a song of Kim's, "I Am Not a Fortune Cookie." If my phone had more charge, I'd call her. Instead, I send her a voice message. It won't reach Kim until I'm back at my mother's place and have mobile data again. If everything worked out, then Kim is in Hanoi with her relatives by now. She visits them at least once a year.

HOW OFTEN DO YOU VISIT YOUR RELATIVES?

I'm doing that now.

DO YOU EVER SOMETIMES THINK ABOUT THE FUTURE?

Why?

. . .

There are black aluminum blinds everywhere, from the outside I can't look into any of the small bungalow windows. When I arrived here this morning I thought: *This is the epitome of a modern witch's cottage.* Five minutes later I was sitting inside at a table made of dark wood: there, I feel young and out of place, I flip through a TV guide without reading it. My mother takes two tins out of a cupboard and turns on the stove. Until now, I haven't seen a single television, but there's still a TV guide lying around. Colorful thin paper that tears easily, with small square-shaped photos printed on it. Abruptly I say:

You know, whenever I watch TV, I have the feeling that I don't really live in Germany.

    What do you mean?

Well, all that trash TV on cable, the stuff they broadcast there or the soap operas, that all somehow has nothing to do with me. Or with anyone that I know. I mean, there's nothing in between, nothing good. And no one on TV who's supposed to appeal to young people is under forty.

    No one is forcing you to watch that junk.

Are you seriously cooking canned ravioli?

    They're vegetarian.

I had thought you might eat better by now.

    What exactly is your problem?

I just mean . . . we could've cooked something decent.

    You could've bought yourself something decent earlier.

I'd been sitting in the bungalow for barely twenty minutes and already had the feeling that I'd been there too long. But after sending her reproachful emails during my most intense therapy sessions, I owe it to my mother to take the time.

CAN YOU QUOTE SOMETHING FROM THESE EMAILS?

hello, hey, you said i should get in touch now and then. so hi. up to now it's been rather strange. i am taking a walk right now. everything here is green, brown, and harmless, and my phone is almost out of power. i'm a little worried that i won't find my way back, lol. but somehow it is nice to be here. but unreal at the same time. i just don't know what she wants from me. for example, earlier, i arrive, she picks me up from the bus station, we don't hug, but she gives me this look. i don't know, it's as if she wanted to hug. like, as if she needed a hug. later on we ate something together briefly and right away the first fight started. i think she's afraid to ask me how i'm doing. or she's too nervous. in any case, she's somehow agitated. bla bla bla, me me me. have you landed already? send me a photo when you're heading into the city. you said there's free high-speed internet everywhere there. okay, i'll be in touch again later. ciao.

I try to relax my shoulders. The walk calmed me down. The voice message I recorded for Kim was just sent, the checkmarks tell me she listened to it immediately. I turn off my cell phone and put it in the strange box that my mom provided for it. Then I knock cautiously on the door, in the rhythm we agreed upon; she doesn't have a doorbell. At this moment, a muscular, well-oiled student is running around on the roof of the bungalow in a thong. He smiles with bleached teeth, staring into nothingness, and holds up a sign that says: *Round two! Ding! Ding! Ding!* Behind that, in the form of an owl, my brother sits in the top of a spruce tree. He's staring down at us and turning his head around 360 degrees.

Why did they arrest you back then?

When you ask like that, it sounds as if you're blaming me. I didn't do anything wrong.

You didn't?

That's exactly what they were trying to achieve back then with their "subversion."

> *But you did smuggle some things. From the West into the East, Atari computers and stuff.*

Nonsense. I was eighteen at the time and had just given birth to you two. I wouldn't have had time for something like that.

Then why does it say in your files—

I should never have shown them to you, that was stupid of me.

Okay.

If for weeks, two guys follow you to your apprenticeship every day and you're just sixteen, always the same two shitheads, who never tell you why . . . on the way to an awful apprenticeship that you were forced into because the government doesn't like your attitude, then at some point you'd also start thinking that you've done something wrong. That they know everything about you.

> *But the Stasi didn't spy on you just because you suddenly had colorful hair.*

But they did.

Somehow I don't believe that.

Your generation, yes, the young people of today, you really don't know what kind of freedoms you actually have.

I'm in my mid-thirties.

Do you know what a paranoid government is capable of? Making their citizens paranoid! Cells filled with water, solitary confinement, group isolation in a dark cellar, having to stand around for hours in the snow in the courtyard, intentional malnutrition . . . just because of a few flyers. Or because of a punk concert in a church.

Or because of your parents, who say: "This child is a good-for-nothing, she's psychologically sick, she needs to go."

Grandma and Grandpa never said anything like that.

And I haven't even gotten to the abuse.

Were you abused in jail?

. . . Why are you here?

Because you asked me to come.

And what did you think we would do here?

Have a discussion?

Something happened, do you understand, I don't have much time. I don't need your rooting around in the past right now.

So no discussion.

Where do you even get the idea that you have a right to hear about my past? That was my life, not yours. That has nothing to do with you.

Sounds like everything's over now.

What?

Your life.

And?

Did you really change your name, like officially, with all the bells and whistles?

Yes, my child, I have a new name now, that's right.

A name that belongs only to me.

And what is it?

You know that already.

I mean your full name, with surname.

Even if I told you, you wouldn't find me on the internet.

. . . What's so funny about that?

You're sitting here like the Stasi in the flesh, interrogating me. And I even
invited you here. What was I thinking?

I'd like to know that, too.

Are you gonna eat that?

. . . No, I'm full.

Okay, then come on, I want to show you something.

Are we going outside?

Yes.

And can I have my cell phone back now?

You really can't survive even three hours without your tracking device,
can you?

*If someone really wants to know where I am, in order to find out
where you are, then they've already tracked me here. You should have
told me beforehand that you didn't want that. Then I would have
gotten a different SIM card for my Nokia.*

I'll give you your phone tonight, okay?

*And what if I want to go for a walk later and I get lost? Without
GPS, I mean.*

Do you actually hear yourself?

*All the time . . . but now please tell me, regarding back then—how
would you explain why they arrested you?*

I've had enough.

Why?

Get out.

Seriously?

I said you need to leave.

Come back when you've got your shit together.

My heart was once a snack machine made of tin. It stood on the platform of some small town, a shining, square-shaped colossus. In the meantime, it's become smaller, lighter, more inconspicuous.

Now the machine is hanging on the wall of a building somewhere in Thuringia or Berlin, it's been tagged with graffiti and covered in stickers. Every day, dozens of people walk by and don't notice it, it's no longer easy to look inside. The red varnish is peeling off, its metal face smiles tiredly.

When I stand in front of the small snack machine filled with chewing gum and bend forward, it evokes a nostalgia in me that might have to do with my childhood or with the founding of the Federal Republic of Germany, at any rate it has something to do with a diffuse vague past. Inside the machine, behind the glass, there's cheap jewelry, toys, and candy in three containers. To the far left: colorful monochrome balls of chewing gum that all taste the same, sweet and old. In the middle: rings made of plastic with ruby-red sparkling diamonds that look expensive on the machine's yellowed advertisements. These fancy rings are longing for my finger, waiting in the machine, encapsulated in a plastic ball that's partly transparent, surrounded by even more colorful gumballs. Then to the far right: toys. Miscellaneous little figures, animals for kneading or blowing up; I can't really tell. In front of every container there's a bolt with a metal latch. Turning it 360 degrees creates a delightful feeling.

WHERE ARE YOU NOW?

It's Wednesday morning, the sun is shining, my mother and I are swimming in a small lake in the woods. It's rather warm for the end of May, the water is framed by deciduous trees and conifers, whose names I don't know. Additionally, there are sandy paths at my feet, on which pinecones are scattered, Coke cans, branches, a lot of shadows, little light, and a flip-flop.

IT'S ASTONISHING THAT THROUGHOUT THE WORLD PEOPLE HAVE A TENDENCY TO LOSE JUST ONE SHOE.

Or one sock.

WHERE ARE YOU EXACTLY?

About a fifteen-minute walk from her bungalow.

I feel inhibited in my bikini, I suck in my stomach, even though I don't want to, even though it's only the two of us. My mother gets into the water naked, submerges her head and resurfaces, swims a little. Then she floats on her back for twenty minutes in the middle of the lake, like a happy jellyfish. I'm already back on the bank, drying myself off, I don't understand why she wants to stay in the water for so long, stretching out nakedly. Why does she always have to do everything to the extreme. Why can't she just go swimming in an opaque bathing suit and then leave the water, and bite into an average apple in an average way.

I wish I could smoke. If I took an f6 from her right now, she wouldn't notice until evening that her package had become empty faster than usual.

BUT YOU'VE DECIDED TO REALLY STOP THIS TIME.

Yes.

EVEN THOUGH YOU LIKE TO SMOKE. ESPECIALLY WHEN IT
BRINGS YOU TOGETHER WITH OTHER PEOPLE.

. . .

LIKE THAT YOUNG WOMAN IN THE U.S., FOR EXAMPLE, WITH
WHOM YOU SHARED A CIGARETTE DURING HER BREAK. THAT
WAS NICE.

What woman?

THE WOMAN WHO DID YOUR MAKEUP.

I don't remember talking about that.

NEARLY EVERY WOMAN THAT YOU SAW IN NEW YORK WAS
COVERED IN A LAYER OF MAKEUP.

Yeah. So? That was years ago.

AFTER THREE DAYS, WOMEN WITHOUT MAKEUP STARTED
LOOKING RAGGED TO YOU. REMEMBER?

. . . Right.

I even felt so unmade-up suddenly. That's why I wanted to try some
makeup in a drugstore. A young Black worker really enjoyed doing
my makeup, with products that she wanted to sell me. She was fat,
firmly built, smelled good, and hummed to herself. I sat on a swivel
stool and let her touch me all over my face. When she applied liquid
eyeliner to my closed eyes, they began to tear up; the procedure took
about fifteen minutes.

AND THEN SHE SHOWED YOU YOUR FACE IN THE MIRROR.

You're officially Americanized now!

I looked like a cross between Amy Winehouse and a white actor in
blackface.

DOES THAT MEAN YOU LOOKED GOOD OR BAD?

First and foremost, ridiculous. But to be polite, and because I thought
it's good that these kinds of products even exist in such a wide range,

I bought the makeup that apparently isn't the right match for my skin tone, anyway.

EVEN THOUGH YOU KNEW YOU'D NEVER USE IT.

If I had gone swimming with a layer of makeup like that on, nothing about my face would have changed, everything would have remained pasted in place. A waterproof visage. Or maybe afterward the entire lake would also officially be Americanized.

WHAT ARE YOU GETTING AT?

Suddenly I'm annoyed about these different things that I perceive as self-evident in my daily life, even though they are images imported from the U.S. meant to compel me to consume. While my mother is floating on her back in the water, I think: *That's just another ad for freedom and happiness, in the German forest, in German tranquility, connected to nature and naked, bobbing up and down.* An ad like the pictures of white American families sitting on checkered picnic blankets in the 1950s, or today the pictures of rapping African Americans with grills in their mouths or those perpetually relaxed smoking cowboys at sunset. I suddenly notice that I long for different images.

AND FOR NICOTINE.

After eating with Henning I smoked my very last cigarette.

IS HE THE FATHER OR NOT?

Since then, I've stopped. Before, Henning told me a lot about his work. He can hold a sustained monologue even longer than me. I understood that he prefers to approach his sculptures based on their titles, which he totally randomly chooses, first just quasi-intuitively, because that gives him more creative freedom.

CREATIVE FREEDOM.

IS THERE ALSO UNCREATIVE FREEDOM? OR CREATIVE BONDAGE?

What?

YOU AND THIS HENNING GUY, ARE YOU STILL IN CONTACT?

No.

WHERE IS HE NOW?

At home.

DO YOU WRITE TO EACH OTHER?

The day after tomorrow, I'm heading back to Berlin, why would we be writing each other messages this whole time?

YOU WRITE TO KIM, LUISE, AND BURHAN.

Kim hasn't answered. Or rather, she always sends me links to images of things she thinks I'd like. Then I respond with a few lines in English that I think of spontaneously; maybe she'll turn them into new songs. I'd rather we just sent each other normal text messages.

In the meantime, she must have arrived at her eldest aunt's village.

WHY ARE YOU MAKING THAT FACE AGAIN?

ARE YOU OFFENDED?

Three days with my mother are pretty long, you know, challenging.

SHE'S LYING IN THE WATER, YOU'RE SITTING ON THE BANK, THE SUN IS SHINING, THERE ARE NO NAZIS IN SIGHT. WHAT EXACTLY IS YOUR PROBLEM?

When I'm in her presence, I simply don't know who I am. I think it's because I've never really understood her character. And therefore it's impossible to be myself in relation to her.

AND KIM?

What about her?

DO YOU KNOW WHO YOU ARE IN HER PRESENCE?

This morning I looked at her photos on Instagram. She mostly posts about food and snippets of conversations with her Vietnamese grandparents. Everything looks cozy. Maybe I should be there too.

WHY?

To experience it with her.

YOU ONLY DO PLATONIC THINGS TOGETHER NOW.

I'm not so sure about that anymore.

BECAUSE SHE'S OUT OF REACH? OR BECAUSE YOU'RE
PREGNANT?

Probably both. Actually, at the moment I don't want to think about
that.

DO YOU THINK IT'S A COINCIDENCE THAT PEOPLE ALWAYS
IMAGINE THAT ALIENS LOOK EXACTLY LIKE HUMAN EM-
BRYOS IN A PARTICULAR STAGE OF DEVELOPMENT?

. . . I am envious of Kim with her family. It's not that everything is
ideal for her. Everyone is waiting constantly for her to marry a Vietnamese man from a first-class family and then promptly have many
first-class children. Only one of her aunts knows that she's a lesbian.
But in her family, there are clear rules, after all, tenacities. In mine
there are none. Everything can drift away at any time.

YOUR MOTHER IS STILL DRIFTING IN THE LAKE.

Yes. Like a corpse.

HOW WOULD YOU FEEL IF SHE WAS SUDDENLY DEAD?

. . .

HOW WOULD YOU FEEL IF YOUR MOTHER WAS SUDDENLY
DEAD?

When she gets out of the water with her wet dyed-red hair, for a moment I'm amazed. Her many tattoos. After my brother's death she began to have herself inked with large-scale images and lettering. Back
then I found it embarrassing; I had the feeling that she was trying
to catapult herself back into her youth, to lightheartedly keep going
there, where her adulthood painfully, abruptly began.

Now I suddenly like the tattoos.

WHICH TATTOOS PROTECT YOU?

I could never decide to let myself be tattooed. By now, it would be too heavy with meaning. Besides, nowadays it's almost more special to not have any.

DO YOU WANT TO BE SOMETHING SPECIAL?

No. During my entire childhood I tried hard not to stand out. My grandmother says that when my mother was in jail and my brother and I lived with her, I apparently used to hide behind the sofa whenever we had a visitor. And there I'd comb my hair for hours with a determined face. Even when I was young, I thought it was desirable to be absolutely average.

SO YOU COULD BITE INTO AN AVERAGE APPLE IN AN AVERAGE WAY?

Meanwhile, clouds have moved in front of the sun, I have goose bumps on my arms and legs. My mother is drying off with a black towel, first her limbs, then her hair; she throws on a wide black dress, sits down next to me, and starts to eat some bread. While I continue to shiver, we talk. For some reason, I'm still sucking in my belly, for a second I wonder whether or not that can harm the fetus, but I remain sitting in my bikini, holding my breath; she starts to smoke. From the outside, our situation seems harmless, maybe even harmonious. Nevertheless, the tension doesn't go away.

DID YOU KNOW THAT MALE DUCKS SOMETIMES DELIBERATELY, AS A GROUP, RAPE A FEMALE ONE?

Before my mother and I leave, she tells me a few too many personal things, casually, as if they were amusing anecdotes.

WHAT KINDS OF THINGS?

Sexual. I don't know if these things are true or if she's making them up. While she talks, I stare at a small family of ducks on the water. I can't manage to redirect the conversation; I don't have a feeling for what would be appropriate for a mother-daughter relationship and what wouldn't.

After my mother stops talking, I take one of her cigarettes and brush my tongue over my front teeth. Then I sit a little away from her, in a spot of sunlight. What she said resonates, I have the feeling that her words have unintentionally hurt me. I sniff back some snot, take the cigarette, and stick it between my lips. Without lighting it, I breathe in deeply, inhaling some air through the cigarette. Over and over I blow invisible smoke out of my mouth, lie down on my back, and close my eyes.

THE COLD FISH.

What?

YOU'RE LYING THERE AGAIN LIKE A COLD FISH.

Yes.

WHAT ARE YOU THINKING ABOUT?

About the past. What else?

WHY DON'T YOU EVER SAY YOUR BROTHER'S NAME?

What?

YOU JUST ALWAYS SAY MY BROTHER.

It doesn't make sense for a dead person to have a name.

WHAT'S YOUR BROTHER'S NAME?

If I say it now, it will sound hollow. In the sense of being hollowed out. Everything is gone, only his name remains, it's just somehow wrong.

DOESN'T HIS NAME HAVE MUCH MORE MEANING THAN THE FACT THAT HE WAS YOUR BROTHER?

He's still my brother. I don't understand the question.

THE WORD BROTHER REDUCES HIM TO HIS RELATIONSHIP TO YOU.

...

WHAT'S UP WITH YOUR EYES?

Nothing.

WHAT'S UP WITH YOUR EYES?

I think lately that so many of my veins have popped because I've been under more pressure than usual.

PRESSURE—VERY GOOD.

WE CAN WORK ON THAT.

On what?

ON YOU, ON YOUR PRESSURE, ON YOUR ARROGANT FACIAL EXPRESSION, ON YOUR LINGUISTIC EXPRESSION, ON YOUR PSYCHOLOGICAL STRAIN.

Just recently, when I was babysitting Milli in Berlin, she sat on her potty chair for a really long time. While she was squeezing, I held her hands and was worried that she might accidentally squeeze her big eyes out in the process. Afterward she insisted that she clean her bottom herself. I helped clean up afterward with a baby wipe, but she was still proud of her attempt. Triumphantly she asked me:

Are you already able to clean your volvo all by yourself?

For some reason, she confuses *vulva* with *Volvo*. I kept myself from correcting her, instead I answered that I was able to wipe myself, *of course*, and I thought about how my mother showed me how with a wet washcloth when I was eight. Susanne's movements were rough, afterward my vulva hurt, and I felt dumb, because I didn't know that I was supposed to wash this spot differently than the rest of my body.

Suddenly, my mother says, *Now put on some clothes, this is unbearable.*

 Everything's fine, I say and ask: *Are we leaving right away, or do you want to go in again?*

I still have to take care of something in the city. But you don't have to come with me. As far as I'm concerned, you can go home.

Go home—that would be heading back to Berlin, not back to the witch house.

BACK TO HENNING.

And our roommate.

THE THREE OF YOU LIVE TOGETHER?

Yes, but she's only staying for a few months. Every morning, she says she has a mission and then she distributes flyers all day for an event with her spiritual master of Happy Science. He'll soon be coming from Japan, for his first visit to Germany, to spread his religion from the Ritz-Carlton, for a fifty-euro entry fee, a donation.

AREN'T YOU A BIT TOO OLD TO HAVE ROOMMATES?

What counts as too old for roommates?

HOW LONG HAVE YOU BEEN LIVING THERE?

A few months. The first time we met each other was friendly and strange: we were sitting with Henning in a spacious kitchen. After the usual small talk, she starts showing me scenes from a German TV show on her laptop.

HAS YOUR GRANDMOTHER EVER VISITED YOU THERE?

What?

No.

My roommate recites the show's dialogue along with the actors and she laughs shrilly at predictable funny jokes—together with the laugh track of an imaginary audience. Henning observes everything, looks through his wineglass, squints alternatively with his left eye, then his right. I briefly have the feeling that my sense of humor is being tested. Later he tells me that this sitcom was filmed only so that foreigners could learn German from it. I notice right away that Henning likes explaining things.

Have you lost track of your thoughts or something?

What?

My mother throws her towel at my face. I sit up. She's already standing, and her things are packed.

You can find your way back alone, right?

Yes, I say, and wonder where the cigarette I didn't smoke has disappeared to.

And then my mother leaves, I sit alone at the lake and suddenly start laughing like crazy. It's one of those laughs that—if you take it too far—turns into crying. The kind of laughter that comes with being an adult.

DID YOUR LAUGHTER CHANGE AFTER YOUR BROTHER'S DEATH?

I think we had a very similar sense of humor, which my mother sometimes found godawful. Like when we'd call her the whitest cracker on earth. Back then we didn't know how we meant it, why we said it. Nowadays I don't think it's funny anymore. When we were twelve, my mother, my brother, and I once went together to Grand Canary for a vacation. Nearby there was also—

STOP, STOP, STOP. PLEASE STICK TO THE TOPIC AT HAND.

Which one?

ALL THESE DIVERSIONS:

MAKEUP, TATTOOS, CLEANING VULVAS—WHAT ARE YOU ACTUALLY TALKING ABOUT?

. . .

WHAT IS THE TOPIC?

. . .

YOU'RE STILL SITTING AROUND AT THE LAKE, FREEZING AND MAKING AN AMBIGUOUS GRIMACE.

. . . I think it's about my body and shame. Or the feeling that the way your body is isn't right. Seeing my mother again means remembering all that with full force, including physically.

REMEMBERING WHAT?

How I felt growing up.

THE EXPLODED VEINS IN YOUR EYES, THE PRESSURE, YOUR
HIGH BLOOD PRESSURE—ARE THEY ALL RESULTS OF THESE
FEELINGS?

The thing with my veins has been going on only a short while.

BUT YOU'RE STILL TAKING THE MEDICATION?

Yes.

WHY HAS YOUR STRESS LEVEL INCREASED, THEN?

I think it has something to do with the pregnancy.

HOW DOES IT FEEL TO BE PREGNANT?

. . . grueling, idiotic, and inconceivable.

HOW DOES THE WORD *ABORTION* SOUND TO YOU NOW?

Less inviting than before . . . like an email newsletter invoking a
demonstration from which not even the organizers anticipate any
political consequences.

. . .

At that time, on vacation, I got my period for the first time.

WHICH VACATION ARE WE TALKING ABOUT NOW?

In Grand Canary. I was confused, frustrated, and couldn't figure
out how to use tampons. My brother quickly befriended some boys
his age on the island. Even though he didn't understand any Spanish, he went swimming with them and high diving. I was impressed
by his courage, proud and envious at the same time: He's twelve
years old, daringly doing somersaults from thirty feet up, while
I'm sitting at the pool's edge in shorts, a T-shirt, and a thick maxi
pad between my thighs, barely daring to stand up. I'd like to know
whether, years later, his jump in front of the train looked just as
graceful.

NO ONE LOOKS ELEGANT WHEN THEY DIE.

THAT'S AN INVENTION OF THE FILM INDUSTRY.

Nonsense.

DO YOU SOMETIMES IMAGINE HOW YOU'LL LOOK WHEN YOU DIE?

I have a very precise image of that in my head, yes.

PLEASE DESCRIBE IT.

Funny, really, that there isn't an app for that yet—a death app. For years now, you've been able to use software to predict how you'll look when you're older.

PLEASE DESCRIBE IT TO ME.

On vacation my brother and I once had a laughing fit at our mother's expense. She was in the middle of enthusiastically describing a building, holding a travel guide in her hand, when she stepped into a pile of dog shit. We couldn't stop laughing. She was so offended that she swore she'd never travel with us again. She kept her word; to this day, I don't know a more resolute person. When my first boyfriend once neglected to show up for a job interview that she had arranged for him, she didn't speak with him for over a year. At the time I was sixteen and impressed and overwhelmed by her severity. When we accidentally ran into each other on the street in Erfurt, she crossed the street without looking at us.

WHAT WAS YOUR FIRST BOYFRIEND'S NAME?

Rollo. He wanted to be an electrician.

HOW LONG WERE YOU TOGETHER?

Too long.

DOES HE KNOW HOW YOU'D LOOK IF YOU WERE DEAD?

He should be able to imagine it.

ARE YOU AND ROLLO STILL IN TOUCH?

No.

COULD YOU USE HIS NAME FOR YOUR EMERGENCY CONTACT?

I haven't seen him in years. Essentially, we didn't have anything in common.

But back then, to be loved unconditionally by Rollo was important.

HOW WAS HIS RELATIONSHIP WITH YOUR BROTHER?

Cocaine, low rider, a demonstrative propensity toward violence; my brother thought he was dumb and admired his ego. Somehow it was the same for me.

Anyway, I don't think I will ever have a noteworthy case of emergency in my life, even if I often feel differently. That's why I don't need to name a contact. Nothing will happen to me. Or to the baby.

EXCUSE ME?

Because enough things have happened to me already.

Because I deserve everything to be good for a while.

Because I'm not in the mood to continue working through my past.

Because I'm not sitting in prison. Because I'm free to shape my life.

Because I have every reason to be happy. Because starting now everything can only get better. Because I know that I can lead a good life. Because I lead a good life. Because the universe is on my side. Because God is on my side. Because I am my own goddess. Hallelujah.

ARE YOU BEING SERIOUS?

Those were lines from my therapy that I said to myself, twice daily, in front of a mirror, for months. Having anxiety is actually a permanent case of emergency.

• • •

A short while ago I called the short psychiatrist who wore the much-too-large blazer. I wanted to ask if I could reduce the dosage of my medicine, because I felt relatively stable. And because of the embryo. Burhan thought the idea was good too. Unfortunately, the doctor had died shortly after my last visit. The nurse on the telephone sounded strangely neutral when she said:

Pneumonia, no one could have expected it, he even less so. Does Thursday at eleven work for you?

I wonder if he saw the world through a pathologizing lens until the very end: borderline here, anxiety there, depression everywhere. If he couldn't see the people for so many diseases.

WHERE ARE YOU NOW?

At the train station. I arrived by train and am waiting for a regional bus that will take me to the edge of the forest. To my surprise, I'm excited. My mother and I haven't seen each other for years, I wonder whether she has gray hair by now.

In the station hall, I buy flowers—three pink lilies. They don't suit her at all; I look forward to handing them over without comment. While I look for change, the saleswoman, who might be from Vietnam, scrutinizes me in a friendly way. Her gaze focuses on my stomach, which is hidden under a trench coat. She quietly begins to hum the chorus of Whitney Houston's most famous song. For several days afterward, it will echo fanatically through my ears, from then on Whitney Houston and my pregnancy grow together inseparably.

WHERE ARE YOU NOW?

At the train station . . . a different train station.

To travel to Grand Canary back then, my mother, brother, and I had to first take the train to the airport: We're in good spirits and excited, we wait, full of anticipation. There are a few people standing with us on the platform, all of them white. If I had known Rollo at the time and if he'd been with me, everything would have gone differently.

BUT AT THE TIME, YOU DON'T NOTICE THAT THE OTHER PEOPLE ON THE PLATFORM ARE WHITE.

Pale by the rail . . . yup.

Our mother is standing on another platform within sight; she has just met a friend whose train will arrive earlier than ours. The two women talk conspiratorially. My brother and I see how her friend laughingly gestures as if she were screwing in a lightbulb in the air. Suddenly I notice that a man and woman, perhaps in their thirties, are staring at us. The man takes a step toward us and then turns away again; my brother and I are sitting on a bench, unprepared. All of a sudden, the man starts screaming with his back to us, it's early in the morning. He screams that we need to get away and then yells descriptions of our bodies that I'll never forget. Words that sometimes rumble around in my head when I'm drunk, making me wish I could throw them up. During his tirade, he turns to face us every now and then, keeps screaming, then turns away again, so we can't understand everything but we understand enough. For example, he says we belong in a concentration camp, that we will be gassed there properly, and that soon the right train will come for us. We see how he repeatedly holds his arm outstretched, we see his wide-open eyes, his enraptured grin, his intoxication from his own voice, and from his transgression, his gratification from liberating himself from an inner pressure. My brother starts crying, I take his hand and sit there, rigid and still. The woman next to the man—his voice now drowns out a passing train—starts to smirk, the other people on the platform have turned into mannequins. Suddenly our mother is there. She screams back that he better shut his fucking mouth, otherwise she will hit him. Both of them stare at each other. Then the man turns away, hisses *red witch*, something we don't understand, because our mother had blond hair back then. Not much later, our train arrives. I'm relieved that it's a completely normal train; we get on at different ends. During the trip, I'm worried the entire time that the man will come over and do something to us. My brother stares at his sneakers, swaying his legs back and forth; behind him treeless, beige-yellow fields zip by. Every now and then I look around, the fear has settled in; my mother says, with a forced calm:

We'll be on vacation soon, it'll be beautiful.

BUT IT WON'T BE BEAUTIFUL.

At least not for me. After I menstruate for three days, awkwardly in Grand Canary, I cry and scream for hours that I can't take it here anymore, until my mother finally can't take it along with me and prematurely ends the vacation. I'm sorry about that to this day. I knew how important it was for her to get out of Germany, how long she had saved for that vacation, how much my brother liked it on the island.

THE WHOLE THING IS PRETTY REDUNDANT.

What?

AT THE TRAIN STATION. THE NAZI.

ALWAYS THESE STORIES IN WHICH SOMETHING ALMOST HAPPENS, BUT ULTIMATELY NOTHING DOES. AND IT'S ALWAYS TRAIN STATIONS.

Something did happen to me.

The problem isn't that my recollections repeat themselves.

RATHER?

The problem is that these things themselves keep repeating, perpetually, that they never stopped.

WE'RE NEVER GOING TO REACH OUR DESTINATION THIS WAY.

What destination?

WELL, YOURS.

WE'RE STILL TALKING ABOUT YOU, RIGHT?

AND ABOUT YOUR DESTINY, HOW YOUR LIFE ENDS, WHAT YOU WILL ACHIEVE ON THE WAY.

Aha? What do I want to achieve?

IN LIFE?

Yes.

TO LIVE?

... Yes.

OH.

WELL, BACK TO *YOUR* PSYCHOLOGICAL STRESS: YOUR EYES.

HAVE YOU BEEN TO THE DOCTOR YET?

I don't have a problem with my eyes, those are just a few veins.

WELL, WHAT ARE YOU HAVING PROBLEMS WITH?

... I don't know, you tell me.

WHERE IS MY MOTHER NOW?

Your mother?

YES, MY MOTHER.

What's that supposed to mean?

EXACTLY THAT. I'M RELIEVING YOU.

YOU'VE HAD ENOUGH FOR NOW.

... Okay.

WHERE IS MY MOTHER NOW?

... In the city.

AND I?

You are alone in the forest, in a bungalow, you're looking at some things.

HOW DO I FEEL?

You feel as if you shouldn't be here.

GOOD.

GO ON, GO ON.

... Like seashells brought from distant beaches that have been laid in decorative glass, together with a disgusting-smelling scented candle?

I MEANT: WHAT AM I EXPERIENCING? WHAT AM I THINK-ING ABOUT?

...

AM I TRYING ON HER CLOTHES?

No. But you touch some of them: the few pieces of clothing hanging on the closet rod, the rough material of her half-full overnight bag, the two hot water bottles in her bed, the picture frames over the bed. EVERYTHING IS IMPECCABLY CLEAN, NO DUST ON MY FINGERS.

The framed photo shows your mother and a man kissing. The photo immediately caught your eye as soon as you arrived. You tried to ignore it, you tried not to show your disturbance over the fact that you were seeing it for the first time in your life, how your mother is giving a man a kiss. Now, alone, you are looking at the photo a little more closely. *The guy doesn't look so fucked up*, you think. *Does he taste like vodka during the day, too?*

In a large box, you find more photos. They're older and sometimes show you and your brother. In that moment, you don't know yet that your mother will send you these photos two weeks later, all of them, that she won't keep a single photo. You don't know yet that she's in the pedestrian zone of a nearby town right now to ask about package sizes and permissible weights at the post office, because she doesn't have the internet and is too proud or too paranoid to ask you to look for the information on your smartphone.

PRIDE AND PARANOIA PLUS A PINCH OF ANGER ARE THE MAKINGS FOR A GREAT COCKTAIL.

What?

A TASTY MOLOTOV COCKTAIL.

DO I THINK IT WOULD BE GOOD IF MY MOTHER WITHDREW INTO A LEFT-WING TERRORIST UNDERGROUND?

. . . And planned attacks against Nazis from there?

FOR EXAMPLE.

You wouldn't put it past her, but you think she might be too old for that.

AND WHAT'S UP WITH ME?

You are much too harmless, that's always been your problem.
UNFORTUNATELY.

Yes.

And unfortunately, your mother doesn't know anything about the pictures that you brought along and that you would have liked to show her. Copies of negatives the photographer gave you. Negatives that he never developed. Images that don't seem as iconic as *Susanne's Dream*; rather, they are more personal, and partly blurry. Pictures that show your mother as a teenager, smiling, running, acting silly with friends in a field, a barren building in the background. In one picture, one of her earrings seems to be tangled in her Palestinian keffiyeh; it looks as if she's trying to untangle it with her head bowed down. In another image, three friends are standing on a small hill bending forward, with their backs to you, speaking about something secretive. In a third image, a young punk smokes a cigarette, smirking, while your mother and a third person appear to be scuffling, they are roughly grabbing on to each other. These are pictures that show your mother beyond you, in a way that you could have never seen her and never will. Pictures that bring your mother closer to you and make your grandmother's eyes water.

Like I said, yeah, I closed the door, but I didn't lock it. If Susanne wants to come back one day, I'm here. But I'm not waiting any longer for her to show up. I'll no longer look intently through the spyhole with a heavy heart every day.

I HAVE ANOTHER PICTURE WITH ME, ON THINNER PAPER, BUT ALSO IN BLACK AND WHITE. THE IMAGE OF A PERSON WHO DOESN'T EXIST YET.

Unfortunately, you'll never find the time to talk to your mother about her box full of photos or look at them with her. Sadly, you will never show your mother any of the photos you brought. You won't manage to tell her about your pregnancy or to give up your defiance, which once protected you from her and that now, in your mid-thirties, just seems silly. Only when you're sitting in the intercity bus and driving away will you notice how sad you actually are about this encounter. How much you would have liked to tell her thank you.

FOR WHAT?

For everything that she did for you and your brother and everything she put up with.

Besides me, no one knows who mounted the chewing gum machine on the wall or who keeps refilling it. Some people think a chubby man with back problems and the sniffles is responsible for it. A man who sometimes sneezes and, in the process, inadvertently spreads his bacteria on the colorful plastic balls and gumballs. Others suspect that a carefree girl with shimmering hair services the machine. A girl who appears only when there's a full moon, and unseen by the world—sleepwalking in the night—always pours new colorful balls into the square metal box. Until midnight strikes and she turns back into a junkie.

It's gratifying that only the machine and I know the truth.

You picture this:

While your German-to-the-core great-grandmother, heavy with child, has zero desire to go use the cold outhouse, just to wipe her butt with torn newspaper after she takes a shit, Charles de Gaulle has no desire to accept the end of colonialism. While French troops once again occupy Vietnam and refuse to give up their colonies, refuse to let go of their big, beautiful Indochina, your great-grandmother's fetus refuses to wait any longer, and will be born three weeks before her due date into a damaged postwar Germany—feet first and head last, a breech birth. While your little grandmother Rita experiences her childhood in the newly founded GDR, tormented by countless marches to the ice-cold outhouse, in the U.S., a young Martin Luther King Jr. leads the Montgomery Bus Boycott; a few years later hundreds of thousands of people will march with him. While a white university in Mississippi admits a Black student for the first time because of the Civil Rights Movement and he is protected by more than five hundred marshals, in the streets of Saigon a monk picks up a match from the ground and sets fire to his body, which has been doused with gasoline to protest against the unscrupulous rule of the Catholic minority over the Buddhist majority, and he burns. While years later in Hanoi, Uncle Hô becomes aware that Uncle Sam is not delivering democracy but genocide, your German-to-the-core great-grandfather beats your pubescent grandmother unconscious with the shaft of a hunting rifle—by accident, he was actually aiming for her cheek, not her temple; Rita's two brothers had bad grades again. While, in Karl-Marx-Stadt, your youthful grandfather (a jovial, quiet teenager, who has never thought anything bad about the GDR) bites into a piece of brown bread, the U.S. sends more ground forces to Vietnam. While Black people, who have been accepted into the white U.S. Army and want to fight for their country, because they believe by doing so they can steal the Vietnamese thunder from the threatening world domination of communism, are told: *Thanks for your body, but this isn't your country. It never will be,* your good-looking grandfather learns how to play the accordion at camp and sings socialist songs of his country. He reminds some girls, who are deeply enamored with him, of Elvis. While Elvis is stationed in West Germany and starts taking drugs, in the U.S., despite his absence, new hits of his are still being released. While hundreds of GDR citizens try to flee over the wall, *This shall no longer be my country, from now on I will be absent,* your grandparents fall in love at the Leipzig Agricultural Convention (a portly uncle had taken Rita along against her will so that he wouldn't have to indulge in his love for plows alone, but now your grandmother is indulging in her love, *love me tender*). While hundreds of American soldiers impregnate Vietnamese women, almost without exception against their will, your mother is born in the GDR. While thousands of Vietnamese women migrate (first from South Vietnam to West Germany, later from North Vietnam to the GDR, always from one divided country into another), for the first time, your sweet eleven-year-old mother is plagued by doubts about her country: *Is the West really that evil? We're always excited about packages from the West.* While your youthful mother, a few years later, sneaks out of her parents' apartment for the last time, safe in the knowledge that she won't get an abortion (*Bento and I, we really love each other, what could go wrong, maybe one day we can live in his country*), dioxin sneaks into the bodies of hundreds of thousands of born and unborn Vietnamese children, so it can one day grow up big and strong—as cancer in their cells, as defects in their nervous systems, as severe physical and mental disabilities. While hundreds of thousands of American war veterans are compensated in the billions by chemical companies for the effects of Agent Orange, not a single Vietnamese person receives compensation, despite countless lawsuits. While the U.S. bombs Benghazi and Tripoli in Libya (*Vietnam has long been checked off the list, forget it*), you and your brother learn to walk. While you walk ecstatically through the streets of New York, with three hot dogs and three bananas under each arm, your mother tries hard just to remember her life before the wall fell. While you, bloated with food in Manhattan, contemplate the English word *longing* in the word *belonging* and think about the German word *Gehör* in the word *Angehören*, about the relationship between ownership (*This country belongs to me*) and national belonging (*I belong to this country*), your water breaks prematurely. While your four-year-old son asks you how the formation of personal identity correlates with national consciousness, skin color, and a capitalist mentality, you suck anxiously on your e-cigarette and look for drones in the sky.

WHERE AM I NOW?

In an intercity bus heading for Berlin. Your train was canceled.

WHAT AM I THINKING ABOUT?

When you look at your cell phone, you see two voice messages from Kim. Besides those, your grandmother sent you an empty email with a photo attachment and the subject heading *Sweater Number 3*.

WHAT DID KIM SAY?

A lot of banal stuff about the weather, food, and about how she is hanging out with her cousins, aunts, and uncles in the country, and that she misses Berlin a little. You naturally choose to interpret from this that she misses you a little, too.

OF COURSE. WHAT ELSE?

You feel more tender than usual, something appears to be breaking away.

THAT'S NICE.

Yes.

AND PLEASANT.

Very.

You find it touching that despite her arthritis, your grandmother immediately began to knit so much, took photos of the finished pieces afterward with a digital camera, and spent several minutes loading them onto her computer.

IT WAS THE RIGHT DECISION TO TELL HER DURING MY LAST VISIT.

It's better for her to enjoy it for just a month, rather than not at all.

DO I THINK IT WOULD BE GOOD IF SHE ALSO KNITTED SWEATERS FOR REFUGEES?

For which refugees?

I TRIED ONCE TO VOLUNTEER.

Yes, but when you stood in the school gym and were supposed to tell the people forced into a line which donated clothes they were allowed to look at, you felt bad about it. Your grandmother's knitting has nothing to do with that.

SORRY, PEOPLE! I'M SO MORALLY SUBLIME THAT I CAN'T HELP YOU. BYEEE—SEE YOU NEVER!

Sweater Number 3 is gold with a lot of pink lines. You're surprised at how trendy it looks. Hook by hook, a small, chic outfit is emerging. Hook by hook, an intricate path of wool.

I CAN NEITHER IMAGINE THAT A CHILD IS SUPPOSED TO COME OUT OF ME NOR THAT IT WILL ONE DAY WEAR THESE THINGS. IT FEELS AS IF I WILL SOON STOW AWAY SWEAT-ERS I–3, OR EVEN I–33, IN A BOX THAT WILL END UP IN THE BASEMENT. WHETHER I WANT TO OR NOT.

Nonsense. Tiny socks, cute hats, wonderful rompers—the more clothing you collect, the more real it will become, and you'll soon choke to death on happiness!

I GET A VOICE MAIL FROM LUISE:

hey, i had that dream again, the one where the man is baked in the oven covered in cheese . . . whatever. about tomorrow: everything is set, we're looking forward to it! oh, and milli wants to know what your favorite di-nosaur is, this child is obsessed, i'm telling you. say, actually, how big is the fetus now? or do i still have to call it an embryo? do you know that anima-tion where you can see how your insides get pushed around by the baby, what an absurd squeezing! back then, i always used to look at this website that compared the fetus to different fruits and vegetables, first it was an olive, then a grape, a lemon, etc., at some point it was a cauliflower, then a pumpkin. at the time i couldn't even imagine milli as a person, because i always had to think about those dumb vegetables. i'll look that up for you, okay? like i said, nine o'clock is great, we'll bring bread rolls. safe travels home, see you soon.

ANOTHER MESSAGE APPEARS:

. . . hey, tell me, do you think if a piece of broccoli sees cauliflower, it gets scared and thinks: "oh no, a ghost!"?

I'D LIKE TO KNOW WHAT IT WAS LIKE FOR MY MOTHER TO BE PREGNANT.

Why?

WE HAVE THAT IN COMMON NOW.

Actually, you don't. Being pregnant with twins is totally different. Every mother of twins in Western Europe will tell you that, in her own arrogant way.

WHAT'S WRONG?

A woman who is sitting across from you has caught your attention.

I ALREADY NOTICED HER WHEN I GOT ON THE BUS. I SAW HER AND THOUGHT: URSULA. WITHOUT KNOWING HER.

Large physique, oily salt-and-pepper hair, perhaps late forties. Now and then she mumbles things to herself, arranges pens on a tray attached to the seat before her. A young man with dark hair is sitting in front of her and listening to music with earbuds. When he pushes his backrest a little, two of the woman's pens fall on the floor. Grumbling, she picks them up, clasps them in her hand, and doesn't let go of them for the rest of the trip. You have the feeling that something's not right. The young man notices you watching him, he turns around to look behind him and understands the situation. With an accent he says in German: *Excuse me, please,* and turns back around. The woman snaps that she has no use for his apology. You don't know if he hears her.

PLEASE, NO MORE STORIES WITH A POINT ABOUT RACISM.

Eventually, you focus on your phone again, you look at *Sweater Number 3* once more, and think about all the people that you know and like who could help you with what may soon come, or not come. In your head, you go over their names and faces. When the bus arrives in Berlin five hours later, the woman stands up first. She approaches the driver and the front door. Suddenly she turns to the young man and punches him in the face with her fist. He jumps up and kicks her in the stomach. She stumbles back a few steps, toward the driver. Everything happens fast, the young man and the woman are standing across from each other gasping for breath, staring at each other, suddenly you hear your own voice:

I NEED A BREAK.

You call out: *Are you two stupid? What are you doing?*

. . .

I REALLY NEED A BREAK.

THAT'S WHY I'M NOT GETTING INVOLVED. THIS INCIDENT DOESN'T CONCERN ME.

The woman turns to you, the young man doesn't, she snaps: *You'd better stay out of it, pumpkin.* You say that you're not a pumpkin and that if she's gonna pull shit like this, you have the right to get involved. The woman says: *Oh, now I guess you want to get everybody on your side,* then she looks back at the young man. You hear your shaky voice again.

I REMAIN SILENT AND STAY SEATED.

You two apologize to each other, otherwise I'm calling the police!

I STARE OUT THE WINDOW AND CAN'T HEAR ANY OF THE ALTERCATION THROUGH MY HEADPHONES.

The woman screams that she didn't do anything, the young man attacked her unprovoked, you get louder, you yell that she should stop lying, you witnessed everything. You can feel the eyes of the other passengers on your back and begin to sweat, asking yourself if this situation can harm the embryo.

A MAN BEHIND ME AND THE BUS DRIVER SUDDENLY INTERVENE.

The bus driver doesn't say or do anything, besides finally pull over.

THE MEN INTERVENE CONFIDENTLY, BEFORE ANY MORE PHYSICAL ALTERCATIONS ENSUE.

All of you reach the bus station, the situation quickly resolves itself. When the doors open, the woman storms out, the young man turns and faces you briefly. Then he picks up his bag from the rack and also gets off, together with the other passengers. When you finally also want to go, the bus driver holds you back.

HE SAYS: *YOUNG LADY, PLEASE EXCUSE ME. BUT THAT KIND OF STRESS ISN'T GOOD FOR AN EXPECTANT MOTHER.*

You expect he'd like to thank you for preventing a fistfight, but he just has a question:

Young lady, excuse me: But that young man—what country is he from?

EXCUSE ME?

What country is he from?

You're astonished that you could respond to the situation. But you don't know how to answer the bus driver's question.

BECAUSE I'M USED TO FEMALE AGGRESSION?

What?

COULD I REACT SO QUICKLY BECAUSE I'M USED TO FEMALE AGGRESSION?

No. But you apparently have a better intuition for when violence is looming than other people do.

AND THUS THE ANXIETY?

Maybe.

DO I THINK MY MOTHER IS INVOLVED IN A VIOLENT CRIME?

Yes.

DO I WANT TO KNOW WHAT SHE'S HIDING FROM?

No.

DO I BELIEVE MY MOTHER WILL EVER BE HAPPY?

No.

DO I BELIEVE SHE WAS EVER HAPPY?

She looked stable when you left. Smiling through the window, she said goodbye, with her outstretched hand askew, first on her forehead, then in the air.

WAS THERE EVER A HAPPY PERSON HIDING BEHIND HER RIGIDITY?

Maybe when she was a child?

If you were to believe your grandmother.

AND IF YOU BELIEVE MY MOTHER?

Your mother only seldomly spoke about her childhood. And when she did, it was always negative, everything was overshadowed by moments when your grandmother made her life a living hell, manipulated the people around her with her whims, and debased your grandfather.

MY GRANDFATHER WAS A SOFT MAN.

She would do so, for example, by climbing up a tall ladder and threatening to jump if he didn't take care of some random things for her. Or when she threw her wedding ring out the window in a tantrum and a few minutes later, your grandfather was outside, down on all fours looking for it on the precisely cut lawn in front of the newly constructed buildings. Or when your grandmother made your grandfather hit your mother with a wooden spoon for her insubordination until the spoon broke. With each passing day, your grandmother increasingly stripped him of his competence until he wasn't even able to decide by himself which clothes to wear or whether to answer the phone.

I DON'T KNOW IF MY GRANDMOTHER WAS EVER HAPPY.

Or your grandfather.

OR MY MOTHER.

Maybe sometimes, with her friends.

JUST LIKE ME?

As happy as you?

HAPPY ONLY WHEN SURROUNDED BY FRIENDS.

HOW DID I SAY GOODBYE TO HER?

You tried to hug her and to justify your premature departure with complicated lies.

I TRIED TO HUG HER.

Both things felt right. Both didn't work.

Aren't you cold?

Back in the day you used to be a real river rat.

You've forgotten, haven't you?

    . . . No idea.

What's wrong?

    Nothing.

Why are you making such a sour face?

    I'm just a little cold, that's all.

Then take off your wet things.

    Please stop trying to mother me.

Mother you . . .

Do you remember when you told me that I'm not really the mothering type?

    Yes.

Well, see.

    I was twelve at the time and you agreed with me. I had the feeling that you were kind of proud of it.

Nonsense.

    But you agreed with me.

Yes.

Are you hungry?

    Nah.

Do you want some tea?

You look pale.

    Are you serious?

So gray somehow.

    That's because I'm cold.

But I packed some sandwiches.

    I don't want to eat right now, okay?

    Especially not toast with remoulade.

Okay, okay.

Holm always liked my sandwiches.

    Now I have to ask: Who is Holm, right?

Don't act as if you didn't notice the photo.

    Which photo?

Ts.

    So is he your boyfriend?

Not anymore.

It didn't work out with us.

    Why?

It doesn't matter.

    Just tell me.

. . . Holm used to be addicted to heroin. That was ages ago.

But that was never an issue between us. He was unbelievably disciplined.

But it was still difficult.

    Hm.

You know that I've never drunk alcohol, right?

    Well. You did as a teenager.

Nonsense, I've never drunk anything.

    But Grandma remembers differently.

*. . . If you knew how many things your grandmother remembers the way
she pleases.*

    Like what, for example?

*In any case, in the evenings, Holm always needed an entire bottle of
vodka. Otherwise, he couldn't sleep. At some point, I just couldn't watch
him do that anymore.*

    He sounds even more screwed up than you.

What did you say?

 Sorry, that was dumb.

 I mean: It sounds like he also had a lot of problems.

Yes. He did.

Unfortunately.

 . . .

. . .

 Do you miss him?

If I didn't, I wouldn't have hung up the photo.

 Why did you always try to give us up?

What?

 Grandma showed me the letters.

Of course she did.

 Those letters to different agencies, before and after reunification. When you tried to give Grandma and Grandpa custody. Or rather when you tried to give Bento custody. So you could get rid of us . . .

 Are those all authentic?

Your father would have never taken you.

He was always too busy with himself.

 So you actually did ask him and he said no?

It wasn't that easy back then.

You know, I was so young—

 But if he had said yes, you would have just given us away?

Not just like that, no.

I would've still stayed in touch with you.

 Somehow I don't believe that.

 You always wanted to be as far away as possible.

Believe whatever you want.

You've done that for your entire life.

 Could we maybe switch places?

All the smoke is blowing my way.

Since when does that bother you?

You don't smoke anymore?

  Nope.

And now you're someone who wants to forbid all others from smoking?

  Huh? I just think it's gross is all.

  Sitting here at the lake with your cigarettes, that just seems wrong.

I'll gather up the butts afterward, don't worry.

  . . .

. . .

  And are you still in touch with this Holm guy?

Nope. But I wrote down his address for you. Just in case.

  In case of what?

I'm in deep shit.

  . . . Do you need money?

No.

But it could be that I'll need to go even further underground. And then you won't see me again.

  How come?

  Never again?

. . .

  Did you kill someone or something?

Huh?

  Did you do something awful?

No.

  . . . Do you plan on doing something awful to yourself?

Nonsense.

  I always wondered about that back then.

What?

  Whether you ever tried to kill yourself.

Or whether you ever killed someone else sometime.

Once I almost did.

Say what?

I once tried to kill someone.

Who?

Your father.

. . . Bento? What did he do?

I stabbed him in the stomach with a knife. He sometimes acted really shitty.

Did he hit you?

He cheated, he betrayed me, he wasn't there for you two, pick your reason.

But Grandma tells a completely different story.

Do you think your grandmother knew everything that was going on back then? She didn't even notice how much her own husband, your meek, quiet grandpa, was wrapped up in that whole Atari stuff. Or how he nearly drank himself to death for years.

. . . But yesterday you said that you were never involved in smuggling computers.

Well, fuck it, forget it.

This is really exhausting.

What?

That I never know whether you're telling the truth.

. . . You wanna hear something crazy?

No!

After things were over with Holm, I was really at my wits' end. That's why I thought: Okay, then give chatrooms a try. And after a few days, I started writing to a really cool guy, I really had a good rapport with him. We got to know each other, well, you know how it goes, we started writing more and more private things to each other. I even told him a little about you. And then at some point we started talking on the phone.

What did you tell him about me?

What you study at university, that you work with children, stuff like that.

I've been done with college for years.

In any case, I suddenly realize that I never asked him what he does for a living. So I ask him and then the bomb drops:

The guy's a cop.

Okay.

You can't make this stuff up, right?

But that's not so bad, if he's nice?

A cop?!

Nope, I'm not in the mood for that shit.

And after that, did you write to other guys?

For a while, yes. But I didn't meet anyone else.

Shortly before I met Holm, I had a few dates.

But didn't you say that you started with the chatrooms only after your relationship with Holm?

Did I?

Is this another one of those stories where you leave something out and in the end half of it wasn't true?

Man, you're like a Doberman.

What?

Right after Sammy's death I joined different chatrooms, okay, not like the other romantic stuff.

There were mostly fascists and hooligans in those.

I don't understand what you mean.

I met with them to let myself be fucked and afterward beaten up by them.

   . . .

For Samuel.

As a punishment.

   . . .

Every new black eye, every new bruise, that was somehow—
    How often did you do this?
Three or four times.
One guy even dislocated my arm.
    And you think that's funny?
You don't?
    No, not at all.
You'll really believe anything.

The company that produces chewing gum machines is located in the land of milk and honey. It produces only two machines a year, because the workers there are very lazy. The delivery time usually takes an additional year. A problem that often occurs is that the delivery men can't keep their hands off the products. That's why there are just a few abandoned machines left in our beautiful world. Only someone who strolls through the streets with attentive eyes and a chewing-gum-hungry heart will discover one of these delightful machines now and then.

Just like me, meaning right now:
The chewing gum machine before me has the perfect size. The longer I observe it, the younger I become.

After a few minutes, I'm standing before it as a seven-year-old. For a minute I consider whether I should put a firecracker in one of the three slots, but I decide against it. I'd rather get an intact toy and stay out of trouble, don't want to try any monkey business today. I'm excited, because it's only the second time that I'm buying something with my own money. But most of all I'm excited because I don't know which toy I'll get. As I pick at my skinned knee, I proudly think, *It's my second deliberate capitalist transaction. The little bit of chance, the unpredictability of the outcome makes everything so enticing. But maybe,* I think with my seven-year-old brain, *I shouldn't go whole hog, financially. Maybe I should try for a ring that costs only fifty cents and get married. If it works out, if the metal mouth spits out what I desire, I could propose to Denny Müller from the next class. Or, better yet, my pretty teacher. No, no,* I think, *I want something just for me, I don't want to pass anything along, just don't accept any obligations. So risk it all financially. And stay single privately.*

I take the German mark out of my pants pocket and stick it cautiously into one of the provided slots. As I turn the metal lever from left to right, I hope to get a little troll with blue hair. Or a mini pacifier made of plastic, preferably in pink, that I could wear on a locket chain. The important thing is to not get anything that you have to assemble yourself, I couldn't bear that kind of disappointment.

You're sitting by the ocean in the sand on a peninsula near Sông Cầu, which is almost directly between the hot rural south and the sophisticated north of Vietnam. It's humid, the sky is as gray as the ocean, your skin is sticky. There, where the palm trees and bushes begin to grow densely and there aren't any houses built yet, about twenty meters behind you, four Vietnamese teenagers are sitting and listening to music. There's a loud, confident voice who repeatedly yells over a sort of Goa techno, kind of like at karaoke: *I am. A superstar! I am. A superstar!* Otherwise, there's no one there, you're wearing your headphones, Radiohead whirs around you melancholically. Now and then, you let wet beige-gray sand trickle between your hands, humming to yourself, watch the milky, transparent crabs that spring from the holes in the ground. They can run sideways and forward, with senseless ambition they dig holes in the sand and disappear into other holes.

He who digs a pit for others—

At some point, from the distance, a small shape that you recognize approaches you. It's the woman who collects cans. She walks slowly and crookedly down the beach in your direction, she has a plastic sack over her shoulder. As she gets closer, you gawk anew at her skin, made rough from the sun, her deep, beautiful wrinkles. She squats down next to you, grins, says *Thank you*, and points to the crushed Coke cans. When she was sorting through garbage on the beach earlier, you waved to her and fished the red cans out of the wastebasket in your bungalow. Now the old woman is squatting next to you, in Germany you'd think she was eighty years old. Her *Thank you* sounds throaty

and warm; you take off your headphones and answer: *Không sao đâu.*
She looks at you quizzically. You try again, because earlier you ambi-
tiously crammed in some vocabulary: *Không sao đâu.*

She doesn't understand you, smiles, points to the mountains, and
keeps speaking Vietnamese. You switch to English, point to the
ocean, and say how beautiful it is here, in her country.

*You know, sometimes I think we are so drawn to the sea because the sound
of the breaking waves resembles the sound of our breathing in and out.*

WHAT ARE YOU SAYING?

*Sometimes I think we are so drawn to the sea because the sound of the
breaking waves resembles the sound of our breathing in and out.*

The old woman keeps speaking Vietnamese, now pointing to the sky.

*And because of that we feel that we should be or that we once were part
of the ocean.*

Pensively, you nod. When she walks away, your gaze follows her. At
some point she stops, gathers up her skirt, squats down, and takes
a shit. It doesn't unsettle you; you've often seen this sight here. Old
women who take care of their business while squatting on the soles
of their feet, so uninhibited and flexible, in a way you never will be.
When the woman leaves your line of sight, you think: She probably
experienced the last two wars in this country. And survived. And it
doesn't matter how much you might try to learn her language; you
could never really speak about it with her.

WHY ARE WE STILL SPEAKING, THEN?

. . .

WHY AM I STILL SPEAKING?

. . . Because you can't do anything else.

IT'S TOO HOT HERE.

COULD THAT BE DANGEROUS?

Since you arrived in Vietnam, your skin has never been completely

242

dry. You knew beforehand that the climate would be exhausting for
you. But you said to Luise: *My African genes will be able to take it, no
worries,* and you showed her a victory sign. Now that's no longer a
safe bet.

NOW THE EMBRYO IS NO LONGER SAFE.

As long as you don't have diarrhea all day, it'll be okay.

HOW DO I FEEL HERE, PREGNANT AND ALL?

Surreal. You're still astonished over the fact that you and this word
now have something in common. "Pregnancy," that's something for
other courses of life. Like: "single-family home," "Dow Jones," "hunting license," or "incurable autoimmune disease."

WHERE DID THE FOUR TEENAGERS GO?

You're alone on the beach now. The sun will soon set.

DO I FEEL LIKE GOING SWIMMING IN THE OCEAN?

The idea pleases you that while you are swimming in the ocean, at
the same time inside you there is something small, something becoming human, swimming around, so you're both doing the same
thing simultaneously. But you don't know your way around here
and don't want to risk anything, no one else here has gone swimming yet. And for the fishermen who you sometimes see, the ocean
is their workplace; you don't want to appear so much like a tourist.
Actually, you would really like to know if they believe the ocean can
save the screams that are released inside of it. Your stomach growls,
announcing real hunger. Binh will soon be cooking dinner. When
you stand up and start walking, you're delighted. Tomorrow Kim
is coming, she's actually coming to visit you. You turn up the music
in your headphones, spin around, and try walking backward to the
bungalow, trying to fit perfectly in the footsteps that you left behind
a few hours ago, and thus back to the bungalow.

THE LAST TIME I DID THAT WAS IN MOROCCO.

You pass a group of Vietnamese tourists, who were dropped off by a shuttle bus for a picnic on the beach. A family of four waves you over to them. The approximately five-year-old daughter looks at you secretly, her older brother grins ambiguously, they gesture to you for a photo. You consent, because you think the kids are cute and you want to be friendly. But only the father gets up to let himself be photographed with you. After several snapshots, you want to go, but the small, sinewy man doesn't let go of your neck. He hasn't had enough. When you try to withdraw, he laughs out loud and holds on to you tighter, the balls of his hands push down between your shoulder blades. Finally, you contort yourself, breaking free of his grip. On the remaining stretch to the bungalow, you no longer pay any attention to your footsteps.

HOW DID KIM AND I MEET EACH OTHER?

Why?

HOW WELL DO WE KNOW EACH OTHER?

Luise, your mutual friend, introduced you two more than fifteen years ago, a while after your brother's death.

HAS IT REALLY BEEN THAT LONG?

That doesn't matter now.

TELL ME ABOUT IT ANYWAY.

. . . Back then, the two of you took the train together to friends of Luise's, heading to a theme party in Cologne—why don't you want to stay in Vietnam?

IT'S JUST BECOME UNCOMFORTABLE.

Okay . . . On the train the two of you change clothes several times and put on makeup. You want to look like you're from the 1920s, because you're in your early twenties and you take theme parties seriously. When you start looking in your backpack for some chewing gum for Luise, and Kim is just coming back from the bathroom, you look up and think: *She could be my girlfriend.* The clarity of this thought confuses you, because you're in your early twenties and you also take your heterosexuality seriously.

The party is colorful, loud, and good, the apartment is big, opaque white smoke from a fog machine wafts out of two rooms. For the entire night, Kim is wearing a silly cylinder hat and a fake mustache. You're wearing a beige-gold cocktail dress whose left strap keeps sliding down your shoulder. The two of you become drunk and destructive rather quickly, you laugh and slur your words a lot. During a song by Britney Spears you hold hands, standing across from each other and bending backward in the light-colored smoke, spinning around in a circle increasingly faster. At some point, you each let go of the beer bottle in your other hand. The brown glass breaks against the photographic wallpaper, coloring the bottom half of a palm tree darker, which you both don't see until you leave the party. Tim, the hostess's boyfriend, comes over to you. He has a shaved head and is over six feet tall, grabs both of you by the shoulders in a grand-fatherly way: *Please pull yourselves together, the bottle just barely missed Valerie's head.* You both ask him what's Valerie's head's problem. *Is it stuck up your ass, haha, and by the way—are you the tallest Nazi in Cologne?* Then you both run away, grab four new bottles of beer out of the tub in the bathroom, which you then throw off the balcony while screaming. Five stories down onto the dark asphalt, nothing can stop you. Tim's girlfriend, the hostess, suddenly plants herself in front of you.

Tim just got back from chemo a month ago, this is his welcome home party, and both of you are disgusting. You'd better leave now.

On the subway, Kim has to throw up. For two whole stations, she keeps the vomit inside her mouth. Then at Friesen Square she spits it into a trash can between people getting on and off the train, passengers who are a little less drunk. You're impressed, within just a few hours you have actually fallen in love; your abysses are similar. The next day, on the way home, Luise doesn't speak to the two of you, because she's mad. You and Kim don't speak to each other, because you wouldn't know how.

I ONLY KNOW HER AS WELL AS SHE ALLOWS IT.

Yes, it's the same for her when it comes to you.

WHERE AM I NOW?

In front of your bungalow. Every evening, Binh, Lothar's Vietnamese wife, says to you, grinning, *Lotsa veggies!* when she serves you dinner. You eat what she's cooked for you and three other guests, while sitting at a plastic table, on a camping chair. In the morning, after one guest had ridden his motorcycle up and down the beach, he flew a drone over the ocean, oblivious to all around him. You never actually talk to anyone else. *Anyhow,* you think, *at least I'm no longer in tourist hell.* Earlier, you were on the island of Phú Quốc, a kind of Vietnamese Mallorca, moaning under the burden of affluent foreign tourists. You had the feeling that even the apes that you saw once by chance in the forest were annoyed about how their habitat is being commercialized.

AM I A LITTLE LIKE THE PEOPLE WHO SIT IN A TRAFFIC JAM AND CURSE: *FUCKING TRAFFIC JAM!*

What?

Bon appétit!

THAT'S WHAT BINH SAYS WHEN SHE WALKS BY AND WINKS AT ME.

What traffic jam?

Lotsa veggies! With lotsa lotsa veggies!

Your hosts, Binh and Lothar, have been living together for five years. During this time, Binh has learned German, because of the guests;

Lothar can speak about eight words of Vietnamese. Their son is three years old and already richer than any family within a distance of sixty miles.

WHAT AM I DOING?

You're lying in bed with a full stomach, the food was good. Three small octopuses, you imagine, will slide in a few hours through the umbilical cord to Baby X—surfing on carrot sticks and bamboo sprouts, with your heartbeat as the beat in their ears and tasty vitamins on their tentacles.

I DON'T KNOW A LOT ABOUT BIOLOGY, DO I?

While the sweat on your back refuses to dry, you watch YouTube videos you found by searching for "insemination" and "the creation of human life." First a five-minute clip, elaborately animated and set to classical music. As countless sperm try to force their way into an egg to an epic tune, you think this reminds you of a gang bang.

THAT'S NOT TRUE.

. . . As countless sperm try to force their way into the egg, you're reminded of a gang bang in a porno.

NO, THAT'S NOT TRUE EITHER.

As a few sperm try to force their way into the egg, you think about the magic ball from the *Mini Playback Show*. Enter as something small, irrelevant—come out as a grand human.

ON THAT SHOW, DURING THE NINETIES, CHILDREN REGU-
LARLY WORE BLACKFACE. ONCE, THEY WORE FATSUITS ON
TOP OF THAT, TO PORTRAY THE WEATHER GIRLS. THE REAL
WEATHER GIRLS WERE ON THE SHOW AS A JURY AND CALLED
OUT SALACIOUSLY TO THE THIN WHITE GIRLS HIDDEN UNDER
LAYERS OF MATERIAL AND MAKEUP THAT THEY WERE DOING
A GREAT JOB SWINGING THEIR HIPS. ONE OF THE WEATHER
GIRLS HAD HER SON WITH HER. THE LITTLE ONE—WHO WAS

A LITTLE YOUNGER THAN THE GIRLS IN COSTUME—SEEMED
EQUALLY BORED AND DISCONCERTED WITH THE SHOW WHILE
HE DREW ON A PIECE OF PAPER.

What does that have to do with you?

NOTHING.

Is that an analogy for your time in the U.S.?

EXCUSE ME?

There you also wore a pretty African American costume.

HUH?

And all day you pretended to be part of the Black community.

I DON'T UNDERSTAND WHAT YOU'RE GETTING AT.

Do you remember how you fell asleep for an hour in the sun on a
bench near the Hudson River? It was pleasantly cool.

THAT WAS A FEW WEEKS BEFORE THE FEAR, WHEN I COULD
STILL SLEEP.

You're coming from a shopping spree and your feet hurt. You use your
bag as a pillow, you wrap one of the straps several times around
your wrist to keep it safe, then you fall asleep on the bench. When you
wake up, you realize that you urgently have to go to the bathroom
and the Statue of Liberty has been within view this entire time, way
off in the water.

AND?

When you return three days later in the evening, the view of the water and the statue no longer seems so inviting, not so free, everything
is somehow dim. You walk toward the end of a narrow street to catch
a glimpse of the skyline. The bench that you slept on during the day
is about sixty feet away from you and there are no people anywhere.
There's only a police car at the end of the street, with blinking headlights. It looks like the cars you've seen in hundreds of action films,
and therefore fake. While you walk past it to get to the water, you

take your hands out of your coat pockets, to be on the safe side. Only when you're standing by the water, with the police car behind you, do you realize what you just did.

WHAT DID I JUST DO?

And suddenly you understand: This warm community of Black people, here in the U.S.A., is possible only because for centuries it was necessary in order to survive. The basis upon which these people meet and empower one another was and is bloody, unjust, and torturous. You can be thankful that you are just a welcomed guest in this community; a tourist of this Blackness born of pain. You should feel lucky that your heart attempts a few somber beats only while you're here.

... PERHAPS BACK THEN IN NEW YORK I FELT A LITTLE AS I DO NOW THAT I'M PREGNANT?

Fatter than usual?

NO.

Hungry, and still feeling as if you could puke?

NO. MORE LIKE THIS: THE POSSIBILITY OF EXPERIENCING AN ALTERNATIVE SELF-IMAGE BECOMES TANGIBLE.

... Hm. Nice idea, but no, that's not how you felt.

TOO BAD.

AND NOW?

What?

HOW DO I FEEL NOW?

You're sitting next to the empty plate that Binh will clean up later. You search the internet with your cell phone.

I OWN AN AVERAGE OF FORTY-FOUR SLAVES, INDIRECTLY. THROUGH MY LIFESTYLE AND MY CONSUMER BEHAVIOR.

That's what you find out on a website. Then you watch more videos on YouTube about the many wars in Vietnam, the Khmer Rouge in

Cambodia, the reasons Hollywood no longer casts Wesley Snipes in films, life hacks about caring for a baby. One suggestion is not to cut the nails of newborns with nail clippers, rather to just bite them off, so the new edges aren't too sharp. Brimming with a collage of arbitrary knowledge, you lie down in bed and fall asleep. The mosquitos leave you alone; you've sprayed yourself with German products and are lying reliably isolated under a mosquito net.

I'M THE SWEATY TILSIT CHEESE UNDER THE CHEESE DOME.

Before you fall asleep, your thoughts wander, they revolve around Uncle Sam and Ho Chi Minh, Elvis in West Germany, your grandmother at the agricultural convention, Agent Orange in embryos, and your grandfather's accordion.

And what are you planning to do now?

What do you mean?

Well, do you want to keep living like you always have?

Do you think I have to change something?

. . .

What should I change?

And the father?

He doesn't know about it yet. I barely know him.

But he's okay, I think.

And I'm not expecting him to be there.

But maybe he wants to take part in it all.

That would be okay too.

But I don't want to suddenly play happy hetero-nuclear family now.

Is he white?

Yes. Why?

Well, I just thought . . . Oh, never mind.

What did you think?

. . . That's not going to make it easier.

What do you mean?

Your child will probably also be seen as white, don't you think?

That depends on how they look, right?

Although, yeah . . . they probably will.

Exactly.

Fuck, I hadn't thought about that.

I mean . . . that won't play a role in your love for your child or your relationship.

How awful would that be: When the whole shit starts from the beginning *again, just differently. And some random people constantly think that it's not my child, but that I'm the nanny or something.*

You won't be able to avoid that.

If I stay in Germany I won't.

Do you want to leave?

I've had the desire since I've known about the pregnancy.

But I wouldn't know where to go.

First, I'd prefer to just hang around here on the beach for half a year and not think about all that for a while.

Then do that.

It's not safe enough for me. I want to have my child in Germany.

Do you think the doctors here are not as good or something?

No.

I didn't mean that seriously.

And it would be much too expensive to stay here.

Besides, my return flight is already booked.

Your dad can pay. He'll be so excited when he hears that he's gonna be a grandpa. Maybe he'll finally come and visit you.

He's already got six grandkids in Angola.

Or you just stay here, your father comes by, and you live together happily on the beach, eternally, and Lothar is the happiest of all. Now, that would be something.

You think that's really shitty of me, don't you?

That I've rented a place here owned by a German.

That guy bought up half the beach.

But the Vietnamese government wanted that, with the change in the law, right? They wanted foreign investors to really get going.

You know, the kids who play soccer or listen to music here without a care, ten years from now they won't be able to set foot in the new beach resorts. Unless they're employed there.

Hm.

Lothar might be nice, but this neocolonialism that he's involved in here is not okay. These bungalows look like miniature row houses in Germany. They have nothing to do with the people who live here.

I was just looking for German cleanliness.

And relaxation.

I know.

. . .

   . . .

Kim, if you were pregnant, would it be important to you . . .

That they look like me?

Yes.

Definitely. And I'd rather have an athletic daughter than a smart son.

What?

You want to talk about race without saying it, right?

Do you think that's dumb of me?

No, it's understandable.

Hm.

I think that in your life, the fact that you've been labeled a non-white person by society definitely plays a role. That's a huge topic for you.

So of course you want it to somehow connect you to your child, right?

Well, I wouldn't like my baby to have to experience the same shit that I have.

Of course.

But if there's something I could pass on to my child and share, out of everything that I have had to understand over the years—that would be nice.

So do you think it would be better if your child was at least a little darker than the father?

I don't want to think about the baby in that way.

Why not? Just tell me.

. . .

   I knew it.

Can you imagine it?

   What?

Me. As a mother.

   Sure.

And you, too?

   Do you mean in general or us parenting together?

Both, I think.

   Mhm.

When I held the pregnancy test in my hand, that was my first thought.

That I can imagine that with you.

And you've always wanted one.

   Hm. I think it's nice that you're thinking of me.

   But things between us have gotten so entangled. I can't respond to that

   off the cuff. I really can't.

Because of your girlfriend?

   No, because of you! You can't expect that you can just fly here, drop

   that information in my lap, and I clap and yell: I'm all in!

I'm not expecting that.

I just wanted to tell you in person.

   This is an intense, exceptional situation that will change everything

   that has happened up till now.

Yes, I know. I think it's already changed everything.

That's why I've come here.

   Sorry, I didn't want to sound so reproachful.

I know.

   I just need some time to think it over.

   You know, think about what that would mean for you and me.

I'm still here for another week.

   . . .

That was a joke. You have all the time in the world.
Well, at least another six and a half months.

   . . .

That was also a joke.
   . . . Would you also do it alone if necessary?
I think so.
If my mother could manage it, I can too.
   And do you want to tell her?
Not right now.
Not before I've decided what I actually want from her. Besides, right now she's going even more underground. Maybe it won't even be possible to tell her anytime soon. Maybe I saw her for the last time last month.
   Okay . . . but she might be completely different as a grandmother.
   Like maybe somehow better, you know? That's often the case.
I don't know. There's a no-trespassing sign in my head, I can't think about that.
   Do we maybe want to take a walk?
Through Lothar's kingdom?
Do you want to know how he initially made his money?
   Yes.
He published a book in Germany: The 1000 Best Addresses on the World Wide Web. It became a bestseller.
   Really?
Yeah, no joke.

I'm still standing in front of the snack machine.

I didn't get what I wanted and now my coin is gone, I only have sixty cents left, confound it and damnation.

A sticker that is partially covering my view of the chewing gum catches my eye. An ad for a dance event in the northern part of the city, in the new development zone. It says they play "soul music" and other "hot grooves." "Soul" means "spirit," I understand that much at least. But it beats me what "grooves" means. And that's why I don't understand why the sticker depicts a woman with an afro. There are no such women in the new development zone; actually, none in the entire city. There's just me, but at the moment I'm seven years old; I'd need stilts to gain entry to the party.

Once again, I grope the change in my pants pocket. I can see five capsules containing rings in between the chewing gum. *My chances are good*, I think, because luckily I've never heard of stochastics and I'm utterly enthusiastic about the beautiful jewelry hidden behind the glass. When I blow on it, my breath steams it up. Bit by bit, fingerprints become visible more and more. On the snack machine's glass and beyond, on the handles, on the coin slot, and on the shimmering, scratched metal corners of the machine. Grease stains with itty-bitty delicate coils, left behind by thousands of dirty fingertips. Maybe those are the fingerprints of all the children who ever bought anything at this snack machine. Children who by now are of retirement age, unemployed, or dead. Or they keep on living overworked lives, and don't experience any excitement anymore when they buy something. Children who buy something every day, sometimes without noticing, sometimes illegally, sometimes online or via the QVC hotline, sometimes even buying other people. People who work for them without payment, who carry their future children in exchange for payment, or who blow them without a condom in a car. *One day, when I'm grown up and have much more time than I do now,* I whisper, *I will come back and I will overlay every single one of these fingerprints with my own.* Hopefully, the time until then will pass quickly.

Oh boy, maybe I should just try proposing marriage to my pretty teacher, I mean no one wants to grow old alone. Hastily, I put my fifty cents into the machine, turn the lever once in a circle, and hold my hand beneath the metal mouth. Please, please, be a ring with a beautiful jewel. Or even a ring without a jewel.

WHERE AM I NOW?

It's your second-to-last night in Vietnam, you're lying on a hammock on the veranda, swinging gingerly. The screams of two geckos who have somehow managed to enter the nicely air-conditioned bungalow are keeping you awake. At first you thought you were hearing pan-icked birds. Kim keeps sleeping, the cries don't disturb her. While, above the terrace, you dangle a cigarette pretending to smoke, it seems like everything, truly everything, suddenly doesn't matter at all.

HOW DO I FEEL IN THAT MOMENT?

A fisherman walks along the ocean in the darkness. His headlamp il-luminates the nets lying in the wet sand, revealed by the ocean, which is at low tide. He crouches down, checks the contents of the nets. Even though it's night and dark out, it smells like fire.

I LIKE MY LIFE.

IS THAT POSSIBLE?

You had forgotten how to. But now you've remembered.

CHILDREN ARE THE BEST ANTIDEPRESSANT THAT EXISTS.
What?

THAT'S WHAT THE GYNECOLOGIST SAID WHEN SHE GAVE ME THE OKAY TO TAKE THIS TRIP.

A blonde with straight teeth, who's about five years older than you.

I NODDED POLITELY AND THOUGHT:

Wrong, Barbie—Children are the best jail that exists.

But now you almost have the desire to believe her.

The fisherman turns off his headlamp. Your cell phone vibrates, you pull it out from beneath your butt, which has sunk so far into the hammock it's almost touching the ground. Burhan sent a photo. It's in the middle of the night where he is, he's five hours behind you. The selfie shows him next to an old, ash-colored version of himself, both men are smiling inauthentically, the subtitle reads: *Started chemo again.* You don't know what you should answer. You send him a yellow thumbs-up, then you correct it to a brown thumb. You decide that in a few days when you're back in Germany, you'll stop by Burhan's and offer him your help. At the same time, you sense that you don't really have the energy for that right now.

HOW LONG HAVE I KNOWN ABOUT BURHAN'S FATHER?

For about three weeks. Shortly before your departure for Vietnam, you two sat together in an expensive restaurant in West Berlin. You actually wanted to invite him to the TV Tower, but he thought it was too silly. Instead, you unironically chose high-class cuisine.

WHAT WERE YOU CELEBRATING?

Twenty years ago, Burhan lived in Australia for a while. He didn't do well there. One of his friends had just died in a car accident, and a few years before that his best friend from school died from a rare disease, ALS.

I THOUGHT ONE OF MY OLD SCHOOL FRIENDS SUFFERS FROM ALS?

Abruptly Burhan tells you about it again in the restaurant, while you're both eating a bouillabaisse. You've already spilled food on the upscale apricot-colored tablecloth twice now and you find Burhan's tone of voice oddly enthusiastic. Back then, after the two deaths, at age twenty-seven of all things, he had swum out into the ocean near Melbourne. He wanted to be alone and to scream in silence underwater. After everything had just gotten to be too much for him. There's no better place for screaming than the ocean. In case things don't go well in Vietnam, you should definitely try that out. Well, even if things do go well.

You had imagined that meeting him at the restaurant would have been more positive. After you tell him about the pregnancy, awkwardly following his story about Melbourne, he hugs you tightly and says:
Wow, that's intense, now I need a cigarette.
When he comes back, you think briefly that he just did cocaine. Then he tells you unexpectedly about his father's illness, as if your topic had been discussed conclusively. He talks fast and doesn't look at you as much as usual. He says he has to go to Duisburg soon to take care of his dad. His father has been sick for months and had hidden it all. He had put off any visits and stopped going to chemo. That apparently hurt Burhan's sister so much that now, during the last remaining weeks or months of his father's life, she's unable to stand by him. While Burhan speaks, you're overwhelmed by your disgust for the invisible cloud of nicotine that his mouth is emitting.

I WON'T BE ABLE TO BE THERE FOR HIM HALF AS MUCH AS HE HAS BEEN THERE FOR ME IN THE LAST FEW YEARS, RIGHT?
Yes. And you both know it.
DO I THINK OF MYSELF AS A GOOD FRIEND?
Sometimes.
But also an ungrateful one.
AND DO I THINK OF MYSELF AS A GOOD MOTHER?
Not yet. No.
DO I THINK MY MOTHER EVER LOVED ME ENOUGH?
There's not a single photo of you two laughing or smiling.
NOT EVEN WITH A FAKE SMILE, LIKE BURHAN AND HIS FATHER?
No.
. . . THAT HUG MY BROTHER GAVE ME ON THE DAY BEFORE HIS DEATH.
What about it?

IT WAS JUST A LITTLE LONGER THAN USUAL, A LITTLE
TIGHTER.

PERHAPS MY MOTHER WISHES SHE COULD HAVE HUGGED
ME LIKE THAT?

. . . Yeah, maybe.

God, I love that smell.

WHAT?

It's early in the morning, the sky is unusually clear, your feet and hers
are not touching each other in the sand. Kim has been there for only
a day, breathes in ostentatiously and doesn't yet know about the tiny
person inside you. A stray dog is keeping you both company, sniffing
a tubby coconut with small holes in it. The two of you occasionally
drink cold Coke out of a plastic bottle while sitting in the sparse shade
of a palm tree. You're wearing a swimsuit with shorts, Kim is wearing
a long-sleeved linen dress that doesn't make any sense.

Suddenly the woman collecting cans comes by, without her plastic
sack. She calls over to Kim, waving at her, and points to you, then
both of them laugh. You don't ask what she said, you finish your
Coke and spit a tasteless clump of ice in the sand.

After the sun has set, you and Kim listen to one of many storms.
During lunch, she played a new song for you, you told her about the
pregnancy, and afterward you both went for a walk. Now, in the se-
cure darkness of the bungalow, the two of you lie together and stroke
each other's palms. Suddenly Kim says that the due date is a good
day. Promising and lucky. Then she asks if she should go to a shrine
in the coming weeks, for the baby. You look in the direction of her
voice, squinting, but you can't spot anything. She's being serious; you
weren't prepared to discover this superstitious side of her.

IF I'M BEING HONEST, I ALSO HAVE A FEW SUPERSTITIONS
MYSELF.

Oh really?

IN THE WEEKS FOLLOWING MY BROTHER'S DEATH, HUNDREDS
OF LADYBUGS FLEW INTO HIS ROOM; FOR YEARS, I THOUGHT
THEY WERE A GREETING FROM THE BEYOND, RATHER THAN
A PLAGUE. EVEN NOW, A COZY FEELING TAKES HOLD OF ME
WHENEVER I SEE LADYBUGS. WHEN WE WERE YOUNG, WE
USED TO CALL THEM PLUMBLEBEES.

And squashed them.

The quiet cracking of chitin pleased you.

WHERE AM I NOW?

You're lying down in the night bus to Saigon. Illuminated by the pink
interior lighting, and wedged into a reclined seat made for people
who are five feet tall, you're feeling incomplete. Kim is going to stay
another day at Lothar and Binh's beach and will return to Hanoi
afterward. The same film is playing on several small monitors without any sound: Asian men are fighting and making rabid faces at
each other. The bus keeps honking, your legs, which you've pulled in
tightly, have fallen asleep, but the rest of your body hasn't. At some
point, the bus stops on a well-trafficked street. There's a pickup truck
waiting off to your left; the bus driver and truck driver get out, greet
each other with a nod, and transfer white sacks from the larger to the
smaller vehicle. In the meantime, in the movie numerous vampires
are fighting one another, which one can tell because the actors now
have two pointy teeth that stick out of their mouths. You think to
yourself that some imaginary figures are the same all over the world;
vampires and witches, Negroes and mermaids.

At one point, a vampire in the film catches a cobra with his hands
and Henning appears. How he holds two sweet potatoes and a pint
of organic milk in his hands, grinning. How you accidentally ran into
each other in front of the supermarket and then, on the way home,

went for a walk in order to spend more time together alone outside the shared apartment. Your conversation worked out well, because you put in the effort and asked a lot of questions.

DOES HENNING HAVE DREADLOCKS?

What? No, you think dreadlocks are gross, especially on white people.

... THAT MIGHT HAVE SOMETHING TO DO WITH MY GRANDMOTHER.

When you look out the window of the night bus, the highway suddenly freezes over. Two pale people are sitting in an ocher Lada. They're driving at a crawl, the night bus passes them by without a sound.

IN VIETNAM?

In Thuringia.

MY GRANDPARENTS.

I WINK AT THEM AS WE DRIVE PAST.

After they learned from a neighbor that all the borders are open, two hours later they're stuck in a traffic jam. An unfortunate stagnation that takes hours and is overcast with a snowstorm; your grandparents' teeth are actually chattering. Years ago, your grandfather's nephew hadn't returned from a wedding hosted by relatives in Hessen. The only thing your grandparents knew for three years was that he was once seen in Frankfurt am Main and that a lot of poor, young male prostitutes end up there. That's why your grandparents persevere hungrily in the midst of the snow, they are hopeful. But then: no reunion, no glamour, no happy, historic moment. Only the debilitating waiting to move forward just a mile, in an unheated car, in an impalpably new country. And the worry that their nephew is being fucked in the ass by rich West Germans at the Frankfurt train station stays with them for the rest of their lives.

WHAT'S THAT SOUND?

. . . The resigned sighing of your grandparents?

NO.

The sound of the ocean?

SOUNDS MORE LIKE THUNDER.

Or like a deep inhaling and exhaling.

FROM AN ENRAGED ANIMAL?

Underwater.

BEAUTIFUL.

Wonderful.

MAYBE THAT WAS THE BABY'S FIRST NOTICEABLE MOVEMENT?

Yeah, maybe.

WHAT WILL MY CHILD DESIRE WHEN THEY HIT PUBERTY?

Unclear. It's enough for you to think: *Hopefully my child will outlive me, and not the other way around.* That's what you desire.

AND HOPEFULLY THEY WILL LIKE ME.

They have no choice but to love you. But we'll see if they will like you.

WHEN?

When they start puberty. Then you've got the day of reckoning four years long.

I THINK I'M GETTING CARRIED AWAY AGAIN.

Maybe.

I'M NOT GOOD AT STICKING TO ONE TOPIC, AM I?

Your father once wrote to you on Facebook that that's typical for an African, taking all these detours before actually getting to the point.

DID HE REALLY MEAN THAT?

There was a yellow smiley face in his message that was sticking out its tongue.

I THINK I'LL CALL MY FATHER SOON.

Good.

MAYBE ON HIS BIRTHDAY.

Have you ever wished him a happy birthday?

NO, NEVER.

I HAVEN'T WISHED MY MOTHER A HAPPY BIRTHDAY IN YEARS EITHER.

When you and your brother were nine years old and should have long been asleep, she once celebrated her birthday extravagantly: You secretly peek at the hallway through the crack in your bedroom door. In the bathroom, which is diagonally opposite your bedroom, your mother has poured sand all over the tile floor and decorated the walls with green crepe paper. Besides that, she filled the room with a lot of plants, palm trees and ivy, she even installed a hammock. Some of her friends greet each other or say goodbye with a balled-up fist held over their heads from time to time, as they yell "Druzhba." A few of the guests smoke, others slurp drinks out of coconut shells with straws. Songs by Bob Marley, Sinéad O'Connor, Lenny Kravitz, and Nena play on the record player. You and your brother would like to be a part of this magical green room; you enjoy the atmosphere. The next day, at school, other children ask you questions about the party, to which neither they nor their parents had been invited, but about which they can still report crude details. None of them saw your mother, how beautiful she looked that night, how she laughed and radiated in the green bathroom. Like a weightless center of gravity, surrounded by pierced and tattooed guests who enjoyed standing under palm trees.

WOULD I LIKE TO REMEMBER HER THAT WAY?

Yes. But it's not possible. When you think of your mother, you remember especially the moment when you two honestly touched each other for the last time, sixteen years ago.

**RIGHT BEFORE WE TOLD MY GRANDPARENTS ABOUT MY
BROTHER'S DEATH.**

At the time, you placed your hand on your mother's shoulders and
nodded at her before she rang the bell. Then she placed her hand on
top of yours, and for a moment you both had peace. Not long before
that, you had tried to call an ambulance for preventative reasons:
you're familiar with your grandparents' weak hearts. But the man
who answers the emergency hotline says it isn't possible to do that,
only in the case of an actual emergency. *But the emergency already
happened,* you say patiently. *You were there this morning and picked up
my brother. When we tell my grandparents now, at least one of them is
going to have a heart attack. I promise you that.*

There's no use. Ten minutes later, you both tell them in separate
rooms. You don't know anymore how this separation came to be: You
speak to your grandmother in the living room, your mother speaks
to your grandfather in the bedroom. Both of them begin to breathe
heavily simultaneously, they gasp for air, stagger into the hall to find
each other, falling into each other's arms. Your grandmother swal-
lows, trembling, your grandfather grips his chest and buckles over,
you call the paramedics again, now, finally, in accordance with the
regulations.

AND THEN?

And then the future begins.

WHAT DO YOU MEAN BY THAT?

At the airport in Saigon. You sit on an aluminum chair that is welded
to identical chairs to make a bench. Outside, behind glass that is
twelve feet high, the palm trees appear to melt, shimmering in the
heat. When you start to panic, you don't hold your ribs. Your hands
wander as if independently onto your belly and remain there, until
the fear subsides.

WHAT AM I THINKING ABOUT?

You haven't gotten anyone a present. No Vietnamese coffee, no sea-shells from the beach, no cheap baseball caps.

HOW DO I FEEL?

You'll soon stand up and get in line to check in. With a small carry-on and a glance at your cell phone, you will start walking. While you go, you won't see a puddle of water left behind from mopping the floor, you'll slip and fall down. The mouth of a cleaning person will silently form a zero; while you fall, for a glowing moment you will be so worried about everything in your belly that there's no oxygen. Lying on your side, on the floor, with your eyes wide open, you'll check whether you've hurt yourself.

HEAD?

Okay!

BACK?

Okay!

ANKLE?

Slightly twisted, but not bad.

At this moment, in the airport in Saigon, you will get up and with radical clarity you'll know that you will have this child, that you must have this child (as long as nothing has happened to it just now). That you will be capable of loving it with a kind of love that you reserve only for your brother. And while you'll lift yourself off of the seamless floor that's smooth as glass, virtually rising into the high, conditioned air of Saigon's terminal, you'll understand that you'll have to share that spot reserved for your brother inside your-self, that you are allowed to share it, pretty soon. And that this will not cut his share in half, but rather maybe something inside of you will double or spread out or heal. Something that comes with letting a new healthy fear into your life—namely a fear that is deeper, warmer, and more disruptive than any fear about yourself, your life, or your identitarian sensitivities could ever be: a fear tied to a love that's as strong as everything that you have ever known, times a thousand.

WHERE AM I NOW?

Your eyes are shut. With one eye you're looking into your stomach, with the other you're looking into your grandmother's custom-made kitchen.

SHE DID IT.

What?

SHE'S FULFILLED THE WISH SHE'S LONGED FOR IN THE WORST WAY: TO HAVE WARM RUNNING WATER IN HER VERY OWN APARTMENT.

When she was a young girl, she always had to take baths in the large dining room, which had the only washbasin.

I ALREADY SAID THAT.

Her father would sit there all day with eggnog and his hunting friends: men who twenty years earlier, at the peak of their physical condition, had served in the Wehrmacht, and whom in the meantime beer had bestowed with soft stomachs. Silently and unashamedly, sitting before their guns leaning against the wall, they watched your young grandmother as she washed herself. When you showed her *Susanne's Dream* about two years ago, she told you that she would often wait until midnight, until all the men were gone, before washing her private parts.

WHY DID I NEVER DARE ASK HER WHETHER ONE OF THESE MEN ALSO DID MORE THAN "JUST" WATCH HER?

It makes you happy that today your grandmother has three different kettles, each allowing her to adjust the temperature. She can even watch from the outside how the water in the glass container—illuminated with blue, yellow, or pink LED lights—begins to bubble.

In the months after the death of her grandson, these vibrant kettles helped her.

I HARDLY BELIEVE THAT.

It's true. Sometimes, for an entire night, she would listen to the triad of kettles heating up. Even today, on holidays when the loneliness threatens to blow up her small, newly built flat, she boils her tears in her fastest kettle. Afterward she cleans the other two with vinegar.

SOMETHING'S NOT RIGHT ABOUT ALL THESE STORIES.

Why?

AM I HOLDING BACK INFORMATION?

No, not really.

BUT MAYBE I SHOULD?

Hold back information? What for?

WELL, I HAVE TO HOLD ON TO A FEW THINGS FOR MYSELF.

. . .

. . . DOES IT MAKE A DIFFERENCE WHETHER OR NOT MY BROTHER WAS IN ANGOLA WITH ME AND SAT IN THE BACK SEAT WHILE OUR UNCLE SHOWED HIS AFFECTION?

In Angola?

WE'RE STUCK IN A TRAFFIC JAM IN LUANDA, BECAUSE THERE'S NO OTHER WAY IN LUANDA, EMBEDDED IN SOFT LEATHER SEATS: MY UNCLE IS TWENTY, JUST A YEAR OLDER THAN ME, MY FATHER'S YOUNGEST BROTHER. THE TAPE DECK IS CHEWING ON A CASSETTE, WE'RE SHARING A CIGARETTE. SUDDENLY HE SAYS, DURING A BEAUTIFUL PAUSE:

We have loved you even before you were born. Everybody here loves you so much.

I START CRYING, AND STUTTER AFTER A FEW MINUTES:

I guess I am . . . I am not equipped to be loved that much, haha, sorry.

When was that, exactly?

MAYBE IF MY BROTHER HAD COME ALONG TO ANGOLA AND
HAD HEARD THESE WORDS TOO, HE WOULD STILL BE ALIVE
TODAY.
So he wasn't there?
IS THAT IMPORTANT?
IS IT IMPORTANT WHETHER MY GRANDPARENTS DROVE A
LADA OR A TRABI?
It depends on the context.
WOULD YOU FEEL TRICKED IF I TOLD YOU THAT MY MOTHER
WAS NEVER IN A PSYCHIATRIC INSTITUTION?
. . . Yes.
MAYBE NOT EVEN IN PRISON.
WOULD YOU BE HAPPY IF I TOLD YOU THAT SHE AND I ARE
STILL IN CONTACT, TO THIS DAY?
DOES IT MATTER WHETHER I WAS IMPREGNATED BY HEN-
NING, DUANE, OR A RANDOM ONE-NIGHT STAND?
. . . No.
IS IT WORTH ASKING THAT IF MY BROTHER HAD BEEN
WHITE, WOULD HE HAVE DARED TO LEAVE THE LIGHT ON
DURING SEX WITH HIS GIRLFRIEND? WOULD YOU LIKE IT
BETTER IF MY FATHER WEREN'T WEALTHY AND COULDN'T
HAVE FINANCED A SINGLE ONE OF MY TRIPS? WOULD YOU
BE DISAPPOINTED IF MY PREGNANCY AND MY MOTHER-
HOOD TURNED OUT TO BE A REAL, COMPLETELY "UNAMBIV-
ALENT" SOLUTION TO ALL MY PROBLEMS?
Are you really even pregnant?
WOULD YOU BE RELIEVED OR ANNOYED IF I HAD INVENTED
HALF OF ALL THE RACIST EXPERIENCES I SHARED?
Are you asking me, or . . .
YES, YOU.

BUT, ESPECIALLY, I'M ASKING YOU:
DO YOU UNDERSTAND THE IDEA THAT EVERYTHING I TELL
YOU FITS INTO A SINGLE LIFE AND THAT THIS LIFE IS NEVER-
THELESS SOMETHING ORDINARY AND GOOD?

Where am I now?

Back in Berlin. When I arrive at the airport, I think: *I had forgotten how expensively dressed and simultaneously ugly many people are here.*

And how much I like cheese and yogurt. How am I doing?

I'm sitting at Imren's in Neukölln. After eleven p.m., I can still get something to eat here. An exaggeratedly friendly clerk takes my suitcase at the entrance and shows me to a table, as if we were in a restaurant. While I'm waiting for my food, he brings me light morsels swimming in hot water. *You have to eat it together with the tea.* Halloumi cheese, strangely sweet; I feel cordially received and not hit on.

Did anyone miss me?

At home, Henning shows me a notification from the mailman. Henning had tried to pick up a package for me from the corner store, but they had said that they never received it. On the other hand, the post office claimed that the package had been delivered to exactly this store. Henning's detailed report with subsequent speculations about where my package could be bores me. While he's speaking, I gaze out the kitchen window, the end of a crane looks like a dinosaur's head, then Henning and I start to kiss.

Why am I nervous?

It's three in the morning, I can't sleep, I'm chewing the nail of my right ring finger, a half-moon made of keratin sails down to the parquet. The blue trash bag. I quietly leave Henning's bed, put on his T-shirt and boxer shorts, go into the hallway, and take the smallest key from the rack. The cellar smells like damp stone. The light is broken, I use my cell phone to light the way through low passages, angular shadows follow me, my life a 1920s horror movie. Rustling, I open the trash bag containing discarded pieces of clothing, I rummage about for a moment until I have the firm fabric in my hand.

I picture this:
In a park, a large field without trees, I unfold the material and pull it over my shirt. The dress reaches to my feet and feels like a costume; I'm disguised, and I don't know what as. I use my cell phone to put a song on repeat, so that it starts over as soon as it ends. Then I lay it on the grass, some of the blades fold down reverently. I stretch, throw my head backward, bend my knees. Whitney Houston sings "You Light Up My Life" perfectly. I think: *Poor Bobbi Kristina*, and I hold a sleeve of Saida's dress under my nose. It smells like curd soap and cellar. Saida and I got to know each other in a vacation house in Essaouira. She had run the household daily, which made Kim and me feel uncomfortable. Kim tried to take washing the dishes off Saida's hands all the time. In the beginning, I did too at first, but then I got lazy. When Saida found out that Kim and I would continue on to Sidi Kaouki and I would spend a few days there alone, she invited me to her house. The day after the threesome with the Swiss guys, I went to visit her.
    Why did she invite me?
The older a woman is, the more kisses on the cheek you give her as a greeting. Saida's younger sisters got two kisses at the doorstep, Saida three, her mother four. The mother looks cute and tough. Smiling, she brings a tagine full of couscous, turkey, and vegetables into the living room. I eat as much as I can. The mother keeps saying I've eaten hardly anything. We make small talk in French, then we watch TV, with Arabic subtitles, for two hours. A young Anne Hathaway is really a princess and has to learn how to comport herself accordingly.

I'm lying on a couch with strangers, stuffed with food and relaxed, as if I belonged to the family. They don't want to know anything about me, not about my ancestry, my job, my intentions, they answer my questions about these topics politely and curtly. Suddenly, the mother gets up from the sofa, leaves the room, and returns beaming with joy. A mountain of fabric is stacked on her forearms, she says: *Un cadeau pour toi*, and gives it to me, grinning. I unfold a purple dress with gold stitching and adornments. Stunned, I pull it over my body, and turn around shyly in front of a mirror in the hallway. The women around me clap and say I should spend the night.

Will I dream of my child first, or will my child dream of me first?

This carefree, uneventful, communal sitting around. It was like that in Vietnam, too. Sometimes I walked along a street and glanced into a living room attached to a shop, house fronts like open sardine cans: in the smallest spaces, close to one another, at least three generations of people would sit on and in front of the sofa. The only thing that moved were the rotating blades of the fan and the images on the television; no one seemed to want anything from anyone. Maybe that's the most beautiful way of being together. A totally unambitious kind of being together with clearly defined roles. Maybe one day my child, my grandmother, my mother, and I will sit together like that. In affectionate ignorance, without making any kind of effort to talk to one another, to understand one another, or to convince one another of anything.

I turn myself slowly in a circle. The dress is making dry creaking noises, crinkly, as if someone is stepping on fallen leaves. *Henning is basically okay*, I think. Okay enough for everything that may come. My mother's voice, at the bus station, after we have hugged each other, and I wanted to get on the bus, is layered over Whitney Houston's voice. All of our Christmases, all of our summer vacations, and all of our birthdays are gone now. If this dress weren't so valuable, I would fall backward onto the field and make a snow angel in the grass. Instead, I start running toward the apartment. Suddenly I stub my foot on something hard. On the dark field, something is lying in my way. I bend over and grope around carefully for the object: cold, angular metal. My fingers greet the snack machine with a caress, for a moment I press my forehead against its scarred tin skin. When my child is grown, these machines won't exist anymore. My child won't have any memories of what it's like to exchange a coin for something sweet, and not quite free of germs, from a metal box. Maybe my child won't remember any sweets or any snacks; rather, they'll just remember their first time online banking or their first trip on a ship. Or their first grueling fight with me or the overalls that they wore on the day the war ended.

I grin. There's a brief rumbling inside the chewing gum machine, then a green ball is lying behind the metal flap. Hop hop, straight into my mouth. I begin to chew, the sweet-and-sour taste quickly fades. I keep chewing until it feels crumbly. Then I stick my tongue into the gum and through my lips and begin to blow. A bubble curves out of my mouth. I pinch the pale shape at the end so that it's sealed. Content, I take it out and I hold it in the weak light that my cell phone casts in the night, to look at it from all sides.

The bubble is perfect.

Slowly I raise it high over my head until it covers the moon. *Farewell, my friend*, I think, and let it go.

Leisurely, the bubble climbs into the night sky.

Whitney Houston grows quiet for a moment, a message from Kim appears on my phone. Just one sentence: *I'm all in.*

I swallow and hope that the bubble will carry my breath as far away as possible. Maybe to my brother, maybe to my mother. Maybe to a ladybug who's been traveling for a long time and is therefore happy to rest on the sticky, soft ball of breath for a bit.

Acknowledgments

The author thanks the Berlin Senate Department for Culture and Europe for the "Arbeitsstipendium Literatur 2019."

Dear Anh & Philipp,
dear Sören,
dear Lilli & Klaus,
dear Gereon,
dear Schnippi,
dear Adrian,
dear Albert:

I am incredibly fortunate that you wonderful people exist, and will be forever grateful for the many ways in which you supported me so I could write this book. 1,000 Millionen Dank!

©Juliane Hahn

OLIVIA WENZEL was born in Weimar, Germany, and now lives in Berlin. Her dramatic works have been staged in Munich, Hamburg, and Berlin. Wenzel also works as a musician and a performer. In 2022, she is leading a series of multi-disciplinary workshops for young adults of color at the Haus der Kulturen der Welt in Berlin.

PRISCILLA LAYNE is associate professor of German and adjunct associate professor of African, African American, and diaspora studies at the University of North Carolina at Chapel Hill. She is the author of *White Rebels in Black: German Appropriation of Black Popular Culture*, and her current book project is on Afro-German Afrofuturism.